OUTSIDE LOOKING IN

A BROWERTON UNIVERSITY BOOK

A.J. TRUMAN

OUTSIDE LOOKING IN

By A.J. Truman

❀ Created with Vellum

ACKNOWLEDGMENTS

Cover: GoOnWrite.com, Editing: Jayne Rogers

Thank you also to Paula and Maureen for beta-reading and helping me whip my blurb into shape. (Blurbs are hard!) And thank you to the readers who have continued to support the Browerton boys. Sorry for the long wait between books! I couldn't have done this without your enthusiasm and encouragement, Outsiders!

What's an Outsider, you say? Oh, just a cool club where you can be the first to know about my new books and receive exclusive content. Join the Outsiders today at www.a-jtruman.com/outsiders.

PROLOGUE

NATHAN

Nathan liked celebrating his birthday—not for the presents, but because it was one of the few days of the year when he knew he'd see his dad. They didn't see each other that often, what with Nathan off at boarding school most of the year. And when Nathan was home on breaks, his father was usually away on business, with his current wife, stepmum number three, tagging along to hit up the local boutiques.

"Where you going, Ginj?"

Nathan rolled his eyes. Two of his classmates walked up to him in the lobby of their boarding school, snickering to each other. There always had to be at least two. It was like that light bulb joke: one person to make the stupid comment, and another to laugh at it.

"Don't call me Ginj," Nathan said. This was England. Had they really never seen a redhead before? Apparently, Nathan must've been the first ginger student accepted to this school.

The dipshit duo cracked up behind him.

"Don't make him angry," dipshit number two said. "Gingers go crazy when they get angry. Like an Orange Hulk." He could barely get that lame joke out before laughing again.

Nathan gave them the finger.

"You're an hour late," Nathan said when his dad pulled up in his Porsche to the boarding school.

"We said seven-thirty, didn't we?"

"Six-thirty. I do have curfew here."

"Which you've been breaking. I got another email about it from the headmaster," his dad said. "What've you and your friends been getting up to?"

"They're not my friends." Nathan narrowed his eyes at the road.

"He heard suspicions of gambling. Have you been organizing an underground casino?"

"For fuck's sake, I'm not a bloody pit boss. It's a poker game. I've wiped the floor with my classmates. They bluff about their hands as well as they do about their heterosexuality."

His dad turned a shade of red. Nathan had recently come out to him over Christmas holiday, but his dad seemed to have as much interest in that as he did the rest of Nathan's life.

"I can't afford to find yet another school who will take you, Nathan..."

"The headmaster has only heard rumors. We haven't been caught."

"...because they won't hesitate. They will throw you right out if you cause trouble."

"All right!"

"I don't know why you insist on acting out like this."

Nathan rested his head against the window, looking out

on a neighborhood of little cottages, wondering if the families in them fought as much as they did.

"'Hi, Nathan. How are you doing? It's good to see you. Happy birthday, son! Blimey. I can't believe you're fifteen,'" Nathan said to the window in his father's voice.

His dad softened his grip on the steering wheel and ran a hand down his thinning dark hair. "It is good to see you, son. I'm sorry I haven't been able to make it up to see you sooner. I've been extremely busy. My clients have been quite restless of late."

Nathan nodded along. These excuses were as overplayed as a pop single.

"How's school?"

"It's fine."

"That was a good impression of me," his dad said. "You should try out for the school play. Do they do that here?"

"They do. I got the lead. Again."

"Oh. I remember that."

"You had a trade show in Japan that weekend." Nathan's dad had told him that after the fact, leaving his son searching the auditorium on opening night and coming up empty.

"I wish I could've been there."

"Sure," Nathan said and continued feeling jealous of these cottages. "I wish mum were here."

"She couldn't make it, but she sends her regards. She had a—"

"Not stepmum. My real mum."

Silence hung in the air for a full minute until his dad pulled off to the side of the road. Nathan got very still. His dad turned and looked at him solemnly. Nathan felt a tightening in his chest, afraid of what was to come.

"Why'd you stop?" Nathan asked.

"Nathan, you're almost an adult, although I think you're mature enough now." His dad gripped the steering wheel. "It's time you know the truth about your mum."

"Truth? She died when I was a few weeks old of an aneurysm. That's what you told me."

"I lied." His dad looked away.

"What?" Every ounce of air was knocked out of Nathan. "Dad?"

"You were too young to know the real truth."

The world spun on its side. It reminded him of the few times he'd gotten drunk, where the ground sloped until it took the place of the sky and he couldn't find his balance.

"What's the truth?" Nathan wanted to keep pushing, but was also afraid to find out more.

Sweat prickled at his dad's temples and curled through his hair. "The truth is, your mum was a one-night stand. I haven't seen her since we...made you."

"What?!"

"Fifteen years ago today, there was a knock at my door and a baby on my doorstep. I had a DNA test conducted, and I am your biological father, but your mother...I have no idea."

"You have no idea? How is that possible?" Nathan could feel his entire face get red like a comet breaking through the earth's atmosphere. He was all fire and heat.

"I remember meeting this bird with a terrible Cockney accent at an Oasis concert about nine months before that."

"Oasis?"

"The band. *Wonderwall.* 'Cause maybe, you're gonna be the one—'"

"Stop singing. I know who Oasis is. Why are we talking about them?"

"That's where I met your mother. We were on mushrooms and wound up shagging in the men's toilet, but I never got her name."

"Dad!" Nathan clapped a hand over his mouth. This had to be a joke. A terrible, terrible joke.

"I'm being honest with you."

"What about the woman who died of an aneurysm?"

"You had asked about your real mother, and I needed a story."

"What about the pictures you showed me?"

"They were of a girl I went to university with. She was the only redhead I knew."

"I can't fucking believe this. You never tried looking for her?"

"How could I look for her? I didn't even know her name." There was minimal effort on his dad's part. This wasn't an actor whose name he couldn't remember. This was Nathan's mother! Nathan had wondered if there was another family out there, one who could save him from the cold embrace of his parents and the demonic turds who comprised his extended family.

"Today isn't even my real birthday then."

"I suppose not."

I don't know my own birthday. That realization more than anything else made Nathan feel like a walking fraud. It was as if he didn't exist.

Nathan turned slowly to his dad, who smiled weakly.

"Do you still want to go to dinner?"

"Actually, I'd much prefer to go to a pub."

"But you're not—"

Nathan whipped out a Fake ID from his wallet.

"Nathan!"

"Please. Just drive," Nathan said, before his dad could try to parent with another lecture.

Chapter 1

SEVEN YEARS LATER

NATHAN

"How are you feeling? It's the big day," his counselor said, as if it was graduation day. For a woman who espoused peace, relaxation, and mindfulness, her hair was pulled back into an awfully tight bun. The tightness made her eyebrows arch up, as if they were getting sucked into the bun, too. It was something Nathan had noticed during all their sessions together over the past thirty days. He had needed something to focus on, since she loved to repeat herself. What other advice did she have besides don't get sloppy drunk?

Her heels, meant more for climbing the corporate ladder than a posh rehab facility, clacked on the stone walkway around the sculpture garden.

"It's just one day. One day at a time," Nathan said, knowing she would like that. Before he could leave, he had to take a stroll with his counselor through the garden of eternal peace and talk out any final fears. They passed people meditating and doing yoga on the grounds.

"And what do you mean by that?" she asked.

Nathan resisted the urge to roll his eyes. She was always doing this, asking him to explain something she already knew, thinking it would take on extra significance if he broke it down. People in here loved to talk talk talk. (Fortunately, Nathan had also discovered a few guys who also loved to fuck fuck fuck.)

"I'm going to attend AA meetings every day and be mindful in my decisions."

"And what do you mean by mindful?"

"Present. I will think before I act. Every time I want to drink, I will think about what's causing this decision, isolate those feelings, and make a better choice."

She paused at a sculpture of a teal rectangle perched on its corner with a circular cut in the middle. "Nathan, cut the bullshit."

"What?" Nobody ever cursed in rehab, especially not the counselors. "What happened to the flowery, hippie-like language?"

"I used to be a VP of marketing. I know how to level with people when I need to." She arched one of her already arched eyebrows at him so that it looked like an upside down V. "You've obviously been listening in our sessions, but have you been *listening*?"

"I have. Every word."

"*Really* listening, though." She peered into his eyes, searching for something. "You're an actor, Nathan. I hope this past month hasn't been a performance for us. I know you're somewhat of a pro."

"Does it count as being a professional actor if you get fired from your first role?"

"I wasn't talking about your motion picture career. This is your second time here in six months. You did so well last time, but then you were back here three months later."

"I missed the artwork. It's very Delia Deetz. You know, from *Beetlejuice*. Catherine O'Hara is my redheaded sister-in-arms." Nathan dragged his finger along an octopus-looking sculpture and pushed down the feelings rising in his chest. He didn't like to be reminded of his failures. There were too many.

They rounded the trail and strolled under a thicket of pine trees. "For sobriety to stick, you need to take this seriously and put in the work. I don't want you to wind up back here, or in jail."

He held her hands and squeezed them as he peered back at her as earnestly as he could muster. "I won't."

He would not be back here. Because rehab was for people who were actual addicts. Nathan had drunk a little too much last November and had gotten into a bar fight, like one does. His father decided to be a parent for the first time in his life and shuttled him off to this place. That did not make him an alcoholic. Nor did winding up passed out in the alley behind his flat a few months later.

So he would drink too much sometimes and got a bit belligerent. So did any Manchester United or Arsenal fan! Rehab was simply the quickest way to get the authorities and his father, when he did decide to care, off his back.

"When is your father picking you up? I wish he and your mum could've attended for a family session."

"Stepmum," Nathan said.

"Sorry."

"Unfortunately, he had to attend a conference this weekend. He's delivering the keynote, and I told him he shouldn't miss it. It is a massive opportunity." Right about now, his father and stepmother were tanning themselves silly on a beach in Hawaii. The only keynote he was delivering was asking a hotel waitress to refill his mai tai.

She pulled a business card from her suit jacket pocket. He admired her for not giving into the crunchiness of this place and dressing in baggy, rumpled clothes like the other counselors.

"This is the information for a therapist in London. Besides going to meetings, I think it would benefit you to talk to him. We never got a chance to talk about your real mum."

"Sadly, I don't remember her. Like I told you, she died of an aneurysm when I was an infant, but I like to think she's watching down on me from heaven."

"That's exactly what you said when I first brought her up. Nearly word for word."

Nathan bit back the pain crawling up his throat. He shrugged his shoulders. "Because that's all I know."

Like fuck was he going to tell her or anyone the real truth about his mother. Any therapist would get a massive hard-on at that sordid little story. What was there to talk about? He was conceived in a porta-potty at an Oasis concert. Nine months later, she left him on his dad's doorstep and wanted nothing to do with him. No good would come from rehashing that history. He was going to care about her as much as she cared about him, which was not at all.

His counselor studied his eyes again, but too bad for her, Nathan's storytelling ability could beat her bullshit detector every time.

"Nathan, you need to take this seriously. Rehab is only a first step." She held onto his hands again, much like a mother would, Nathan thought. Well, other people's mothers. Her penetrating gaze cut through the armor he needed to survive such a touchy-feely place like this. "I see a part of myself in you. I had money and success and a sarcastic sense of humor, but there was a hole inside me I kept ignoring. I didn't think I had a problem. And then I lost everything."

She looked away for a moment and composed herself. Nathan rubbed her shoulder, then gave her a hug. He appreciated that she'd shared about her divorce in a session once. He wasn't the type to be open like that.

"I'll work on myself. I'll go to meetings and keep doing yoga. I promise."

"Nathan..."

"I'm telling you the truth."

"It's time you start telling the truth to yourself."

He put on a smile even though his insides were charred black. He swung her hands back and forth like their arms were jump rope. "I'll be fine. One day at a time, right?"

"LANDING IS ALWAYS THE HARD PART." Nathan dipped his olive into his vodka martini a week later. Sobriety had been incredibly boring. "Think about it. You're in a tin can careening to the ground at three hundred kilometers per hour. It's bound to be bumpy. But I pride myself on having the smoothest landings."

"Wow." The guy across from Nathan shook his head in disbelief. "I could never be a Royal Air Force pilot. It sounds terrifying. I'll gladly stay behind my camera."

"It's nothing." Nathan shrugged and took a sip. "I live for the excitement."

He wasn't too impressed with this new bar. It looked like every other trendy place in Soho. Dark lighting and red curtains and plush couches. At least the bartenders weren't just eye candy; they could make a decent drink.

"So do you wear those flying hats?" The guy asked. "You

know. The ones with the brim that goes out to here and they're round on top?"

He tried shaping it above his head. Nathan would never play charades with him.

"Yes, a captain's hat. I'm aware of what they are." Nathan tacked on a laugh at the end.

"Have you flown in combat?"

"Several times, of course. I was part of the unit that captured one of the heads of ISIS."

"Really?" The guy's eyes nearly flopped out of his head. His brain might not be that big, but by the look of his large hands, something more important was.

"Our unit was caught in a dust storm, and it was hard to see our target on the ground. Hell, I could barely see out my windshield. My mate...he wasn't so lucky. His plane was shot down and..." Nathan put a hand over his eyes. "Excuse me. This is not proper bar chatter."

"Don't be." The guy rested his hand on Nathan's knee. "You are a hero."

"Am I though? What is a hero?"

The guy's mouth puckered with concern. "Let me buy you another drink."

"No. I shouldn't. I shouldn't try to dull the pain."

"Well, maybe there's something I could do to cheer you up."

It was almost too easy.

THE NEXT MORNING, Nathan skillfully untangled himself from his latest sexual encounter without waking him up. The guy slept soundly in Nathan's bed, his baby arm of a cock sticking up under the sheet. Nathan gave it a salute and headed into the kitchen.

The entryway had been rimmed in gold, or something painted gold. His stepmother loved the Palace of Versailles aesthetic, even if her design budget couldn't compete with royalty. She set out to turn their flat into a tacky monstrosity filled with gold and marble and lots of things from catalogues. Nathan found a note on the kitchen table from his father.

> *Here is the name and number of the hotel in case you need to reach us, but only for emergencies please. Don't eat the lasagna in the freezer. We are saving that for when we come home. Love, Dad.*

"Happy to be back, too," Nathan said to the note. His father had been bought out of his company for a tidy sum and was enjoying an early retirement visiting every cruise and five-star resort in the world.

They never talked about his mother, his real mother. Whenever Nathan used to ask, his dad would just tell him to forget about her, even though he was the one who dropped the bombshell on his son. "What she did...she's not worth looking for," his dad had told him, his voice going cold at the mention of her.

When Nathan had first found out the truth, he tried finding her. He looked on YouTube for recordings of the Oasis concert in Knebworth and searched the footage for his father. It was the largest outdoor concert in the UK, with over 250,000 attendees, but Nathan pored over each frame he could find, hoping to locate his maternal needle in a haystack. Needless to say, it was a giant failure, and soon,

Nathan took his dad's advice to heart. She wasn't looking for him, and he wouldn't look for her.

Nathan could never get fully on board with this plan, though. He hated her, yet he also felt a connection to his real mother. Maybe she had a good reason for doing what she did. It was a possibility that squatted in the darkest corner of his mind and was impossible to evict.

Why am I thinking about this now? he asked himself. He'd been thinking about her more in the past week than he had in years. Stupid counselor getting into his head. Maybe that was part of the plan. Purposefully screw up recovery to ensure repeat business.

Nathan beelined to the liquor cabinet, but it was locked. His father never locked it. "What? You think I'm some addict who you can't even trust?" he said to the cabinet. His dad never attended a performance or major event in his life, yet because he dropped Nathan off at rehab, he thought himself fucking father of the year.

He was going to find that key. He didn't even want the alcohol anymore. Sure, he could go to a nearby liquor store, but he wanted to take from his father's precious stash, as a very personal and special kind of fuck you.

Nathan rummaged through the kitchen drawers with no luck. He took out his parents' precious lasagna and ate it during his search. *Oops.*

Over the fireplace was the same enlarged photo of his extended family taken at Christmas when he was nine. Nathan and his uncles, aunts, cousins, grandparents. The sick taste entered his mouth as if on cue. They all looked the same, with their thick chestnut brown hair and chocolate chip eyes, their stocky builds. And then there was the literal redheaded stepchild Nathan kneeling beside the tree, his light hair and pale skin practically glowing. Before they took the picture, his cousins shoved him around in a circle outside, calling him Ginger and asking if he knew the Weasleys, like they loved to do. Their lack of creativity ceased to amaze him. Nathan's insults weren't that much more creative. He called them a bunch of braindead cock-suckers (ironic in retrospect). His eldest cousin punched him in the stomach before pushing him into a puddle of mud, where he landed on his ass. Hence the kneeling position.

Still a bunch of braindead cocksuckers.

Nathan stormed into his parents' bedroom and tore through their dresser and nightstand drawers. He came up empty. He recoiled at the canopy bed with thick drapes and the gold sparkly walls of the bedroom. His stepmother had a gay stepson at her disposal yet still churned out rooms like this.

Next, he searched through his father's desk drawers in his office. He leafed through papers and envelopes and files. Steam filled his head, and the whites of his eyes glistened with purpose.

"I know you're in here," he muttered. Nathan popped open the locked bottom drawer of his father's desk, like he'd done as a teenager when he needed some cash.

He found the cabinet key sitting atop an old checkbook. Whenever he broke into this drawer, he always went for the checkbook. After forging his father's signature on permission slips, it was only a natural progression. Not like his father cared or even noticed the money Nathan had taken from him. When he did discover the stealing, Nathan thought he'd be in for it. Yelling. Punishment. Wondering about what kind of downward spiral his only son was on. But all his father did was get him his own credit card. "That should make things easier," his father had told him before going out to some swanky benefit.

Nathan picked up the checkbook. He had this urge to rip it into pieces, or sign all the checks and hand them to homeless people on the street. Something else far more interesting grabbed his attention. At the bottom of the drawer, the corner of a paper peeked out from under a stack of more important documents. Or at least it looked like paper, but thicker. Nathan had never noticed it before, since his attention had always been drawn to the checkbook.

He pulled out the important documents and folders piled to the top of the drawer. They stacked up to his calf muscles. His dad never liked to throw anything out. This delicate paper wasn't a paper at all. It was a Polaroid photo, weathered and frayed from being stuck down there for so long, but the image was still clear. A young man and woman smiling at the camera in the middle of a gigantic outdoor concert.

The photo began to shake. That was Nathan's hand, and his body, quivering with a realization. The young man was his father. He had far less hair now, but his gumball-sized eyes hadn't changed a day. And the woman...with her red hair...Nathan just knew. He knew it in his heart, in every synapse in his brain.

"Mum?"

"Nope." Mr. Baby Arm hung on the doorframe wearing nothing but boxers. His sexiness did nothing for Nathan. "But I can be your daddy."

"Hey, I'm sorry about this, but I have to cut our morning short." Nathan could barely get the words out. His fingers traced the picture over and over. "I have some business to attend to."

"Early flight?"

Right. I'm a pilot.

"I have to file a flight report. It's the unglamorous part about my job. Can you see yourself out?"

The guy's face dropped. Nathan didn't mean to be so sudden. But playtime was definitely over. He gave him money for breakfast and a cab and promised to call him, whatever his name was.

Nathan stared at the picture, stared at her face. That was his fucking mum!

He had spent the past six years trying to follow his dad's instructions. Forget about her. Push the sad feelings down. Nathan had taken the extra step to cover them with a thick layer of sarcasm, sex, and alcohol. But the wound pushed through.

Maybe this was a sign. He found this picture for a reason. In rehab, they talked about signs. Well, they were referring to signs of addiction taking over your life, but signs nonetheless. There had to be a better family out there for him, one with redheads or just people who cared about him, and he intended to find them.

Chapter 2

LIAM

When Liam went to sleep last night, he had made a promise to himself. No going on Facebook. He didn't even like Facebook and believed it to be one of the worst inventions known to man.

The next morning, he threw on the same pair of weathered jeans from yesterday with his boxers peeking above the waistband and got his day started. As he cooked himself scrambled eggs while brushing his teeth, careful not to get any foam in the skillet, he thought of other things. More important things. He had a lengthy to-do list, just as he did every morning. Perhaps he should add "clean the house" to his list. Though it wasn't that dirty, more just old.

He walked past his computer en route to the kitchen. No stopping. He scratched at his thick beard as he cooked himself some eggs. Liam had always been clean-shaven, but after the major life overhaul of the past year and a half, he decided to grow it out. He needed the change. He was a rancher now, not a city boy. He was living out in the wops, practically the middle of nowhere, with lush, rolling hills of green grass laid out before him. His shaggy black hair puffed out in wild bushels, making his eyes appear even bluer in contrast. With the beard and his muscular chest, not to mention the thick arms and legs that came from manual labor, he was the definition of rugged.

Liam lived in a shed that he and his oldest brother converted into a studio apartment for him. The bedroom was next to the kitchen, which flowed into his living room and the corner where his computer resided. He was only one guy. He didn't need extra space.

It was during breakfast that Liam *just happened* to remember that he had to email one of his buyers. Right that instant. It had nothing to do with it being Kelly's birthday yesterday.

Liam went on his computer, emailed the vendor, and...

"Fuck," he said under his breath. "Fucking Facebook."

He clicked onto Kelly's page. She smiled at a dinner table in a fancy Wellington restaurant surrounded by their mutual friends, their faces aglow from the birthday candles. And Craig was sitting right next to her, his fucking arm around her fucking shoulders. Liam wished he were born one hundred years ago, in a time without social media, in a time when if your girlfriend left you for your best friend, you didn't have to keep seeing pictures of them. You wouldn't be able to compare social media updates to determine if they'd been having a long-term affair. They could be truly out of sight and out of mind.

Liam couldn't escape it. Even after defriending them, Kelly and Craig kept popping up as "People You Might Know." Their pictures showed up in their mutual friends' statuses.

He heard familiar yelling coming from outside the shed.

"Yeah, I know!" he yelled back. "I only went on to email someone."

The yelling continued in its constant dull tone.

"I really did!"

The yelling gained voices and volumes. They sounded more desperate than usual. Liam stuck his head out the window into the dark of early morning. Five of his nosiest sheep baaa'd up at him. He looked out on a sea of wool.

"Fine. I checked." He shook his head. "Be lucky they haven't invented Facebook for sheep."

Some ranchers had roosters crowing to wake them up. Liam had sheep. He came from a line of sheep farmers here in New Zealand, a country where sheep outnumbered people. After being cheated on in the most unbearable fashion, he found refuge in the sea of non-judgmental wool.

He put on one of his flannel shirts, buttoned halfway up, and greeted his Greek chorus. One of them, Matilda, named by his nephew after his favorite book, seemed to shake her head at him.

"Don't pack a sad," Liam told her. "I didn't wish Kelly a happy birthday."

He patted Matilda's distended belly. "It's almost that time, isn't it?"

She let out a short bleat and walked away.

"Don't be embarrassed! You're glowing! You're all glowing!" he called out to his bevy of pregnant sheep. "Lambing season is just around the corner."

He knew on some level that animals were not this perceptive, but when you worked with sheep all day, every day of the year, you started to wonder.

The sheep continued baaa'ing, though. Usually they stopped when he approached, but their noises still rang with desperation.

"What's wrong?" he asked. Like with any relationship, over time, he'd become an expert at deciphering what sound meant what. And he recognized this baaa. "You're hungry?"

Liam ambled into the hoof house, which was a large greenhouse-looking structure with a half-moon roof where the sheep ate. It reminded him of those large tents under which he'd attended weddings with Kelly or craft beer festivals with Craig. He mixed together the feed. Every spring, he mowed the grass when it was most nutrient rich and saved it for the rest of the year. Dozens of sheep watched him with anticipation. He poured the food into the feed troughs, and they descended upon him like he was their god.

Liam had a small farm of about eighty hectares. When his parents passed away, he and his four older brothers inherited their much larger farm, which was divided equally, King Lear-style. Minus the murders and intrigue. Three of his brothers rented their land to other farmers with dreams of selling, while his oldest brother Mark lived on his share in their parents' old house.

Liam had originally thought of selling, too, but held on for years even as he worked as a visual effects artist for movies and lived in Wellington. He had always looked up to Mark, who was twenty years older, and Mark wasn't selling, even though he wasn't a farmer. Something inside Liam told him not to sell, that it was his birthright.

It turned out to be fate when he decided to leave the bustling metropolis of Wellington behind a year and a half ago to get away from his breakup. Mark let Liam use his land to expand his farm. He used his savings and took on freelance graphic design projects to supplement his income until the sheep farm turned a profit, which other farmers warned him could take years. Liam would wait. He had no intention of going back to the city. Kelly and Craig could have Wellington. He preferred sheep.

LIAM HAD BUILT an outdoor shower attached to the shed to avoid tracking dirt into his home. He let the water cleanse him after another long day in the fields. Every muscle inside him cried for mercy. He had to work double time in anticipation for lambing season in July, which was only a few weeks away. He had barely survived his first lambing season a year ago and wanted to be more prepared, repairing the sheds and equipment, making sure he had enough supplies.

He washed the smell of mud, hay, and sheep off him as best as he could, though after eighteen months of full-time farming, it was baked into his natural scent.

He put on clean clothes and walked across the field to his brother Mark's house. It was nice having family just across the field, and in a bigger, more updated house for those rare times when the shed got to be claustrophobic.

"Gidday, how ya going?" his niece Franny said to him when he arrived. He remembered when she was a little girl, screaming his name and running into his arms whenever he came over. Now she barely looked up from her phone. We were all teenagers once, Liam thought.

"How is my favorite niece?" He mussed her hair, which he knew she hated. Mark bemoaned how much time she spent in the bathroom every morning.

She smoothed her thick waves of brown hair back into place. Franny had the tall, gawky look of puberty. She was becoming a woman, which was so strange to the uncle who held her in his arms when she was born.

"You can't say that, Uncle Liam. You can't pick favorites!"

"Says who?"

"It's the rule."

"Weren't rules made to be broken?" He sat down on the tan couch; its weathered, lumpy cushions could put him to sleep faster than his own bed. Franny hopped on, too, though she was too old for his lap.

"Uncle Liam!" Walt ran in and punched his arm a few times. With his bright red hair and pale skin, he reminded Liam of a lit match, which was an appropriate description in more ways than one. At ten, Walt was at the age just before it became uncool to like your family.

Liam hauled him over the couch and lobbed soft punches at him.

"Uncle Liam, can I help you when you shear the sheep?" Walt asked.

"You're a little bit too young, but maybe next year."

"I'd be really good at it. I cut my own hair!" Walt pointed to his head and uneven lops of hair missing. He was at that age just before he thought about trying to look good for girls. Liam remembered those high school mornings where he put a gallon of product into his bushy black hair.

"Dinner will be ready in five," Mark called out from the kitchen. "Walt, why don't you set the table tonight?"

Walt hit Liam once more in the stomach, with more force than he was expecting, and buzzed off to the kitchen.

"How's school?" Liam asked his niece.

"All good." Even glued to her phone, he noticed her expression change slightly.

"Is it?" He made sure the kitchen door swung shut. "I won't tell your dad."

"There's just these popular girls. They like to say mean stuff."

Mean girls. Some things never changed. Liam didn't know them, but he hated them.

"What kind of mean stuff?"

"About my hair." Franny touched her roots self-consciously. Her natural red hair was starting to grow back, giving her head an awkward two-toned look.

"I like your hair. Red, brown, you're beautiful."

"Thanks," she said, unmoved. "They also call me the farmer girl who lives in a barn. They all wear these designer clothes and shoes and live in nice houses in town."

Some things really never did change. Even though they live on a farm, the school district is part of this posh suburb. When Liam went to school with those rich kids, he was also teased for being a farm boy, as were his four older brothers. Except they called him Sheepfucker.

"They're stink girls. They wish they had this view." Liam pointed to the flowing fields and cresting mountains just outside their window. "Bullies like to get a reaction out of their targets. Don't give them that satisfaction. Just ignore them."

"Nah yeah," Franny said with a flash of hope before returning to her phone.

Liam wished he could tell her to beat the shit out of them, but that was not proper uncle advice.

Mark stepped out of the kitchen with a piping hot tray of fajitas. "Who's ready for dinner?"

AFTER DINNER, Liam washed the dishes. He looked forward to the quiet of his shed and his bed, except for the occasional sounds from his sheep, though he slept through those now.

When he left the kitchen, he glanced around the room. Mark had done big renovations and redecorating after he moved in, but Liam still noticed tiny parts that reminded him of his childhood. A black mark just above the door from when his brother Callum threw a marble at him. The creaky step on the stairs that alerted him when someone was coming.

"Going home?" Mark asked. He wiped down the dining table. The kids were upstairs doing homework.

"Another day awaits."

"Have you begun lambing season yet?"

"Soon. My ewes are about ready to burst." Whenever one of them sat down, he worried that they would start giving birth right then and there. Ewes couldn't be moved once their water broke. If a farmer tried to move them, the ewe would risk her life to return to that original spot. Liam had had to deliver lambs last year in pouring rain, in mud puddles, and at the top of hills. Lambing seemed like a chain reaction. Once one ewe gave birth, others followed.

"Have you given anymore thought to hiring a new farmhand?" Mark asked.

"I don't need one. It's a small farm. I can manage the season on my own."

Mark gave him a look chocka block full of doubt. "You're still new at this. You can't do it alone. And I would help if I wasn't a single dad with a full-time job."

"What about all those years helping Mum and Dad on the farm? Last year was rough, but I can handle this."

"It can't hurt to bring on a farmhand for lambing season."

"Yeah nah." Liam said in acquiescence. He didn't know where he would find a farmhand this late in the season.

Most of the good ones were snatched up, or they wanted too much money.

"Just looking out for you. Plus, it wouldn't hurt to have someone to talk to who can talk back."

"Here we go again." Liam took the sponge from Mark and continued cleaning off the dining table. "It's eight-thirty. Almost my bedtime. So I'll finish the rest of this conversation for you. 'Liam, you should really think about dating again.'" Liam made sure to use a high-pitched voice for his brother, just to annoy him. "'Mark, I don't feel like dating anyone. I want to focus on building up the farm.' 'Liam, that's just an excuse. Not all girls are evil bitches like Kelly.' 'Mark, I told you not to use such coarse language.'"

"I never used that word." Mark swiped the sponge out of his hand. Liam remembered the days when Mark used to have a dirty mouth. Until he had kids.

"I'm doing great. I'm working with my hands and doing something I love." Liam really didn't have time to think about dating. Or looking up exes on Facebook, but he *barely* did that.

"I reckon you've really taken to sheep farming. It's great. But it might be nice to have someone to come home to, don't you think?"

Liam cocked his head at his brother, letting him know exactly what he thought.

"I haven't heard of you going on one date. It's been two years since you and Kelly broke up."

"I was cheated on, Mark. Kelly and Craig were sneaking behind my back and lying to me over and over for months. I don't want to go through that again. If I try to be with someone, that's all I'll ever think. I trusted Kelly completely. I had no bloody idea." The pain lanced his heart all over again.

And I don't know if I want to date a girl next time. The

words stopped on his tongue, just as they had done plenty of times before.

"I know you don't want to go through that again," Mark said, taking a different set of words out of his mouth. "But there's someone out there worth the risk for you. I know there is."

Liam remained doubtful, but he didn't shake off his brother's remark completely. "Have a good night. I love you."

"Love you, too. Say hi to the sheep for me."

Chapter 3

NATHAN

The rest of the day was a string of dead ends and hangovers for Nathan. He didn't mean to drink again so soon after rehab, but searching for your mother called for a libation backup. He tried reaching out to hospitals in London to find out if there was a single woman who gave birth around his birthday twenty-two years ago, but he was met with long, awkward pauses followed up by standard responses about how they cannot give out that information, even if they had it. Nathan didn't have a real birth certificate. In England, his father just had to take him as a newborn to a register office within forty-two days, something Nathan had looked up when his dad first dropped the bombshell on him. He tried Google reverse image search, but the only results that came back for the photo was a Wikipedia definition of *lady*. He looked through more footage online of the Oasis concert, but anyone who wasn't a Gallagher brother was a blur on screen.

From his balcony, Nathan watched the sun slip behind the buildings of downtown London, as if it were playing hide and seek. He drank Bombay Sapphire straight from the bottle. Alcohol didn't make him happier or sadder. It made life one constant, dull, barely bearable blur.

This time, though, the Bombay dared him. He lit a cigarette and reached for his laptop. Right after his father had first told him the truth about his mother six years ago, he found a website for missed connections both large and small. It was more extensive than the typical Craigslist page, as people posted about strangers and lovers they'd met on global travels, mostly for one-night stands. Nathan had never seen a post that went back over twenty years, and when he used the site six years ago, nobody responded. But he was out of options. His gin was tinged with desperation.

He uploaded the picture and typed the post:

> *Had one of the greatest days of my life with this woman over twenty years ago and then never saw her again. I can't stop thinking about her all these years later. Does anybody out there know who she might be?*

"Idiot," he said to himself when he reread the live post. The only thing the internet was good for was shaming and ridiculing someone. He had nothing to lose.

Nathan drifted off to sleep, one of those drunken, hazy sleeps that were like being under anesthesia. He did have one dream he remembered, one where he was at a dinner table with his mom and her family, and they were his family, too. Loving and accepting. It was very Hallmark, like some tacky advertisement, but it was real.

When Nathan awoke, he discovered that he was not as much of an idiot as he thought.

THEY FOUND HER. The Internet found her. Well, one person found her. But all he needed was one.

> *This woman looked familiar to me, and I think I saw her in* Les Miserables *years ago down in this little community theater in Wellington, New Zealand. Good luck!*

The internet wasn't terrible! Nathan did a Google search for theaters in Wellington that produced Les Miserables and scrolled through cast listings and photos until he found her in a still for *I Dreamed a Dream*.

Mariel Foster.

Her hair was tucked under a wig, but the blazing eyes and button nose matched his Poloroid picture.

There she is! She's an actor like me!

Nathan's life began to make more sense. This was where he got his love of theater, his desire to stand out.

He read through articles about her, but his search stopped cold when he got to her obituary.

She's dead?

It couldn't be. A car accident. Here one minute, gone the fucking next. Nathan broke out crying in his lounge chair. He couldn't remember the last time he cried like this, the pure emotion spilling out of him. If only he had searched for her years ago. If only his fucking dad had showed him that picture and hadn't told him to give up hope. He could've had a mother, someone who loved him.

He kept reading, and his mouth dropped.

She is survived by her husband Mark and her two children.

She has kids. I have half-siblings.

Nathan wiped his tears off his cheeks. He had family in New Zealand. Even though they were half a world away, he felt close to them. They were alive. But did they know he existed?

Eamonn Charles had at one time been Nathan's boyfriend but now transitioned into the role of his Jiminy Cricket, the friend who was his voice of reason and conscience, whether he liked it or not. Eamonn had been a good boyfriend to him. Kind, devoted, loving. Nathan had treated him like an accessory and cheated on him right in front of his eyes. Yet somehow, they had managed to repair the damage and emerge as friends. Eamonn was like a nutrient that Nathan needed in his life.

"No. That is a terrible idea," Eamonn said over the phone. "You cannot go to New Zealand."

"Why not?" Nathan poured himself a glass of wine and traipsed through the living room, flinging his fingers against the plush drapes of the floor-to-ceiling windows. "I have family there."

"Supposedly. Just because one person on the internet says it's true doesn't mean it is."

"I checked. It was her, E."

"So maybe write them an email."

"An email? This is the most momentous news of my bloody life, and you want me to deliver it via email?"

"So what's your plan? Just show up at their doorstep?"

"Exactly." Nathan had a flair for the dramatic. There was some juicy symmetry in that scenario, what with his mum leaving him on his dad's doorstep. "Where's your sense of adventure?"

"If you want adventure, go parasailing."

Nathan knew how this might've sounded, but he'd been

wondering about his mum for the past six years. Hell, for his entire life. His dad had told him that his mum had no family, that she was an orphan, hence why they never did family events with that side of the family. His dad knew how to spin a story, though the apple did not fall from the tree on that one.

"And what about those two kids? It's probably going to be a shock to them. They might not even know you exist!" Eamonn's raspy voice was layered with concern. He'd always worried about Nathan and was the one who got him to go to rehab, even after Nathan had punched his new boyfriend in the face. *Oops.*

"I tracked down an address for her husband Mark Foster. He lives on a farm." Nathan had only been to a farm once, on a primary school field trip. He'd gotten in trouble for pretending to jerk off a cow's udder and had to sit on the school bus for the rest of the day.

"You don't even know their names or genders. You have to be careful with this. You can't be impulsive. Remember how you felt when your dad dropped this bombshell on you? I don't want to see you get hurt."

Nathan slid down the drapes to the floor. His stepmum loved talking about how much she paid for these gold drapes. Nathan blew rings of smoke onto them.

"My mum was killed in a car accident a year ago. Just one year ago. What if I had found this photograph earlier? What if I had found her..." Nathan's voice wobbled with emotion that usually remained smothered in a haze of booze and sarcasm. Tears stung at his eyes. "I could've met her if I hadn't made myself forget, if I hadn't been fucking my life up. I don't want to waste anymore time. I have family out there, E."

"You have family in London."

"It's not the same. You know how they are with me." Eamonn knew. He had almost punched one of his cousins one Christmas for calling them faggots. "Not one of them contacted me when they heard I went to rehab. And my dad just wishes I wasn't here at all. I have real family out there, people who I could connect with, who could make me feel part of something, like the way you feel with your sisters and mum."

Nathan gulped back a lump in his throat. "And I want to know."

"Know what?" Eamonn asked.

"Why them and not me?" Nathan held back his tears. He'd already been mushier in the past twelve hours than he had in the past twelve years.

Eamonn didn't respond.

"E, still there?"

"Yeah."

"What are you thinking?"

"You know what I'm thinking. I'm thinking this is not a good idea, but you're going to do it anyway."

Eamonn might've been his Jiminy Cricket, but that didn't mean Nathan had to listen to his advice.

Chapter 4

LIAM

On his brother's advice, and only on his brother's advice, Liam put up help wanted signs in town. After a week, there hadn't been any bites. He gave Mark a few copies to put up at his office to spread the word.

Liam worked on a freelance graphic design project for a new restaurant opening up that winter night, which was unusually warm for June. Because he was at his computer, he had no choice but to hop over to bloody Facebook for a quick check on Kelly and Craig. They seemed to be enjoying a quick holiday in Sydney. Great. Wonderful. Liam had once wanted to whisk Kelly off to Sydney for a weekend trip to see Neil Finn play at the opera house. She said she was busy with work, but urged him to go with one of his brothers. Who knew what she and Craig were getting up to that weekend?

Liam wiped sweat off his brow. He couldn't feel the window air conditioning unit in his bedroom, and the ceiling fan barely helped. He missed the cool confines of Mark's house, when he wore a light sweater to dinner. He now sat in front of the computer in his boxers with a small fan blowing in the corner, Facebook stalking his ex when he should have been working on a graphic design project for one of his clients. What killed Liam was that he didn't know. He had been completely blindsided when Kelly dumped him and admitted to sleeping with Craig. He had no suspicions. He was too trusting, stupidly trusting. Only little kids trusted people that much.

Baaaaa. His sheep called out from the window.

"Aye, knock it off!" he yelled. "Go to sleep!"

The sheep continued making louder noises. He heard them shifting around in the field when they should be at rest.

"What are they doing out there?" he asked himself. He'd heard of sheep robbers sneaking onto farms and stealing the livestock. With larger, commercial operations around him, Liam's farm was the little guy, and he had to protect himself. Liam grabbed his shotgun, loaded it, and tiptoed outside. He was only in his pair of boxers, but he didn't care so long as his sheep were all right.

He followed the growing chorus of bleats. He stopped at the hoof house and hid against the wall.

Crunch. Crunch.

Those were footsteps. He definitely heard footsteps. Some asshole was on his property. Liam stilled himself and listened to their movement. Wheels squeaked as they moved on the grass. What were they wheeling? A wagon to cart them away?

Liam kept his gun flush against his chest. His dad had taught him and his brothers how to shoot, but all he'd shot were empty bottles and cans, not people.

I'm not going to shoot them. I'll just point my gun and that should be enough.

Liam exhaled a breath and counted to three.

1

2

3

He jumped out from behind the hoof house and pointed his gun at the sheep robber. "Aye!" His yell echoed across the field.

The man in front of him screamed five times as loudly. It was louder than his gunshot would've been, and it sent the sheep fleeing in all directions.

"Shit! Fuck! Bugger!" The man yelled at the sheep who brushed past him in a panic. His posh clothes and styled hair made him a dead-ringer for a city guy. He must've made a really wrong turn.

"Get the fuck away from me!" The man tried shooing them away, but the sheep all went in their own directions, zig-zagging and criss-crossing amongst each other, with the posh guy in the center. He dragged his suitcase through the soft grass, leaving two tracks in his wake.

"What the hell are you doing here?" Liam yelled.

"What the hell are they doing?" The man pointed at the flock with his cigarette. "Shit!"

He slipped and fell onto the grass. Well, what Liam hoped was just grass. Sheep were not potty trained, after all. The man, whose rusty head of hair reminded Liam of his niece and nephew, rolled around trying to get up. He pushed his hand into the ground for leverage, but it kept sinking into the wet grass, slick from a recent rainfall.

"A little bloody help here!" The man yelled. Surprisingly, he managed to keep his cigarette lit and in his free hand this whole time. Liam hated smokers, but he couldn't deny how impressive that was.

He gave the man a hand up, since he obviously could not

be a sheep robber, yet scowled at him the whole time. Grass stains covered his clothes.

"As I asked before, what the hell are you doing?" Liam asked. "You scared the sheep."

His livestock continued to scurry in all directions, and now his sheepdog was out and barking at them. It was as if Liam had fired off his shotgun. In moments, Mark would probably be out here.

"The cab dropped me off at the address, where there should be a front door."

"The cab dropped you at the edge of my field."

"You need to talk to Google Maps. The GPS in this area is all fucked up." The man took a drag of his cigarette.

"Could you not smoke on the premises?"

"I just went through a life-threatening, traumatic experience. I deserve some nicotine." He took another defiant puff.

"That was your fault. What were you doing sneaking through my field?"

"I do not appreciate the tone." The man eyed Liam up and down, blatantly checking him out and reminding Liam that he was only in boxers. "I see farmers' uniforms have changed since the days of Old McDonald."

Liam crossed his arms over his chest.

"Is this eleven Puriri Street?" the man asked.

"It's nine." Many people made that mistake. Liam had only established a residence on the land when he decided to move back, and online maps hadn't caught up yet. Mark lived at eleven Puriri Street, and a spark of worry ignited in his kid brother.

"Is it that house?" The man pointed with his cigarette at Mark's house across the field. The light of the living room glowed in the darkness.

"You're a bit sus. Who are you looking for?"

"Mark Foster."

"What for?"

The man stared at Liam for an extra second. Whatever his reason, he wasn't saying.

"Right. I take it that's his house over there. Thank you for your help." The man wheeled his suitcase across the field. Liam didn't trust him for a second and followed right behind him, not caring how little clothing he was wearing.

Nathan

Ah, New Zealand, the land where half-naked farmers followed you through dark fields at night.

At least this farmer was easy on the eyes, with his thick chest and ropey arms.

Not like Nathan was looking. He was focused on the house in front of him. It beckoned to him like a lighthouse in this sea of farm darkness. Nathan's head was still reeling from the combination of jet lag, Ambien, and mimosas he had on the plane. He didn't know what day it was, not because he was drunk but that whole international dateline business.

"What is your business with Mark Foster?" the farmer asked. Still following him. Still half-naked.

"It's personal," Nathan said.

"What do you mean personal?"

"I mean none of your bloody business." Nathan whipped his head around. "Either you're stalking me or blatantly checking out my bum. Whichever it is, please stop."

That left the farmer gasping for words. The tips of his ears turned red, something that brought the twist of a smile to Nathan's lips.

"What—I—no, I am not checking out anything, just this potential maniac going to see my brother for some mysterious reason."

"Brother?" Nathan's suitcase got caught on a rock. He packed way too much, but he didn't know how long he would be here, and he wanted to make sure he had appropriate outfits depending on how this all played out. He tugged on the handle, but the wheel was wedged and would not budge.

The farmer came around and lifted the full suitcase as if it were no heavier than a paperback novel. Nathan might've glimpsed his biceps at work.

"Thank you." Nathan took back the luggage handle. He looked into the milky grey-blue eyes of this farmer, which reminded him of the cloudy London sky he'd left behind this morning, or yesterday, or whatever time it was. "I come in peace. I promise."

He arrived in front of a modest, two-story house with warmly lit windows that hummed with life on the other side.

You can do this. You traveled halfway around the world to do this.

Mark looked Nathan up and down when he opened the door, not in a sexy way. Nathan wondered if he could tell. Did the hair or eyes give it away that Nathan was his late wife's bastard child?

"Hiya," Nathan said to the widower. He tried to read all the microexpressions creasing his face, but there was zero flash of recognition.

"I found him wandering across the field with my livestock," the farmer said. "He was looking for your house."

Nathan bit his lip. He felt even more embarrassed now. *Thanks a lot, sexy farmer.*

"Thanks, Liam," Mark said. He turned to Nathan. "Can I help you?"

And here it was. This was the moment. This was what his journey was about.

"Yes. You can. I am here because...wow, I just want to say what a beautiful house you have."

It had a lived-in feeling, like people actually liked being in this house. Unlike his dad's high-rise London flat and paternal grandparents' museum-esque abode. A hand-sewn quilt was draped over the couch and the coffee table had slight nicks in the wood, probably from children playing. It was the least posh place Nathan had been in, but it also was the one that felt the most like a home.

"Thank you," Mark said. "It's not for sale."

"Right. Though in this market..." Nathan was stalling for time, but he couldn't figure out why. The words were on his tongue! *Your late wife is my mother!*

"Why are you here?" Liam glared icy lasers at Nathan. He was screwing up Nathan's flow.

"I'm here..."

"Dad, what's going on?" A boy stumbled halfway down the stairs. His red hair swished and slopped across his head. Red hair!

That's my brother!

"Who's there?" A teenage girl followed behind him in a t-shirt and sweatpants and stopped at the step above him.

That's my sister!

"It's nothing," Mark said to them. "Why don't you go back upstairs? It's almost time for sleep."

"It's way past Uncle Liam's bedtime," the girl said with a smile at the farmer, who was in no mood for inside jokes apparently. They returned back into their rooms. Nathan's eyes landed on a family picture that was on the wall where they just stood. The four of them smiled at the beach. His mum had the prettiest smile, full of teeth, full of life.

Nathan had to catch his breath.

Mark turned back to him, waiting for an answer. His heavenly patience was showing cracks, whereas Liam's patience was nonexistent from the get-go. He did that windmill hand motion to get Nathan to spit it out.

Nathan froze with fear. What if they reacted poorly? Nathan had one shot with them, and Eamonn's warnings rushed back into his head. He didn't want to mess this up. The truth was on his lips, but in that moment, all Nathan wanted to do was lie. Lies were easy.

He noticed a stack of flyers inside, on the table beside the door.

"I'm here for the farmhand position."

"What?" Liam interjected.

"I saw one of the flyers you posted."

"It's actually Liam's farm." Mark eyed his designer outfit. "You're a farmhand?"

A spark of inspiration came to Nathan. That one improv class was about to pay off. "Of course not. I'm an actor. I'm researching a new role I'm shooting in a few weeks where I play a farmhand. It's...a gritty reboot of *Babe*."

"The kids movie about the pig?" Liam asked.

"I quite loved that movie," Mark said. "Are there no original ideas left?"

"Mark!"

"The director wants to shoot it almost cinema-verite style, and he tasked me with getting work on a sheep farm to prepare for the role."

"Can we confirm this with anyone?" Liam asked.

"I am a legitimate actor. You can look me up on IMDB." The production that Nathan was fired from hadn't taken down his credit yet. He knew that final credits wouldn't be confirmed until the film was locked and screened for the press months from now.

Mark scrolled to Nathan's page on his phone, which still had his headshot and bio, and nodded approvingly. Liam looked over his shoulder.

"The director for this film doesn't want to announce it to the press. He is planning to bring it as a surprise screening to the Cannes Film Festival."

"Why couldn't you come here in the morning?" Liam asked.

"I'm all screwed up from the time change. It's morning to me." That part Nathan wasn't lying about. He was wide awake, though that was also because of the adrenaline pumping through him.

"Well, this is an interesting development." Mark slipped his phone back into his pocket. "But my brother needs someone who can do the hard work. Lambing seasons gets very hectic. Do you have any experience working as a farmhand?"

"Yes. I gardened at university." The lies spat out of Nathan like bullets in a machine gun of self-preservation. *What the fuck am I doing? The only farmhand I'm familiar with is jerking off a random guy outside a barn!* "You can talk to my former employer, Eamonn Charles. He ran a farm at Uppercross College."

Liam crossed his arms. "What did you grow?"

Marijuana.

"Tomatoes."

"This isn't a tomato farm. Do you have any experience handling livestock?" Liam asked.

"Even better!" Nathan raised a pointed finger in the air. "I've been to some of the hottest clubs in London. I've had to navigate through drunk, sweaty, aggressive crowds. If you think those sheep are a handful, try getting to front of the bar when the line is ten people deep. Try carrying your friends home when they're too smashed to walk." So technically, Nathan was that drunk friend, but he empathized with his friends' struggle to lug him back to the hall.

"This is unbelievable!" Liam ran his hands through his hair, which was as thick as his beard. "You are supremely under-qualified for this job."

"What I lack in experience, I make up for in grit." Nathan had heard that in an inspirational movie before he passed out on his couch. It made the corner of Mark's lip turn up into a smile.

"So you're from London? My wife spent some time there years ago."

"You don't say?" Nathan's voice cracked on the last word.

"She studied at the Royal Academy for Dramatic Arts for a little bit. She was an actress, so I have a soft spot for them. Everyone gives them a hard time, but they are incredibly resilient, resourceful, and thick-skinned. At least, my wife was." Mark seemed to retreat into a fog of memories.

Liam softened just a bit. "I'm sorry, but you just don't have the experience necessary to handle this undertaking."

"So I'll learn!" Nathan felt so close, he didn't want to give up yet. "I've learned new accents and pages of new dialogue in hours. I'm trained in stage combat, too. I can certainly feed some sheep."

"It's a bit more strenuous than that."

"I've done boot camps at my gym. I know all about strenuous."

"There's something about you...you almost feel familiar..." Mark stared at him, and Nathan wondered what he was finding. "I have an extra room you can use."

"Mark!" Liam yelled. "Are you serious? The man could be a serial killer."

"If I was a serial killer, I would've packed lighter."

Mark laughed at the joke. Liam most certainly did not.

"Liam, have you gotten any other applicants?" Mark asked.

"It's only been a week."

"I can work for free," Nathan said.

"And the farm will get some free publicity once the film is released," Mark said. Nathan pointed at him to underline his point.

Nathan took a step toward Liam and was about to put a hand on his broad shoulder before pulling away. Liam was not ready to be friends.

"Like I said before, I come in peace." Nathan gave him an earnest look. He hoped he understood just how badly he wanted to be here without giving away as much.

"Fine." Liam must've realized this was a game Nathan wasn't going to let him win. "I suggest you get some rest then. We have a long day ahead of us tomorrow."

Chapter 5

<u>Nathan</u>

Mark had an extra bedroom where he allowed Nathan to stay. Nathan was exceedingly grateful, since he was a stranger who literally showed up on his doorstep. Liam did another Google check on Mark's computer and reluctantly came to the conclusion that Nathan was normal. How could someone that sexy be so painfully rigid? So he strolled through his sheep field and caused a commotion. Was that really so terrible?

"It has its own bathroom, so you'll have privacy." Mark turned on the lights. The room had the basics of a bed and dresser and not much more. "In the mornings, you can use the back door off the kitchen to go to the farm. It'll be less noisy."

"Thank you for letting me stay here." Nathan beamed at him. "And for advocating for me back there."

"No worries. Liam means well. He's still getting the hang of farming. Above all, he values honesty. So as long as you're straight up with him, there shouldn't be any problem."

"Right. I'm all about honesty." *Except when it comes to why I'm here.*

Mark pulled out two extra pillows from the closet. He showed Nathan how the shower worked and warned him that hot water could take a while. Nathan stopped listening after a moment. On top of the dresser was a picture from Mark and his mum's wedding day. She wore a sleeveless gown, and her hair fanned out under her veil. She could've been a Greek goddess.

"She was the most beautiful woman I'd ever seen," Mark said.

"How did you meet?"

"We grew up together, started dating in secondary school. I attended this parochial school where her father was the pastor. He was terrifying. Still is."

"So you two got together when you were twelve or thirteen?"

"Nah yeah, we got engaged our first year at university." Mark looked at her picture in disbelief, like he couldn't believe the amount of time that was. Nathan also looked in disbelief, because he just realized that his mother cheated on Mark with his father.

How could he ever tell this family the truth about who he was? They would never want anything to do with the illegitimate bastard son that represented one childhood sweetheart blatantly cheating on the other. It would destroy their storybook relationship. That must've been why his mum wanted nothing to do with him. But even so, something stuck out to Nathan. He saw lots of pictures of her on the walls, being such a wonderful mother to the boy and girl he saw on the steps. How could she have been so wonderful to them and then leave her other child on a doorstep? It seemed extreme.

Nathan realized he was holding the wedding picture with both hands, his fingers digging into the frame. He promptly put it back on the dresser. "I'm sorry for your loss."

"How do you know she's gone?" Mark asked.

"I assumed. By the way you talk about her."

"I suppose I'm still in mourning. We all are." Mark watched Nathan to make sure he was being careful with the picture.

"She seems great. From all the pictures I saw."

Mark laughed. "We have heaps of pictures. My wife was always taking on these projects. She'd read an article that said having out physical pictures of family members strengthens relationships and helps us remember them, especially when we get older.

"She was only forty-two years old. Car accident. She got caught in one of our torrential rain storms. It was hosing down that night. She loved driving, too, even though she could never settle on a radio station. It used to drive me crazy." Mark smiled at the memory, but Nathan saw the pain just beneath the surface. Nathan felt the same pain.

"You're crying," Mark said.

Nathan touched the tears on his cheeks. He wiped them away, but another round came. *What the fuck.*

"Are you all right?" Mark handed him a tissue from the bathroom.

"No." Sadly, that was the most truthful thing Nathan had said since he got there. "It, uh, just reminds me of my parents. They both died. Cancer."

"I'm so sorry."

Shit. That was a big lie. Nathan had panicked. He worried if he said that just his mum died, it might be suspicious. He thought about his dad and what he was doing at that moment. Before he took off, Nathan shot him off a quick email, letting him know he was doing some traveling to visit friends and clear his head. His dad wrote back *Have fun*. That was all he had to say. He didn't care where Nathan was going or how he was doing.

They stood in silence looking at the picture. Nathan worried that he made things too awkward with the parental death omission. Mark was going to ask him to leave. That usually happened when Nathan dared express any emotion.

"Fuck cancer," Mark said, cutting through the quiet.

"Fuck cancer in the ass. Without any lube." Nathan shot out. Mark let out a big, deep belly laugh and slapped Nathan on the back.

"You're a real dag, mate."

"Is that a good thing?"

Mark's laugh let him know the answer was a resounding yes. "I'm knackered. I'm going to turn in. Make sure to set your alarm for four. You need to be at the farm by four-fifteen."

"A.M.?"

"Correct."

"I knew that. I thought because we were in the Southern Hemisphere, a.m. meant p.m., like how the water flushes in the opposite direction and June is considered winter. Just want to check."

"Let me know if you need anything." He left Nathan alone in his room. Nathan kept looking at the wedding picture. He took out the Polaroid of his mum and dad from his suitcase and compared them side-by-side. Yep, it was her. No doubt. She was gorgeous.

Nathan crept out of his room, with the wedding picture in hand. He thought about all the wonderful memories that took place in this house, memories he wasn't a part of. He thought of his mum's relationship with Mark and her life here. So many thoughts. So many revelations. It was too much noise in his head. Everything was feeling real, too real.

Mark had gone upstairs, leaving the first floor dark and quiet. Nathan had zero farming skills for his new job, but there was one life skill he had acquired over the past few years that had served him well.

Swiping travel-sized liquor bottles from the airplane drink cart.

Nathan reached into his carry-on messenger bag and took out three dollhouse-sized tequilas. He had never needed anything so badly in his life.

Chapter 6

LIAM

Liam woke up at four and began his rounds checking on the sheep, refilling their food and water troughs. The sheep had calmed down after their encounter with his new "farm-hand" last night. He used air quotes because he was far from sold on Nathan's ability to do any type of manual labor, no matter how many tomatoes he grew and how many people he shoved out of the way to get a drink.

By four-forty-five, the sheep all had food and water and there was still no sign of Nathan. Liam wasn't surprised. He had little faith in his new employ, but he still found it insulting. This wasn't a fun experience for a movie role. This was Liam's business.

Liam walked into Mark's kitchen softly so that he didn't wake his family upstairs. He opened the bedroom door and was greeted by Nathan's ass.

Nathan was sprawled across the bed, completely passed out. His trousers were half off, exposing Calvin Klein oxblood red underwear. One shoe remained dangling from his foot. For a second, he thought the guy was dead, until he heard the sounds of peaceful snoring.

"Time to get up," Liam said.

More snores. They sounded like he was slurping soup through his nose.

"All right now. Get up." Liam couldn't believe the state of the room. His suitcase vomited out clothes across the floor, right next to a tiny bottle of tequila that they hand out on airplanes.

"Nathan."

Nathan reached into his underwear and scratched his bum.

"You were supposed to be at the farm by four-fifteen. It's almost five."

He emitted a long, droning snore and got more comfortable in bed. Or on bed in his case since he hadn't gotten under the covers.

"I know you can hear me." Liam didn't care if he sounded like a hard-ass. This was unacceptable. He couldn't believe Mark had sided with this guy and allowed him a chance. "I'm not going to wait around for you. I have work to do."

Crickets. And soup-slurping snores. Nathan put his arm over one of his ears to block out the noise.

"You have left me no choice then."

Liam walked into the bathroom. He grabbed the empty trash can and placed it in the shower. He turned on the water. Like his own shower, it took a few minutes to get warm and the first gust was pure ice cold. During the darkest winter months, Liam would force himself to take cold showers to wake himself up. He felt the water with his finger and lurched it back.

He didn't warn Nathan when he doused him with a

bucket of cold water. The liquid launched into the air and landed smack on his bum. Nathan jumped up and screamed at the top of his lungs. He tripped inside his tangled up pants and fell to the floor.

"Bloody hell!" Nathan yelled.

"My thoughts exactly. You're late. You were supposed to be at the farm thirty minutes ago."

"I think I have hypothermia."

"That will be the least of your problems if you don't get to the farm immediately."

"You could've tapped me on the bloody shoulder!" Nathan pulled up his pants. He rubbed his temples. "Jesus."

"Keep your voice down. You're going to wake Mark and the kids."

"I think I should. I have to warn them that their uncle is a fucking psychopath." Nathan stumbled to the bed and plopped down. His soggy underwear squished on the sheets, making him leap up again. "Shit!"

"Get dressed and get to the farm. We have heaps of work to do. I will see you out there in twenty minutes." Liam stopped before the left the room. He found a picture of Mariel on a hiking trip on the nightstand. "What are you doing with this?"

"I, uh, the frame was dusty. I was going to clean it."

Maybe Nathan was the fucking psychopath here. Liam got in his face, where he was met with a gust of alcohol-soaked breath. "Have you been drinking?"

"No. That's my antibacterial mouthwash. It's very strong."

"I don't know what you're doing here. All I know is that you came out of nowhere and snuck onto our property yesterday. You have to earn my trust, because right now, you don't have it. Any questions?"

"Yes. Does my twenty minutes start now or once you leave?"

Liam turned and walked out. He wished he had another bucket of cold water.

TWENTY-FIVE MINUTES LATER, Nathan met him at the barn. Liam was going to say something, but it wasn't worth it. He was honestly surprised he was only five minutes late. Nathan almost tripped over a patch of grass. He inhaled a puff from his cigarette and walked with a wobble that reminded Liam of Jack Sparrow in *Pirates of the Caribbean*, or Johnny Depp in real life. How much "antibacterial mouthwash" did he imbibe?

"Are you sure you want to wear that?" Liam gestured to his jeans and long-sleeve T-shirt that had FCUK written across it. That stood for French Connection, a very posh brand of clothing Liam had seen on people in Wellington nightclubs.

"If we're critiquing outfits, can we start on yours next?" Nathan pointed at Liam's mud-splattered jeans and wrinkled flannel shirt.

"You're going to get dirty. You're going to be on your hands and knees today."

"You sound like my ex-boyfriend."

Liam felt his ears get red. He got a flash of what that entailed early this morning, and he might've just thought about Nathan with his pants down again.

Nathan smirked with his cigarette hanging out of his mouth. He put his sunglasses on, covering his bloodshot eyes.

"The sun isn't up," Liam said.

"Yet." Nathan pushed them up his nose. "I'm prepared."

"Are you hung over?"

"Hangovers are for amateurs."

"Are you still munted? Drunk?"

"You ask a lot of questions. We should probably get to work, Liam."

"I don't appreciate your attitude. If you don't want to work here, then leave."

"I'm happy to work here. I guess I'm just drying off from this morning, when I was drenched in a surprise ice bath. That was the *only* thing you could think of to wake me up?" Nathan quirked an eyebrow at him. "I don't see why we have to get up so early. The sheep would still be here at noon."

"Noon? Is that when you get up?"

"Again with these questions." Nathan puffed out a cloud of smoke. "Do you have any coffee? I have a headache like a motherfucker."

Liam was too frustrated to roll his eyes. He had a feeling Nathan would be quitting by the end of the day, and then he could get back to his regular routine. "There's no smoking on the premises."

"Somehow that doesn't surprise me. I'm almost done."

"Not almost. Now, please."

"Just two more puffs. Or three."

Liam nodded and strained to smile. "Those are nice sunglasses. Can I see them?"

"Sure." Nathan took them off and handed them over. Liam studied the sleek plastic frames.

"These are sweet as."

"Sweet as what?" Nathan asked.

"Huh? Just sweet as. We like saying that here. Sweet as, mean as."

"Do they not like finishing similes in New Zealand?"

Nathan exhaled smoke from his cigarette and held out his hand. "Can I have those back?"

"They're designer, I'm assuming." Liam ripped the cigarette out of Nathan's mouth and stubbed the butt on one lens, then the other. The ash burned peepholes through the plastic.

"Those are Dolce and Gabbana!" Nathan yelled.

"I'm more of a Gucci man." Liam tossed them back to him. "Let's get on with it. Are you ready to shovel some hay?"

NATHAN

The answer was no. Most definitely no.

Nathan's head felt like a buoy bobbing in a sea of whiskey. He didn't remember how much he drank. Enough to get him to stop thinking about his mum and his family and feelings that he hadn't thought about in a long time.

Until he was nearly drowned a few hours later by this monster of a boss. Nathan had a lot to process over the past few days, and hours after encroaching on his mother's family, he was being thrown headfirst into farming. It was a bit much.

And now the sun was coming out and he had no sunglasses.

Liam had him clean all the dirty, smelly hay off the barn floors where the sheep rest.

"It's all smells like shit. How will I know which one to remove?" Nathan asked.

"You'll know," he said gravely.

Nathan scraped off hay mashed into the floor, hay covered in things he did not want to think about. He worked and worked until his body could take no more and his muscles wanted to explode in agony.

"Is there a break room where I can get a cup of coffee? I really need some coffee."

"It's not time for a break."

"Aren't there labor laws that mandate I get a break?"

"You've been at this for ten minutes." Liam checked his watch. "Technically nine minutes. We need to get this hay picked up so we can spread new hay."

Liam left to get new hay. Nathan stuck out his tongue at his back as he walked away. "*Technically nine minutes*," Nathan mockingly repeated to himself. He was teased for being too posh yet these sheep got fresh hay like they were staying in a suite at the Ritz Carlton.

Nathan rarely faced the day without coffee. His head was in a ten-point-oh earthquake that wouldn't stop. He couldn't do this without coffee. Fuck, he *was* hung over. Rehab had turned him into an amateur. He would have to rebuild his tolerance, which would be really annoying. His buoy of a head was being slammed by wave after wave of residual liquor. He was so hung over he couldn't even describe it in metaphors anymore.

Fuck.

"You're missing some hay."

"It's good enough. These animals don't even use the toilet. They can live with some dirty hay in their barn."

"Not if it causes infection and disease. I can't be a sheep farmer if all my sheep are dead."

"Well, that's a morbid thought."

"Nathan, I know you like to think I'm being a prick to mess with you, but this isn't about you. This is my livelihood."

"Sorry." Nathan wished there were easier ways to get to

know his new family. But telling the truth still would've been more painful than what he was going through this morning.

He could barely see. The headache, the alcohol, it all sloshed together. Ten-point-oh earthquake and tsunamis. It was basically that movie *The Day After Tomorrow* inside his skull and stomach. "Are you sure there's no coffee?"

"No. We can break in a few hours."

"*A few hours*?"

"If you need water, there's a faucet and refillable bottles in the barn."

"*Water*?"

Nathan sighed and continued cleaning off the rancid hay. Rancid was an understatement. Everything here reeked. It was like living in the bottom of a public toilet.

After another eternity (or an hour, according to his phone), he was done with the hard part. He brought Liam into the barn and showed him the cleaned floors.

"I did it. Break?"

"You did it? I still see moldy hay on the floor. What do you call that?" Liam kicked at a patch of hay that was really stuck on there. Nathan tried but he wasn't Hercules.

"It's good enough."

"No, it's not. If you're going to be a farmhand, you have to take it seriously."

"The sheep won't know the difference." Nathan squinted to ease some of the pain of vision from this epic hangover. Had he ever been this hung over in the past? Probably, but he was smart enough to keep drinking in those instances.

"I'm going to redo it. Bloody…" Liam trailed off.

"This is on you for giving me something so difficult," Nathan said, although he did feel bad. This was the guy's livelihood, after all. The only time in his life Nathan used a broom or a rake was to play Quidditch. "I did try."

"I'll give you something easier then." A smile quirked on Liam's full lips.

"Why are you smiling?"

"Because I know what you're going to do."

SHIT. Literally shit.

Liam wanted Nathan to shovel all the manure around the farm into the manure pit.

"There's a manure pit?" It sounded like the most disgusting thing to Nathan.

"We haven't yet set up indoor plumbing for the sheep. They're demanding bidets. It's going to be costly." Liam smirked. "This is real simple. Anywhere you see shit, shovel it up and put it into the manure pit."

The name was incredibly accurate. Nathan stared into a massive hole in the ground. Flies and bugs buzzed around it.

"Why do you keep this?"

"I use the manure to fertilize the dirt."

"How green of you."

Liam pointed to a piece of manure by their feet. Nathan yelped and jumped back. At least Liam found that humorous. He was more into torture than Christian Grey.

"Let's do a practice round." Liam handed him a shovel. Nathan couldn't even enjoy watching his biceps flex.

Nathan bent over and shoveled it up. It was heavier than expected; the weight crushed his already-sore back and strained his arm muscles. *What were these bloody sheep eating?*

Liam pointed to the manure pit. Nathan's shovel wobbled as he struggled to carry over his load. He had a lean figure carved from hours of spin and pilates classes. He didn't have the musculature for this.

"Now, just toss it into the pit."

The smell of the pit was even worse than Nathan's most treacherous nightmares. It was the nuclear cloud over this whole farm. It choked his lungs and punched at his stomach.

"You don't smell that?"

"I'm used to it." Liam waited for Nathan to do his job.

Sweat poured down Nathan's face. His arms could barely hold the shovel anymore. Every organ cried out for any type of hydration. Coffee, more alcohol. Good Lord, even water.

"Just toss it in," Liam said.

Nathan couldn't hear anything. It was all static. Static in the earthquakes and tsunamis. *That rancid smell.*

But he did it. He tossed his shovel of manure into the pit.

"There you go! See, that was easy."

And then Nathan barfed. Three times.

His stomach wrung itself out. He heaved in air salted with the scent of crap. Liam handed him his water bottle.

"Thank you." Nathan took a sip, then he barfed again. Apparently he wasn't done.

"Feel better?" Liam asked.

Once Nathan knew it was over, he took a sip of water, swirled it around in his mouth, and spat it out. Then he chugged the rest of the bottle. He couldn't recall being so thirsty.

"There's a faucet of clean water in the barn. Make sure to stay hydrated. I mean it. I'll go and fill up a bottle for you. Instead of a cigarette break, take a water break."

Nathan appreciated his concern, which he didn't expect to find from Farmer Tight-ass.

"Sweet as." Liam slapped Nathan on the back. "Don't worry, cuz. Everyone chunders their first time at the manure pit. You'll get used to the smell in no time."

NATHAN ACTUALLY CONTINUED SHOVELING manure that morning. Not pretending. Like, actually doing it. The grossness of the task outweighed the gross feeling of his hangover. The bottle after bottle of water he drank eased his headache and gave him renewed strength. And he hated to admit Liam was right about anything, but he did get used to the smell eventually—or rather, his disgust was subsiding into strong dislike. He puffed out his chest with pride when he looked out on a field free of shit.

By the time he was finished, his arms and shoulders ached so badly he thought they were going to slide off. He discovered new muscles and new kinds of bodily pain. His back hunched with acute soreness. The only respite was that it was a cloudy day. He supposed he didn't need his sunglasses.

Nathan checked his phone. Three hours had passed. Time flew, but when would this day actually end?

He sunk to the floor of the hoof house and rested his head against the opening to one of the sheep sleeping areas. There was an aisle in the center with resting areas on both sides, like a sheep apartment complex. One sheep rested in the fresh hay, hay that he had moved there.

"You're welcome, by the way," Nathan said to her. He assumed it was a girl since Liam had said something about the ewes using this space. "Would it kill you and your brethren to learn to use the toilet?"

She let out a *baaaa*. He found it kind of endearing.

"This is the life, isn't it? Eating, sleeping, shitting. If you add shagging and getting smashed, we could be twins." He looked at the name scrawled on her collar. Matilda. Of course Liam gave his sheep such proper names. That tracked.

"Is it all right if I call you Tilly? Tilly is probably what all your friends call you." Nathan moved a patch of hay closer to her head, so she could have more of a pillow.

Tilly closed her eyes contentedly and nuzzled into the hay. Another surge of pride hit Nathan, something he hadn't felt since the day he aced his first audition at boarding school.

"I see Liam allows you to get fat and lazy. Us farmhands don't have it as easy."

"She's pregnant."

Nathan jumped back when Liam approached. He couldn't stand up, though. His body would not let him.

"I needed to take a break. I'll get back up soon."

"Here." Liam handed him a mug.

Nathan nearly somersaulted with joy when the aroma of caffeine and ground beans filled his nose. "This is real coffee."

He took a healthy gulp and let it burn his throat.

"I have milk and sugar in my house."

"No. This is brilliant." Even though Nathan was desperate for caffeine, that wasn't just what made this cup amazing. It had a mocha flavor with a hint of spice. "This is really good. Pardon me. It's really *good as*. Did I say it right?"

"Hard out. That means yes." Liam's smile sent a pulse of

energy through Nathan. "There's a coffee farm the next town over. I give him wool, and he hooks me up with beans."

Life slowly came back to Nathan. Liam handed him a full water bottle.

"Drink that, too. You need to stay—"

"Hydrated."

Nathan did as instructed. He didn't know water could taste so good. He felt it cool his dry, salty insides. "Is it also from a farm?"

"No. I think you were just very thirsty."

True. It had been a while since Nathan drank plain water. His hydration usually came from coffee and the mixers and fruit garnishes in his drinks.

"Keep drinking. I don't need you passing out on your first day." Liam watched with care as he drank the water. Nathan found it rare for people to be concerned about his wellbeing, and Liam's gaze was both a welcome and uncomfortable spotlight. "You did a good job out there, eventually."

"I've been told I have a talent for shoveling shit. Metaphorically and now literally. When do we stop working for the day?"

Liam smiled at the pure exhaustion in his voice, his full lips peeking out from his full beard. "We'll have lunch soon, then a few more hours and we should be done. I like to work before the sun is strongest."

"Cheers, mate." He handed back the mug. Their fingers touched for a second, like an electric shock, before both pulled away.

"I'll get you a refill of both." Liam walked back to his house, and Nathan watched Farmer Tight-ass's tight ass bounce around in those jeans.

Chapter 7

LIAM

"How did today go?" Mark asked him that night. Liam helped his brother prepare dinner in the kitchen. He had offered to do the cooking, but Mark shot him down every time. He said that after a day in an office, he looked forward to working with his hands and crafting something.

"Today was...not terrible. Though not great, either. He had quite the attitude."

It frustrated Liam all over again, but it also made the beginnings of a smile spark on his face. He didn't know why. He knew there had to be a real farmhand out there who would've done the work without complaining and wouldn't have shown up blatantly hung over.

"Dad!" Franny burst into the kitchen holding the remote control in her hands. "The remote is busted. It's not working."

Mark opened the back and checked the batteries. "Maybe they're out of juice?"

"I thought we just replaced them."

"We'll deal with it later, Fran."

Franny let out a perfectly teenage ughhhh then left.

"It's going to be a very interesting next few years," Mark said with a knowing smile. Liam felt like he was also raising some kind of child, having to follow Nathan around today.

"I don't have the time to train the Brit. I have a farm to run," Liam said.

"He'll get the hang of it, just like you did. This is a new experience for him. It could get you some good exposure if his movie's a hit. Until then, enjoy the free labor."

"I couldn't find any articles about a gritty *Babe* reboot being produced."

"There will be once the movie comes out. I'm glad you're looking up something else on your computer except your ex-girlfriend." Mark tossed vegetables around in a wok.

Liam hadn't been on social media at all today. And this was the first time today he thought about Kelly or Craig.

"He's still on a probationary period," Liam said.

A little bit later, they all sat down for dinner. Mark, Franny, and Walt took their regular seats.

"Is Nathan coming?" Mark asked.

"I told him about it." Liam got up and knocked on Nathan's door. Music blasted from the other side. "Nathan. Are you coming to dinner, cuz? Nathan?"

The door swung open, and Nathan stood in front of him dressed like a total gentleman. He wore a dark blazer, crisp white shirt, dark jeans, and shined black shoes. His rusty hair was combed to the side and the front strands fell into his bright green eyes. He should be at a fancy dinner in Wellington or London.

Liam couldn't talk for a second. He became very aware of his accelerated heart rate. The man was lousy in the field but cleaned up damn well.

"Are you going out?" Liam asked.

"You said there was a dinner tonight."

"It's not *a* dinner. Just dinner. At the house. With the family." Liam was having trouble speaking in complete sentences. He couldn't believe this was the same guy puking on his property this morning.

"Oh, sounds lovely."

"Nah yeah." *Blink, dammit.* "We're ready to start. Just waiting on you."

Nathan waltzed past him, his musky cologne making Liam a bit dizzy.

"Sorry I'm late." Nathan waved to the others. His hand dropped when he looked at Franny and Walt. Liam noticed a quick change overtake his face, shock mixed with something else, like a cloud passing over the sun. And then it was gone.

"Gidday!" Walt said.

"I'm Franny and this is my brother Walt," his niece said.

"Cheers. It's a pleasure to meet you." Nathan shook both of their hands. He was at his most polite, something Liam didn't think he was capable of. "A family dinner. How quaint."

"Wait!" Franny yelped. Nathan stopped himself from sitting down.

"What is it?" Liam asked.

"That's...that's Mum's chair." She and her brother looked to Mark. Nathan held onto the chair, but did not sit.

"I can move elsewhere."

"It's...wait one moment." Mark went into the kitchen. He came back out with a folding chair. "I keep these for extra company. They're a bit rickety, but should get the job done. That's, uh, where their mum used to sit."

Nathan put his hand up and kept the mood jolly. "Not a problem. I get it."

He sat in the folding chair, but Liam noticed that his hand lingered on Mariel's old chair.

NATHAN

"Nathan, do you need a drink?" Mark asked.

Yes, yes, a thousand times yes! Nathan wanted to scream out. His body was a garbage heap of sore muscles from the day that would not end. They had stopped working in the fields at three today, but it felt like midnight. He didn't take a nap. He just lay on the bed staring at the ceiling, willing the pain to stop.

On top of that, he was sitting across the table from his half-brother and half-sister but couldn't say a word. There they were! His siblings! All Nathan wanted to do was look at them, but he didn't want to seem like a creep. He did notice that Franny dyed her hair. The red roots were leeching out. If she let them grow out, with her porcelain skin, her rust-colored locks would absolutely glow.

Oh, and he was sitting next to the chair where his real-life mother used to sit. It was all a bit much. Every part of him cried out for a handle of whiskey, but he didn't want to make a bad impression in front of everyone. Liam had already caught him grossly hungover.

"We're having a beer. Do you want one?" Mark held up his bottle, then nodded his head behind him at the kitchen. "They're in the fridge."

Nathan's eyes darted the other way, to the liquor cabinet. He caught Liam looking at him with a suspicious glint in his eye. He probably wondered how the hell Nathan knew where the liquor cabinet was. He was like a bloodhound when it came to libations.

"I'll stick with water. I need to stay hydrated." Nathan

glanced at Liam, who'd been looking at him a lot tonight. *He was onto me.* Liam went into the kitchen to get a beer for himself.

"Nathan, would I be able to read your script? It sounds like an awesome idea," Franny said.

"There is no script. We're improvising all of it. I'll be doing actual farm work and portraying Farmer Hoggett."

"How can they have animals improvise?" Liam swung through the kitchen door and returned with his drink.

"I will be reacting off of them. It's how the director works. Anything goes. I'm very excited because as an actor—"

"What's the director's name?" Liam asked.

"Jasper Cort. His work has been mainly experimental." Nathan met him out one night and knew he'd be able to cover for him.

"You're so inquisitive, Liam."

"You raise a heap of questions, Nathan."

They locked eyes for an extra moment. *Game on.*

Nathan dug into his chicken and vegetables. "I am famished."

"Stop," Liam said coldly.

"What?" Nathan asked with a mouth full of food.

"We pray first."

"Seriously? Are you part of a cult?"

"We say a prayer thanking the Lord for our dinner every night," Walt said.

"Oh."

"It's a tradition Mum started. Would you like to lead the prayer?" Franny asked. "You get to make a new one."

"Me? Just so you know, the last time I was in a church, I was on my knees but for completely non-religious reasons."

Mark's eyes widened in panic. Liam looked about ready to spit his beer out.

"Because I was cleaning the floors," Nathan added. "Okay, let's give it a whirl. Right, I see we're all holding hands."

Liam held Nathan's hand and squeezed it tight to keep him on track.

"Um, Dear Lord," Nathan began, absolutely at a loss for words. The only time he called out to God was during sex, and considering the lack of stamina of his last few sexual partners, the Lord was not listening. "Thank you for this food. Thank you for being...a friend. You've traveled down from heaven and back again. Your nutrients are true. Lord, you are a pal and a confidant."

"Is that *The Golden Girls* theme song?" Mark asked.

"I...is it? I was just spitballing here."

Liam rolled his eyes and turned to Nathan again. "Can't you be serious for one—"

"We love that show!" Mark said. He and the kids laughed.

"How did you know we liked it?" Franny asked.

"Sofia's my favorite," Walt said.

"You watch *The Golden Girls*?" Nathan asked. "But you're all so...straight. I mean, I didn't know it was broadcast here."

"I don't watch it," Liam said.

"I figured, since you have no sense of humor," Nathan shot back.

The table got quiet. Mark and the kids shared a solemn look.

"My wife loved that show. They rerun it on one of the television stations, and she got us all hooked."

"She even had a pillow with the characters on it. Is it still in the basement with her other stuff?" Walt asked his dad.

"Still there, son. My wife was a bit of a hoarder," Mark said with a laugh.

"So is my dad. Was." Nathan took a sip of water. "Your wife had great taste."

He took it as some kind of sign. Maybe he and his mum could've bonded over watching episodes, like so many gay men and their mothers had in the past. He held up his glass. "For my prayer, let's do a cheers to Mariel, shall we?"

"Hard out," Mark said.

"To a wonderful woman, full of love and mystery and wonder. Mariel, if you can hear us, we think about you everyday," Nathan said, with more seriousness than he expected. His voice got thick, and the table let out a solemn, uniform "Amen."

He looked over at Liam, expecting to find the suspicious glint in his eye, but the farmer nodded warmly at him, his ice blue eyes twinkling in the light. It unexpectedly sent a shiver up Nathan's spine.

"Let's eat," Nathan said.

Chapter 8

LIAM

The next morning, Liam waited for Nathan on the farm. He checked his watch. It was four-thirty-five. No sign of Nathan. The first traces of sunlight cracked through the dark sky. It didn't matter how much this mysterious stranger charmed his family last night. He had a job to do. And that job started at quarter past four in the morning.

Liam stormed across the field. Right before he reached the side door off the kitchen, it swung open, and Nathan popped out. It was a surprise to Liam, who thought he'd have to do the water trick again.

"Good morning!" Nathan said. He wore his jeans, which were matted with dirt and grass stains from yesterday, and a black v-neck shirt that hugged his chest, showing off lean muscles just under the fabric.

"You're late." Liam crossed his arms.

"I don't know what happened. My snooze alarm never went off." Nathan breezed past him to the farm.

"Did you hit the snooze?"

"You have to hit it?"

"Yes." Liam clicked the side door shut. "It doesn't snooze automatically. When your alarm goes off, you hit the snooze button—" Liam didn't waste his breath. Nathan seemed like someone who was always fashionably late. He marched across the field, wobbling a little bit, but that seemed like normal tiredness and not inebriation. Liam clocked his perky bum in those designer jeans and did not mind the view.

Nathan waited for him outside his shed while Liam grabbed gloves. There was no front porch. Liam had put out two turned-over buckets. That was the extent of his outdoor furniture.

"We're starting in the hoof house," Liam said, handing him a pair of thick gloves he remembered from yesterday. "You're going to scrape the hay off the floor, like you attempted yesterday."

"Would it be all right I start off with a cup of coffee?"

"You just got here."

"You've seen what I'm like without coffee." Nathan cocked his eyebrows at Liam, as if he needed a reminder of the mess he was yesterday. "All I need is one cup." Nathan seesawed his head. "Two cups."

"All right." Little did he know, but Liam already had a fresh pot going. He figured Nathan would need the caffeine jolt. But he chose to play the part of gruff boss.

Nathan pulled open the screen door, then front door, and sprinted to the kitchen. He picked up the empty mug next to the coffee pot and poured himself a cup.

"This is the best coffee I've ever had." Nathan took a whiff of the coffee before inhaling half of it. He picked up Liam's mug from the sink. "Want a refill?"

"Sure. I'm glad you like it," Liam said. Nathan handed over the mug and sat on the kitchen island, which should've annoyed Liam, but he let it slide. "I want to thank you for last night."

"Can you be more specific?"

"Mariel's chair." Liam thought about the prayer Nathan said for his late sister-in-law, how surprisingly heartfelt it was. There was more to Nathan than sarcasm, apparently.

"I get it." A wave of seriousness washed over Nathan's face as he shook off the nice words. "She sounds like the dog's bollocks."

"She was kind of a rebel. It's not hard to be when your parents have enormous sticks up their arses." Liam stood against the wall where the kitchen became the living room. "Speaking of...Mark told me, about your parents."

"Right."

"I'm sorry."

"It's nothing. Well, not nothing. Just...in the past." Nathan's face went from normal to red immediately. Liam figured it was hard for him to hide with his light skin. He found it endearing. There was one part to Nathan that couldn't be hidden in charm and bullshit.

"Mine carked it when I was a teenager. Two heart attacks, a year apart. Bloody strange." It felt like yesterday still. Liam never stopped thinking about them. "Do you ever forget that they're gone? Like, you'll be doing laundry or something, and suddenly it'll hit you all over again."

"Right," Nathan said awkwardly. The pain seemed to be coming back to him, judging by the continued blush on his cheeks. Liam cursed himself for revealing that.

"I'm sorry. I shouldn't have brought it up."

"You may want to work on your smalltalk topics," Nathan said.

"I don't find too many people in my position, so I try to connect with them when I can. I know how rough it can be."

"I prefer not to talk about it, frankly." Nathan poured himself another cup of coffee, walked into the living room, and sat on the arm of the couch.

"Finish up your coffee. We should get out there." Liam put his mug in the sink, washed it out, and replaced it next to the coffeemaker in its rightful place. Clouds swirled in the dark blue sky as more of the sun made itself known.

"Why hello," he heard Nathan say.

It was just then that he remembered that he'd left his laptop on the couch last night. After going on Facebook.

Fuck.

Liam darted into the living room and tried to pull the laptop out of Nathan's hands, but Nathan realized that he'd hit on gold. Liam reached over Nathan, who held out the laptop away from him. Kelly's face took up the screen.

"You really didn't want me to see this," Nathan said. "And it's not even porn."

"Just give it back. We need to get out in the field."

Liam's shoe slipped on the rug. He fell onto Nathan, and they both tumbled onto the couch. Liam was right on top of him and could feel the heat of his body. He could feel those lean muscles under that black shirt. He could smell the deodorant under Nathan's arms. Their eyes met, and neither one of them moved for a second.

Kelly and Craig smiled at them from the screen.

Liam shut the laptop and sat up. "Time for work."

NATHAN

Nathan got to work cleaning the dirty hay off the hoof house floor. He was determined to be a better farmhand today, but the raging pain clanging inside his head was making this a challenge. Not drinking seemed to feel worse than drinking too much. He'd been through withdrawal before. He had to work through his pain with farm chores. Nathan wanted to do a good job, especially when he pictured his conversation with Liam about his parents. Here was a guy who legitimately lost his parents, and Nathan shat all over that with a fake story. *Why did I have to say that lie to Mark? Because I wanted him to like me. How fucked is that?*

The lie would keep him safe. He couldn't let on that he was Mariel's son. Not yet. Not when he'd just started connecting with Franny and Walt. Maybe if Liam and his family liked Nathan, then they wouldn't banish him from the farm when they realized he was a bastard child. A redheaded black sheep bastard.

He worked through the morning, making sure to drink lots of water, which eased his headache. He finished by mid-morning and joined Liam back in the barn. He put a smile on his face and proudly proclaimed the farm shit-free. He'd never be able to spend more time with his new siblings and find out more details about his mother's life if he was banished from Liam's farm. This was the acting job of his life, and unlike his real acting career, he couldn't fuck this up.

Nathan stumbled back when he walked in on Liam in front of a line of sheep butts.

"Am I interrupting?" he asked suggestively.

"No. You are just in time. You can help me crotch."

"Crotch? Like..." Nathan pointed to his own crotch. "That kind of crotch?"

"Yes. It's called crotching." Liam used a pair of shears on the backside of one of the ewes.

"Huh. I'm surprised the gays weren't the first to use crotch as a verb."

Liam waved him over with the shears. Nathan kneeled beside him.

"Crotching involves cutting off the excess wool around a ewe's udder and nether regions. If there's dirty wool around the udders, it could pass bacteria to the lambs when they nurse. And cleaning ewes up in the vaginal area makes it easier to check on things when they're giving birth."

"So you're basically giving these ewes a bikini wax?"

"I'm not sure what that is."

"I know women in London who shave their fannies before they go into labor, although they do it because they know their husbands are filming their birth. And some of them have a really cute doctor."

"To each their own, I suppose." Liam shot Nathan a lazy smile that lingered in his own crotch. The ewe bleated as Liam sheared away. "Can you hold the ewe still? This will go much faster if there's two of us."

Nathan stood over the ewe and held her on both sides. His hands trembled slightly as his fingers disappeared into her thick wool coat. He jumped back when she let out a noise.

"You don't have to clamp her in place. Be gentle."

"Right." Nathan put his hands on her body while giving her some personal space, like the time in school he had to slow dance with a girl. "So, who's Kelly Harmon?"

The shear made a *snip snip* sound as it lopped off more wool. Nathan had a feeling he hit a nerve, but curiosity got the better of him. He had a bad habit of egging people on. It might've been another one of his addictions.

"Is she a crush? She's a pretty girl. I'm kind of over blondes, but to each his own."

Snip snip. Liam didn't say anything. The shears spoke for

him. Nathan couldn't see his face, he was practically buried in the ewe's snatch. *Why would Liam be so embarrassed?*

"Is she an ex?"

"Yes, and she's dating my best friend. Former best friend. Now you know who Kelly Harmon is." Liam had a dead serious look on his face as he motioned with his shears for Nathan to move to the next ewe.

"That's rough. Really rough. If you tell me where they live, I'll gladly slash their tires."

"No thank you." Liam snipped away.

"Relationships are bollocks anyway," Nathan said. "It's like here's this person that you say you love and would do anything for, and then the next day it's like 'So long. You're dirt to me. Sod off.' How does that make any sense?"

Liam didn't respond, but Nathan could tell by the softness of his snips that he agreed somewhat with that assessment.

The ewe let out a bleat that Nathan felt vibrate in his hands.

"You're doing great. He's almost done. Don't hurt her!"

"I'm not. She's just being melodramatic."

"It will be over soon," Nathan cooed to her. He found himself rubbing her sides as if he were a parent, and it seemed to calm her down. "Trust me, I know your pain."

"Oi?" Liam looked up.

"I crotch myself on a regular basis."

Liam stopped mid-snip. "You do?"

"I like to keep things neat and tidy."

"I don't need to hear this." Liam focused on shearing.

"You don't trim down there?" Nathan asked.

Liam didn't answer, but the tops of his ears turned red. It was a delightful sight, much better than the grumpy snipper.

"So you're all natural then? Everything is in full bloom down under?"

"Down under is Australia." More red.

"Or do you trim the mound but leave the balls and taint as the Lord intended?"

"You are at work, Nathan! This is not an appropriate conversation."

"I think it's very germane to the task at hand."

"You are crude. Has anyone ever told you that?"

"On occasion."

They moved onto the next ewe.

"Just breathe," Nathan told her. "You may want to buy yourself some pants because you'll be a bit more sensitive to the wind down there."

"I'm going to throw you in the manure pit." Liam tried to sound serious, but he was a shoddy dam holding in water.

"Right. You need to concentrate. I don't want you accidentally chopping off this poor gal's cervix."

Liam tried to fight back a smile, but he couldn't stop. His lips could barely hold in the laughter.

"Is that a smile? I think that's a smile. I think that means you find me funny."

Liam flipped him the bird.

"All right then."

Liam got the silence he requested. Nathan held the ewes as Liam chopped. They made a good team. Nathan liked watching Liam work with each ewe. He was firm in his job, but he showed tenderness in how he handled them. He fixed his steely gaze on shearing, and Nathan imagined that look on him. It was a shame Liam was straight, pining over that blonde on his computer. A part of him thought Liam was going to kiss him on the couch earlier, but Liam bounced right off before anything could lead to anything.

"Looking good bitches," Nathan said to the row of ewes. He waited for a comment from Liam about how unprofessional he was, but it never came. They locked eyes for a split second, and Nathan wondered just how straight Liam was.

He wasn't going to try any funny business, though. As much as he would love to be one of those guys who fucks the boss, he wasn't going to do anything else to jeopardize his relationship to this family. No matter how sexy those shears made Liam seem.

Chapter 9

NATHAN

After showering, Nathan lay on his bed with a warm washcloth on his forehead. His hands kept shaking, his head kept pounding. The aching of his muscles from manual labor amplified its pain. Damn withdrawal. It only got this bad in rehab, but he would eventually tough it out. (Or fuck it out.) It would pass like a storm. Eventually.

He crept into the living room and put his hand on the cabinet. What if Mark or the kids caught him? Or Liam. He couldn't take that chance. He summoned every ounce of willpower to hold out. The withdrawal would pass. He just had to keep busy.

Nathan ambled through the house, up the stairs and past Mark and the kids' bedrooms. With its lived-in furniture and walls piled with pictures, the Foster house was like a family hug in architectural form. The only pictures hanging in his dad's flat were stiff family photos. He stared at the closet in the master bedroom, a closet used by his mum. Was there any of her stuff?

He took a step into the room but stopped himself. His

eye caught a row of framed pictures hung on the far wall. Each frame had one or two theater programs with a still of Mariel on stage.

There she was as Desdemona in *Othello*, and as Nora in *A Doll's House*, and as Elizabeth Proctor in *The Crucible*. *My mum was a star!* She signed each program, her cursive loopy and playful.

She reigned supreme among her castmates. In one picture, she toppled over vases with glee as Stevie in *The Goat or Who is Sylvia?* Another had her Roxie Hart in *Chicago* taking a bow with Velma Kelly. Nathan wondered if he caught the acting bug from her, if she had passed it down in her genes. He definitely considered himself more of a Velma than a Roxie, though.

"You are beautiful," he said to a candid picture of her backstage smiling at the camera. He noticed no program from London hung on the wall. He wondered if she dropped out of RADA before she could act. And then he thought about what she was doing in London for those months. It seemed like she didn't come home to New Zealand or else Mark would've seen her knocked up. *Did she wander through London by herself under I was born, and then left the bloody continent as fast as she could?*

He didn't have time to dwell on this question because he heard the front door open. Nathan scrambled out of the master bedroom. He waltzed down the stairs just as Franny came up them, her face a red, blotchy mess.

"Hiya," he said as she brushed past him. "Franny?"

"I'm good," she said in that mucus-clogged voice one gets mid-cry. She went into her room and closed the door.

Nathan turned to go back downstairs, but paused on the top step. He knocked on her bedroom door. "Franny."

"I said I'm good."

"We both know that's bollocks. Do you want to chat?"

A few seconds later, she opened the door. Her cheeks puffed with redness and were streaked with tears.

"I'm going to get you a washcloth." Nathan darted into her bathroom and pulled a cloth from the linen closet. He soaked it in warm water under the sink.

"A warm washcloth on the forehead is like a bath for the brain," he said as he dabbed her forehead.

"Thank you."

He wiped her cheeks. "Do you want to talk about it?"

"It's these girls at school. They made fun of my hair. I dyed my hair brown because they made fun of me for being a redhead."

Nathan had been there plenty. "Let me guess. They called you ginger, or carrot top, or firecrotch."

"Firecrotch?"

"Because..." Nathan tried to slyly nod south, but Franny was not picking up. "Because down there...it doesn't matter. People are naff." Nathan found, though, that the men who called him firecrotch were the ones who couldn't wait to fuck him. "Some wanker will probably call you it in university, so be prepared."

He smoothed his hand over her hair. The red roots shimmered under her dyed brown hair, reminding him of the first reaches of sunrise. "My cousins loved to make me angry because they wanted to see a redhead lose it. They would hide my mobile, steal food off my plate. When I was little, they told me that redheads were God's mistakes."

"Maybe I should chop off all my hair," Franny said. "Uncle Liam says I should ignore them, but that's difficult when I see them every day."

"If I can give you some brotherly advice. I mean, brother-like advice." Nathan pulled up his feet and sat cross-legged on her bed. "It's not about ignoring them. You have to believe you're better than them. And you are. They're jealous of your natural red hair. Red is in! Amy Adams, Julianne Moore, Jessica Chastain, Prince Harry. They want to keep you down, but don't let them. They can spend their miserable pathetic lives talking about you. You have better things to do. So much better things to do."

"Like what?"

"You need to figure that out. I got into acting in local theater. I focused on that. I made new friends." Nathan also focused on drinking and hating the world. He had to learn this lesson on his own. He didn't have an older sibling to impart this useful advice, but at least it wasn't going to waste.

"Thanks, Nathan." Franny hugged him. Her fruity perfume filled his nose. He hesitated, but then hugged her back. His body vibrated with warmth. He breathed in this moment.

There was something very natural about the hug, even though they quickly realized that they barely knew each other.

"Sorry," she said.

Nathan waved it off. He hopped off the bed. "We *need* to do something about this hair."

"I think it'll grow out in a few weeks."

"A few weeks?" Nathan couldn't let his secret sister go through another day with two-toned hair and a bad dye job. "Nope. Come with me. We're going to do something about that."

THAT NIGHT AT DINNER, all eyes were on Franny. She practically swept into the living room, her vibrant, revitalized red hair swishing about her shoulders in a chic, shoulder-length bob, her baby blue cotton dress fanning about her legs. Nathan could've watched this all night. His heart grew a million sizes. He had once worked at a soup kitchen as part of community service, but he found this much more fulfilling.

"Franny." Liam's stood up from the couch, slowly, as if he were regaining muscles in his legs.

"You look awesome," Walt said, unable to inject brotherly sarcasm into his comment.

"Good as gold," Liam said, still gobsmacked, which Nathan enjoyed.

"Thanks!" she said modestly.

"She could be a model in Paris or Milan." Nathan joined them in the living room.

"Did you dye your hair again?" Liam asked.

"God, no," Nathan said. "I told her the only things she should buy from a drug store in a box are condoms, cigarettes, and pregnancy tests." Liam shot him a look, which gave Nathan a small thrill. "This afternoon, we went into Wellington and got her hair transformed by a professional."

"And then Nathan took me shopping for a new outfit!" Franny twirled in her dress once more. This time, Liam was not gobsmacked. Far from it.

"Is that a Burberry dress?" Liam asked. "It has that plaid pattern."

"Good eye. How do you know Burberry?" Nathan asked. Was Liam not as heterosexual as he presumed?

"My ex was very fashionable."

Oh, right. The blonde who broke his heart.

"Franny?" Mark came out of the kitchen and put the main course on the table. He looked like he was about to drop it when he saw his daughter. The look of sheer joy on his face as he watched Franny bounce around nearly made Nathan choke up.

"What do you think, Dad?"

"You look..." Mark put his hand on his chest for a second, and Nathan realized that with her flowing hair, she looked like her mother. Their mother. "You look so beautiful."

"I feel beautiful." Franny smiled at Nathan, who was still on the verge of choking up.

"Nathan, a word?"

Before Nathan could ask what that word was, Liam was pulling him into the bathroom. It was not the first time Nathan had been in the bathroom with another man, but he doubted things would go the same way this time.

"Did you buy her those clothes and that new hair?" Liam asked. It was a small bathroom, and they did their best to keep their bodies from touching. Up close, Nathan noticed the lighter flecks of brown in Liam's beard.

"I didn't buy her new hair. I fixed her existing hair."

"It looks expensive. It all does."

"So." Nathan shrugged.

"Why are you buying my niece designer outfits and taking her to professional salons? You only met her a few days ago."

Nathan wasn't going to let Liam make him feel weird about this. He didn't care if this was proper or not. "Because I wanted to. She looks smashing. She feels smashing."

Liam studied him for a moment with those probing eyes that could've stripped him naked right then and there.

"Sweet as."

Nathan was not expecting that response.

"That was very nice of you."

"You're welcome. Did you pull me into this bathroom just to tell me that, or was there something else you wanted to do?"

On cue, the tips of Liam's ears went red. Blush even filled up the part of his cheeks not covered by hair. *Gotcha.*

"It's dinner time, Liam." Nathan left the bathroom.

———

AFTER DINNER, Nathan and Walt cleared the table while Liam drank a beer on the couch and Franny searched through old DVDs under the television. Nathan tried not to smell Mark and Liam's beers at dinner. He was not a fan of beer. It just made people burpy and saggy. Hard liquor was for classy alcoholics. But still, beer was better than nothing.

Nathan watched Walt clear the table, stacking the dishes and bundling the utensils. He had never cleared a table before, hadn't even watched the maids do it. He copied Walt's technique.

"Ughhh," Franny hissed from the TV. "The remote still isn't working, and I put new batteries in it, too."

Nathan felt a sinking feeling in his stomach as he got a flash of stepping on it during his drunken haze his first night in New Zealand. It had only been on the floor because he knocked into the coffee table. He was a sloshed bull in a china shop.

"You're turning red," Walt said.

Nathan noticed his cheeks in the mirror. "Let's bring these dishes into the kitchen, shall we?"

In the kitchen, they placed the dishes next to the sink and began loading the dishwasher. Mark wiped down the counter.

"Nathan," he said in a low voice. "Whatever you spent on Franny's hair and clothes, I want to pay you back."

"No, not necessary. It wasn't much."

"I insist." Mark looked back at the kitchen door that led to the dining room. "I haven't seen her that happy in months."

"That's payment enough for me."

Mark cocked his head at him. "I'm serious."

Nathan shot him a firm look. "Me, too. You're letting me stay here. You helped me get this job with your brother, who's a bit of a drill sergeant, but still...I can't accept your money."

Mark grinned with appreciation. He finished wiping down the counter and helped Nathan load the dishwasher. He was an expert at strategizing which dishes went where to maximize space. He began making adjustments to what Nathan had done, but soon took everything out and redid it his way.

"He doesn't mean to be a hard ass," Mark said. "Liam's the youngest of five sons, so he's also been on the defensive. And our other three brothers like to take the piss out of him. They've been that way ever since we were younger."

Nathan could empathize, but he didn't need to rehash anything more about his dreaded cousins. "What do they think of him as a farmer?"

"Honestly, they don't like it. They wanted him to sell. They could've gotten more money if we all bundled our land together to sell, rather than what they're making it renting it now. But I didn't want to give this place away. It's our home."

"He's good at it. Farming," Nathan said. "I've only seen him in action a few days, but he cares."

Nathan wondered if he'd ever cared so much about something, or someone.

"Sorry," Mark said about the dishwasher. "I'm a bit anal about loading it my way."

"You seem to know best."

They returned back to the living room. And there was Mariel.

Singing. Right in front of Nathan.

Franny sat on her knees in front of the TV where the video played. Mariel was dressed at Fantine from *Les Miserables* in a taping of one of her stage performances. She wore a brown wig of short, chopped off hair and a dirty dress.

And she sang. *I Dreamed a Dream*. She sang the ballad beautifully. Her voice filled the room, filled the house, filled all of New Zealand with its longing and melancholy.

It was like she was singing directly to Nathan. There she was. Alive and right in front of him. This was his mother. This was as close as he would ever get to her.

"Franny, what are you doing?" Mark asked.

"I was thinking about what you said earlier." She was talking to Nathan now, but her voice was a bit of a fuzzy blur. "I need to find something to focus on. I want to act. Like my mother."

Like our mother.

The room went silent. Walt and Franny watched with rapt attention. Nathan craned his neck at Mark, and the look he gave the screen was heartbreaking. Nathan wanted to cry, but he held it in. He couldn't let them see. That would lead to questions. Why was this man crying over this woman he'd never met?

That is my mother, and I will never meet her. The bad feelings came bubbling up. *She didn't want you. She ditched you in England because you ruined her life.*

Mariel stopped singing. The audience gave her a standing ovation, but in the living room, nobody uttered a word.

"I'm going to go to bed. I'm quite knackered," Nathan said quietly. It went unacknowledged. He closed the door of his bedroom and lay on the bed.

There was no way he was going to get any fucking rest tonight.

Chapter 10

LIAM

Liam dreamt about Nathan's crotch. His smooth, shaved crotch. He pictured them on his couch again. In his dream, instead of reaching for his laptop, Liam slid a hand into Nathan's jeans, past his tight stomach, and felt his—

The sound of sheep baa'ing lurched him out of sleep just in time. *Did I really dream about that?* He was curious. That was all. That was all it could be. After all, Nathan had been so open about it.

The sheep kept baa'ing, more desperate than before. Maybe it really was sheep thieves this time.

He jumped out of bed and put on jeans. No more half-naked farmer for him. He tiptoed to the kitchen window to get a better look. Before he saw Nathan out there, he heard his voice. His slurred, shouting voice warbling some song he couldn't make out.

Liam ran outside and found Nathan dancing—well, more like swaying and twirling—at the edge of his property. He skipped around and between the sheep, causing them to freak out more. A bottle of some type of alcohol clinked in his hand.

"I dreamed dream dream dream dream dream dream..." He slapped sheep on their asses. His dancing downgraded to a shuffle, almost like a zombie.

"Nathan!" He called out and jogged over to him. Liam's heart began to speed up. He started to worry, which he couldn't stand because Nathan was a pain in the ass. He wasn't supposed to be somebody worth worrying over. "Nathan!"

"Liam, you joined the party!" He took a swig of his drink.

"What the hell are you doing?" Liam knew he wasn't going to get an answer from him.

"Just going for a stroll." Nathan tried to stroll, but just stumbled. Liam had to catch him before he smacked into the ground face first.

He reeked of alcohol. It soaked through his skin.

"Where did you get this bottle? Did you break into Mark's liquor cabinet?"

"Sherlock Holmes! You did it! You solved the puzzle!" Nathan blatantly checked Liam out. It was a lot sexier in his dream. "Hey, you remembered trousers."

"You can't do this, Nathan! What is...what is the matter with you?"

"I'm a piece of shit. A complete, worthless, unlovable piece of shit. Haven't you heard?" Nathan laughed as he said this. It came out so matter-of-factly, even in his drunken state, that Liam's heart broke for him for a second. Just one second. Because the man was still wreaking havoc on his property.

"Come on. I'll bring you back to Mark's house." Liam put his arm around Nathan's waist to lead him back to his brother's. Nathan stumbled along with Liam's guiding arm, which had to work double time to keep him from falling.

"Shouldn't you be firing me? Farmer Tight-ass?"

"I'll do it in the morning when you'll remember it."

Nathan stopped and swung around to face Liam. His eyes were dark and dangerous and in seconds, he was kissing Liam.

It was an awful kiss. Sloppy, angry, like his mouth was trying to take over Liam's face. And the taste of hot breath and alcohol made Liam's stomach seize up. He pushed Nathan away, and the guy collapsed to the ground.

"Sorry," Liam said. "I..." He held out a hand to Nathan, but Nathan smacked it away.

"You know, you're keeping these poor sheep captive. These poor sheep deserve to be free. You can't control their lives." Nathan wobbled up and as if imbued with a lightning spark, he sprinted to the fence.

Bugger.

Nathan opened the gate. "Be free sheepie! Free!"

The sheep rushed for the gate opening. These animals were smart enough to know an escape when they saw one.

Liam ran as fast as he could and shoved the gate closed. "Shit!"

Three sheep trotted off down the road, like old ladies going for a walk around the neighborhood.

"What the fuck!" Liam wrestled with Nathan to get him away from the fence.

"It's freedom, Liam!" Nathan laughed a hearty, drunken laugh. "It's beautiful."

"Get off." Liam pulled at Nathan's hand to get him off the fence. It snapped back and Nathan whacked himself in the face, tumbling to the ground.

"Nathan?" Liam nudged his prone body with his foot, but he was down for the count.

Nathan

Nathan pinched his eyes closed at the daylight streaming in through the window and tried to go back to bed. Only there was no daylight. An outdoor light shined through the window, a window he didn't recognize. He glanced around and realized he wasn't in his bedroom. He was on Liam's couch in his little shed-apartment abode.

He sat up, and instantly pain hit his head like some evil witch dropped a stone on him, and then for more fun, pressed her fingers hard into Nathan's scalp. He must've blacked out. He usually awoke from blackout sleep with a headache. It wasn't real sleep, just his body calling a time out for a bit. *How much did I drink?*

The night spiraled after watching that video of his mum. It hadn't triggered him. It kicked him off the ledge, and he didn't know where he landed.

He rubbed the hair out of his forehead and tried to remember what happened. He wasn't quite sure how he wound up on Liam's couch. Did they have sex? No. Liam wouldn't take advantage of him like that. Something bad happened. Nathan had a sinking gut feeling. Drinking this much never led to good things happening.

Did I tell him that Mariel is my mum?

Panic took over Nathan and flashed his eyes open. He hated drinking. He loved it and needed it, but hated it at the same time. The before and during were always fun, but the after was a nightmare. Nathan wished he had never found Mark's liquor cabinet. Once he figured out what happened, he would make sure to regret it.

The light clicked on in the bedroom area. Liam shuffled out of bed and into the living room, looking exhausted. His jeans slung low on his hips. Had he fallen asleep in them?

"What time is it?" Nathan asked.

"Two in the morning." Liam had nothing but glares for him.

"I am so sorry," Nathan said, unsure of what he was sorry for yet, but figured it was best to get his apology out there preemptively.

Nathan smiled back to ease the tension, and his cheek winced in soreness. He felt his face and wondered if he'd fallen. Until he remembered.

The punch.

That memory set off a chain reaction in Nathan and more pieces of the night came into startling focus. Stumbling across the field. Dancing with the sheep while singing *I Dreamed a Dream* in a beautiful voice. And the punch. The punch that he rightfully deserved.

"What were you doing?" Liam asked.

Nathan wanted clarification. He didn't want Liam to know he couldn't quite remember everything.

"I..." Nathan shook his head. "I may have had a little bit too much fun."

"Because of you, I almost lost three of my sheep, maybe more if I hadn't shut the gate in time."

Nathan put his head in his hands, avoiding his hurting cheek. He had a vague recollection of wanting to free the sheep from captivity. *What have I done?* He asked himself, unfortunately knowing the answer.

"Did you hit me?"

"No. You did."

Another wave of embarrassment crashed on Nathan's shores. Of course he hit himself.

"I think you may have a drinking problem," Liam said with complete seriousness. "I think you need help, Nathan."

Nathan considered telling him that he had sought help in rehab, but realized that would make him sound worse. The ex-rehabber who couldn't stay on the wagon.

"I'll be fine. I won't drink anything else while I'm here."

"About that. I don't think it's a good idea that you work here anymore."

Nathan's head bobbed up. A touch of sorrow reflected in Liam's eyes, and it gave Nathan a sliver of relief knowing this wasn't completely easy for him either.

"I'm entering a very busy season for this farm, and I can't jeopardize it with your recklessness. If you need a few more hours of rest, that's all right. But today, I want you to pack your things and go."

"Liam..." Nathan tried to say more. His throat was so dry it tingled with pins and needles. "I really am sorry."

"That's not good enough." His lips pursed into an equator across his face. Lips.

Lips that I kissed. The one missing memory. It came back. It came back hard and socked Nathan in the face even worse than he did to himself hours ago. *I kissed Liam.* The one thing he said he wasn't going to do, and he did it while completely wasted. *Was it good? Probably fucking not.* Nathan had been kissed by drunken fools before, and it was always a disgusting affair.

Nathan got up. He couldn't look at Liam as he walked out the door. He was a fireball of anger, furious with himself. Using his phone's light to navigate across the field, Nathan retreated to Mark's house. He opened the side door slowly, so as not to even risk making a sound, and tiptoed to his room. He undid the covers and got inside his bed.

Nathan stared at the ceiling. Within two seconds of

laying down, he realized he wasn't going to get a wink of sleep. No use trying, and he wasn't going to count sheep. That would be salt in his wound.

He stared at the ceiling, thinking about how he got here and how he didn't want to go. He thought about Franny's buoyant figure in her new dress, the tears of joy when she saw her fixed hair. And he thought of his mother, naturally. Whenever Nathan used to fuck up, which was often, she would be the first person he thought of. He pictured her somewhere, wherever she was, some vague figure in his mind, shaking her head, thinking, "Well, I dodged that bullet." She knew he was trouble from the first second she laid eyes on him, and she smartly ditched him. He would then think about his dad, who gave up his life to raise Nathan, who no matter how callous he might seen now, had kept his son and not tossed him into an orphanage. And what had Nathan done to repay him? What had Nathan done to help anyone?

He whipped off the covers. The sun had not risen. In his eyes, it wasn't tomorrow yet.

Chapter 11

LIAM

When Liam awoke, it was full-on daylight. Nine a.m. The day was already half gone, while back in Wellington, he would just be strolling into the office. He had let himself sleep in since his night was interrupted. Once Nathan left his house, Liam lay in bed for a while trying to fall asleep. He was angry at Nathan, but he still felt bad about what happened. Nathan had just collapsed to the ground so helplessly. Liam thought there'd be more of a fight when he told Nathan to leave, but he shuffled out, completely defeated.

He sat up and breathed in the peace and quiet around him. It was too quiet, though. He hadn't set his alarm because he figured the sheep would wake him up with hungry bellies. *Why weren't they hungry?*

Were they gone?

He put on a fleece since it was a bit chilly. Heavy clouds hung in the sky. Liam went outside. His sheep were still there, perfectly content. They muddled about the field and grazed.

Liam checked the water troughs and feeders, and to his

surprise, they were all full. He walked over to the barn to check on the ewes, and on his way, he noticed there was no manure anywhere on the ground. He did his usual bobbing and weaving for nothing. *They didn't eat, drink, or shit. Did my livestock turn into robots?*

Over the sounds of bleating, Liam heard Nathan's voice inside the barn. He was talking to someone, and Liam heard his name in the conversation. He stopped at the door so as not to interrupt him. Liam figured he was on the phone.

"This is probably my last day here, and I wanted to say that even though our time together was brief, it was memorable."

One of the sheep baaa'd.

"I don't want to go, but...well, I fucked up. I fucked up real bad, though I appreciate your support Tilly."

Liam recognized her familiar bleats.

"What? You don't like your name? Tilly is a great name!"

Liam rested his head against the barn wall and kept listening.

"Are you nervous, Tilly? Very soon, you're going to become a mum. That's a big responsibility. You don't want to be one of those mums who just leaves. Trust me, it'll fuck your children up for life. And you're going to have a big family. Lots of lambs. You'll never be alone. It's going to be wonderful." Nathan let out a yawn. "You know, Till, you are so easy to talk to. If you ever get tired of the rural life, you should look into becoming a therapist."

Liam smiled to himself. His foot slipped on hay and jerked back, kicking into the wall. *Busted.*

"Hello?" Nathan called out.

Liam strode into the room where Nathan laid with the ewes. As soon as he saw him, Nathan jumped up, his spine rigidly straight. Not a speck of attitude in his demeanor.

"Please don't lay down on the hay. That's for the sheep."

"Right. I was just making sure they were doing all right."

"It's not your responsibility to worry about them anymore."

Nathan nodded with his head down. Again, defeated. It made it harder for Liam to stay mad at him.

"You replenished the troughs and picked up the manure?"

"And I cleaned the feeders, scraped off old hay from the barn floors, and patched up a hole in the barn." Nathan showed him where he nailed a piece of wood over a hole one of the sheep had kicked in.

"I didn't know you were so handy."

"I watched a few YouTube videos before doing so." Nathan fought back a yawn, practically pushed it back down his throat. His eyes were all bloodshot, but there were still flickers of life behind them.

"You didn't have to do this. I told you—"

"—to pack my things and leave. But I'm hoping you will reconsider," Nathan cracked out. "Liam, I am so sorry about last night. I promise to do better. To be better."

Liam exhaled a breath through his nose. "You apologized earlier this morning."

"This time, I mean it."

"I don't know if you should be here." Liam found the anger inside him slipping away, and a surging need to wrap Nathan in his arms took hold, a need he would never act upon. But still, it was there, lingering.

"I want to stay. I will keep giving you one hundred percent. One thousand percent. I can do the work. Let's just pretend like last night never happened. If I mess up again in any fashion, I'll go. But please give me another chance.""

"You were a complete disaster. Why did you get completely munted?"

Nathan thought for a moment, then shrugged his shoulders and put on a smile. "I think the last remnants of jet lag got to me."

Bullshit. Liam knew it. Nathan knew it. He studied Nathan's face, waiting for him to be honest. They were in a mental tug of war over it, but Nathan kept smiling, kept pulling.

"I'll think on it," Liam said. He turned around and walked away.

"I was in rehab." Nathan said when he reached the entrance. Liam put his hand on the door frame. "Before I came here."

Liam pivoted back to Nathan, who was stripped of all artifice, his pouty top lip quivering. It was a peek behind the curtain for what felt like the first time.

"Nathan, why do you want to stay here? There must be other farms where you can do research for your movie."

Quiet took over the barn, and Nathan kept looking at him. "Because I like who I am here. Loads of times, so many fucking times, I get this objective view of myself, and I hate what I see. I'm like a car crash in slow motion. But I'm becoming a better person here. It's better than rehab, I'll tell you that. In rehab, guys wanted to treat me like a piece of ass to help them forget about drugs for a few minutes. Staff workers who were supposed to help me tried selling me shit because they knew addicts would pay anything for a fix."

Liam wanted to take back his punch of Nathan and use it against every person at that facility he was at. Maybe the farm was better than rehab. Nathan was away from most temptation and working through his addiction with manual labor.

"What do you say, Liam?"

Damn, he wanted to hug Nathan so bad, but something held him back. Liam gave him a terse nod. "One more chance."

"Thank you. And please, let's just forget everything that happened last night. *Everything*," Nathan said.

Liam knew what he meant. It was a terrible, gross kiss, one that Nathan seemed to fervently regret. But Liam deflated just a bit. He wondered just how much Nathan wanted to erase it from his memory.

"Forgotten," he said.

"Great." Nathan fought back another yawn.

"I can cover things from here, if you want to take a nap on the couch."

"No. There's still work to be done." Nathan looked like he was going in for a hug, and maybe Liam would've tried to reciprocate. He felt some type of force trying to pull them together, but they both stopped themselves.

Liam tipped his hat at Nathan instead.

Chapter 12

NATHAN

Over the next week, Nathan was a model employee. He was on the field by four-fifteen every morning, and Liam was there with an extra mug of coffee in hand. He didn't complain about the tasks Liam gave him. He shoveled shit with a smile on his face. And it did feel good, doing actual work and being helpful.

Liam asked him if he was going through any withdrawal, and Nathan cheerfully told him he was absolutely fine. Which was an absolute lie. The week was filled with killer headaches and nausea. Next came the shaky hands as the last bits of alcohol clung to his skin. In those times, he gripped his shovel or whatever tool he was holding extra hard, willing the poison out of him. For those times when he thought about having a drink, or about all the liquor available to him in Mark's cabinet, he pictured Liam naked, shagging his brains out. Hell, even just picturing Liam walking towards him on the field, his jacked arms and broad chest getting closer, a half-smile on his face that peeked at his white teeth, was enough for Nathan. He gripped his own tool in those cases, masturbating like he was a teenager again. Lusting after one's boss and the uncle of one's secret siblings wasn't an ideal situation, but it did the trick.

Nathan knew that nothing would happen between him and Liam. That kiss was a drunken mistake, even if Nathan had secretly wished he'd done it when sober. But he was already on shaky ground. He couldn't risk getting booted from the farm and getting on the bad side of his siblings. Even though it set him on that alcohol-fueled tailspin, Nathan wanted to see more of his mother. He wanted to watch more videos and look through more of her things. He wanted to be closer to her, as hard as it would be. There had to be more to the story about why she abandoned him. Mariel seemed like a sweet, loving mother and wife. How could she do what she did to Nathan all those years ago? It didn't jive, and perhaps in her personal belongings, there was a clue as to what happened.

"Once more, from the top." Nathan sat on Franny's bed and cued her to start singing again.

She stood up straight, jutted her neck out softly, and the words of *On the Steps of the Palace* flowed from her mouth. There were some bumps in the musical road, times where she yelled the words to wring emotion instead of sang them, but overall, she had natural talent. Mariel had blessed both of them with abilities.

"How was that?" she asked.

"It was all right." Nathan refrained from going Simon Cowell on her. But he wasn't going to lie to her. "It needs work, but the base is there."

"Do you think I can master this song by the audition next week?"

"It's possible. You're going to have to work hard. We'll need to practice everyday."

"I will. I remember Mum would sing scales and practice lines to herself as she cleaned the house."

She smiled at the memory. Nathan found himself picturing the memory, too. Now that he had a better idea of what she looked and sounded like, he could envision Mariel. It was a small comfort. No longer was his mum a complete enigma. Just a large one.

"It would be awesome if I got cast in the show." Franny was auditioning for the local playhouse production of *Into the Woods*. It was the same theater where their mother had performed. "Do you think I'd get cast as the baker's wife like Mum?"

"You're probably too young for that role, but I think you could be Rapunzel or Cinderella. Doesn't every girl want to be a princess?"

"I'd rather be the witch, the one causing all the trouble," Franny said with a sly smile, one that would've looked right at home on Nathan's face.

"Nathan?" Mark knocked on the door.

"It's open."

"Did you want to go get Liam for dinner?"

"Will do."

Nathan walked across the field. He thought about how wonderful these nightly dinners were. Mark had discovered Pinterest and was trying new recipes. There was good food, good conversation, and after dinner, they'd watch an episode of The Golden Girls together. It was a perfect cap on the day.

The air was chilly and thick tonight. He paused for a second to admire the night sky full of stars. They didn't have skies like this back in London.

He yanked open Liam's screen door so that it thwacked

against the house, then the front door. "Liam, dinner's ready. Shit!"

And there was Liam, wet and buck naked.

He was in the middle of toweling off from the shower. Fortunately for him, and maybe for Nathan too, he had been drying his nether regions, so Nathan had glimpsed everything but the *piece de resistance*. From the looks of his blooming pubic mound, Liam had not been inspired at all from their conversation about crotching.

"Shit. I'm sorry."

"I think the proper thing to do is knock." Liam didn't try to run. He kept toweling himself off. "What did you storm in here to tell me?"

He wrapped the towel around his waist where it slung low on his hips. Droplets of water glistened on his chest hair and cascaded down his abs. Nathan remembered to blink. It would provide good fodder for fighting off the alcohol demons later.

"Dinner's ready." Nathan took a breath. He didn't know why he was the uncomfortable one here. If Liam was an unfazed straight dude, then he could be the unfazed gay guy. "I said dinner's ready."

"I'll get dressed." Liam seemed to be enjoying this, much like Nathan liked making his ears turn red. He went into his bedroom area, his round ass moving under that towel effortlessly.

"You didn't make me uncomfortable," he called into the bedroom. "I've seen plenty of naked men. Plenty!"

"Congratulations," Liam deadpanned.

"And if you think I'm going to get naked to make things even, well then you have a fucked-up sense of fairness."

Liam came back out wearing boxers with sheep on

them. Against all odds, Nathan found it attractive. "Have a seat. I'll be dressed in a minute."

Nathan waited on the couch, facing the wall in front of him. On the coffee table was Liam's laptop, once again open to Facebook. Fortunately, he wasn't looking at pictures of his ex-girlfriend as far as he could tell. His feed refreshed, and Nathan found something much more frightening.

The picture of his mum and dad.

One of Liam's friends sent him a Facebook message attaching a link to his missed connection post and wrote *Isn't this your late SIL?*

"No. No no no," Nathan said. Liam couldn't see this. It would blow Nathan's cover and expose that Mariel had fooled around behind Mark's back. He couldn't let his mother be sullied.

Nathan quickly logged onto his original missed connection post and deleted it. But the FB message remained.

"What are you doing?" Liam was behind him moments later, jerking his laptop back. "You deactivated my Facebook account? You had no right to do that! Why would you do such a thing?"

Nathan pulled the laptop back from him, a story forming in his head. "You don't need to be on it. I know what you were doing on here. Stalking blondie and your ex-mate. Am I right?"

Liam hunched his shoulders. The guilt was written on his face.

"For a man who prefers country life, you are surprisingly addicted to social media."

"Am not. I like to connect with friends I don't see very often."

"Two in particular."

Liam reached for the laptop, but Nathan snatched it back.

"You have a beautiful night sky and lovely animals and a lovely family in the real world, right now. You don't need the false sense of camaraderie of Facebook. I want you to go on a Facebook cleanse. If I am abstaining from alcohol, you will abstain from social media. Deal?"

Liam gritted his teeth, but then stuck his hand out for a shake. "Deal," he sighed.

"Is your brother or Franny and Walt on Facebook? I don't want them to tempt you."

"Mark has an account but never goes on. And Franny and Walt think I'm a dinosaur for being on there."

"You are." Nathan handed back the laptop and breathed a stealth sigh of relief when Liam placed it on the table without a fight. He sat on the couch and rested his elbows on his thighs.

"I don't know why I keep checking their accounts," Liam said.

"Maybe you haven't quite come to terms with it. How did it happen? Did you catch them *en flagrante*?"

Liam shifted uncomfortably, hinting to Nathan that this would be quite a story.

"You can tell me." Nathan considered himself a good listener. He had learned something from all those counselors at rehab. "All you have to do is talk. I'll just listen."

Liam paced in the small space of the living room. He seemed to be having quite a conversation with himself.

"If I tell you, would you promise not to breathe a word of it to anyone, especially my family? I haven't told a single person."

"Of course. The benefits of being a stranger."

"I also want to get your opinion," Liam said.

"Then stop pacing and start chatting."

Liam plunked down in his desk chair and leaned forward. "Kelly, Craig, and I were close for a while. We all used to work together at Weta, the special effects house. We worked on the rebooted *Planet of the Apes* films. When Kelly and I were dating, he never felt like a third wheel. It was great." Liam ran his fingers through his beard, then through his hair. "One night, we were drinking, and we decided to have a threesome."

"And now it just got interesting. I think you need a drink."

"I don't have any alcohol in the house. I got rid of it."

"Because of me?" Nathan found it sweet how much he cared about his sobriety. Now he couldn't fuck things up. "How about some water?"

Nathan poured them two cups of water. He returned to his desk chair and motioned for Liam to keep talking.

"We figured it would be fun." Liam shrugged. "We're going at it, and I keep noticing Kelly and Craig getting very involved. They're all over each other, and she's moaning for him, and then I feel like a major third wheel. I tried to join in, but they were not into sharing the love. A few days later, Kelly broke up with me, and two days after that, she and Craig changed their status to 'in a relationship' on Facebook. I later discovered from other friends and through my own snooping that they'd been having an affair for close to a year. That night, they were pretty much flaunting it in my face.

"I feel like I can't escape it. We have mutual friends, and their pictures pop up, and Facebook keeps suggesting I friend them. I know I should block them or just get off the internet."

"But you can't. We are all gluttons for punishment in some way."

"I think that if I block them or if I leave the site, then in some way, I'm admitting defeat. I'm admitting they won."

"There are no winners in relationships. You're either trying to get in one because you don't want to be sad and single, or trying to get out of one because you can't stand coming home to same person." Nathan tapped at the bottom of his glass. "I cheated on my last boyfriend."

"Aye." Liam raised his eyebrows but then tried to play it cool.

"Are you really that surprised?" Nathan said with a detached shrug. "And he was a good guy, too. I could see myself fucking up in real time, but I couldn't stop. I'm not good at relationships."

"It's hard to be when you know the other person could be lying to your face."

"Or they could pick up and leave at any second."

"Poof and gone." Liam opened his hand like a magician revealing a magic trick.

"Cheers to shitty relationships." Nathan held up his glass. Liam leaned over and clinked it.

"To shitty relationships."

They chugged the rest of their water. There was no liquor, but Nathan still felt drunk on something.

"So what made you do a threesome with your male friend? Don't straight guys prefer two girls?"

The tips of his ears turned red. Nathan waited with anticipation.

"I thought it would be fun, and I think...well, I'm realizing that I'm not completely straight."

"You're bi?"

Liam nodded yes. "I proposed the threesome because I

wanted to have sex with Craig and Kelly. He has a good body, which I hate admitting."

"A bisexual sheep farmer with pubic hair. You continue to intrigue me, Liam Foster."

"Please don't use any of this for your character."

Nathan was confused for a second before remembering he was an actor doing research. He held up his hand. "Promise."

Liam stood up. "Ready to go to dinner?"

"Can you get me another glass of water? I'm still a little parched." Nathan handed his glass over. Liam went into the kitchen.

He was not thirsty, but the thought of Liam getting it on without another guy made him sprout major wood, and now was not the time to show off the tenting in his pants.

Chapter 13

LIAM

Liam had less and less to correct Nathan on. He showed up at the farm every morning on time and did his chores without too much complaint. His eyes seemed clearer and skin brighter without the fog of alcohol.

But he still did not like cleaning up manure. "It's built my character up enough. Can we trade off maybe?" he had asked.

"No. I have my own share of responsibilities, too. One day, when you buy your own farm, you can hire a farmhand to manage waste collection."

"Stop calling it 'managing waste collection.' It's shoveling shit." Nathan quirked an eyebrow at him that sent a rush of excitement to Liam's cock.

He still couldn't believe he'd told Nathan about the threesome. He hadn't breathed a word of it to his other friends, although since they all stayed friends with Kelly and Craig, he wondered if they knew, if it was a common joke among all of them. It'd been two days since Nathan forced him to forgo Facebook. Going cold turkey was making his hands twitchy around the computer, but if Nathan could give up alcohol, he could give up social media.

Nathan was easy to talk to. And all the farm work had started to add more heft to his frame. His shirt sleeves tightened with new muscle, and his thighs thickened in his pants. Which made something thicken in Liam's pants. Nathan bent over to shovel a glop of manure. Liam made himself avert his eyes.

"I'm gonna go..." Liam pointed at the barn and went to check on Matilda. She was humongous, so close to lambing. She could go at any minute. It was like sitting at the top of a roller coaster, just waiting for the drop.

He heard his phone ringing in his house and told Nathan he would be right back. He maintained one landline in his house since he couldn't always count on cell phone service where they were. The ringing of the old telephone pierced the quietude of his home.

"Hello?"

"Hey there, Piglet."

Callum. Liam sighed. "Hey, brother."

His older brothers loved calling him Piglet when they were growing up, based on his small size and the stuffed animal of Piglet from Winnie the Pooh that he used to sleep with until he was nine. Like all embarrassing things from our childhoods, the name stuck. Mark stopped calling Liam that once he became a teenager, but his three older brothers, Oliver, James, and Callum, refused to stop no matter how much Liam insisted they call him by his actual name.

"You must be getting close to lambing season." Callum was a born salesman. He had that slick way of talking that made Liam believe there was always a deal percolating under his words.

"Just around the corner. Any day now."

"Exciting. You scared? I remember last year it nearly destroyed you."

"I can handle it. I hired someone to help."

"I didn't know you had the money for that."

"I do." Liam gritted his teeth. He hated his brothers knowing his business. They never cared about his privacy. They never knocked when they all lived together, and their parents' house didn't have locks on the doors. Liam learned to take shits with one hand pushed against the door and masturbate with speedy efficiency. Even when their parents died, his brothers' attitudes didn't change, save for Mark. He was still Piglet, still tailor-made to be teased. Tragedy did not bring them closer when Liam needed them. He got the feeling that ragging on their baby brother was a constant for them, a way to deal with the pain no matter how it affected him.

"What do you want, Callum?"

"Feisty Piglet," Callum said defensively, which he did whenever Liam pushed back the slightest bit. "I have a tantalizing offer for you."

"What kind of offer?"

"A friend of mine is a real estate developer. He wants to buy our plots of land. Wellington is running out of housing!"

Liam had heard about some farmers selling their land to real estate developers who were building planned communities, but he didn't expect the building boom to reach this far out of the city.

"Real estate developer? He wants to build houses here?" Liam glanced out his window at the beautiful rolling hills and mountains in the distance. It was nature unbridled.

"It's going to be a mix of houses, townhomes, and condominiums. There will be three pools and a tennis court. He showed me the plans he drew up. It took my breath away."

Callum wanted to turn his birthright into suburban sprawl.

"What about the farmers you're currently renting your land to?"

"It's peanuts compared to what we can get paid. This developer, Harold Grates, has fantastic plans for state-of-the-art suburban communities."

"He asked you to talk to me...are you getting a cut?"

"A fee for facilitating, yes." *Classic Callum.* He didn't help people unless there was a cash incentive. He was the one who convinced James and Oliver to rent their land eight years ago. "And you, Piglet, you would be swimming in heaps of money. Your piece of land has some of the best topography and views."

Callum gave him an estimated offer. Liam had to take a seat. Holy shit. He'd never imagined so many zeroes before.

"Still there?" Callum asked.

"What did Mark say?"

"We haven't told him yet, but I know if you sold, he wouldn't hold out. He and the kids are practically screaming for a better, more modern house. He'd only be holding on so you wouldn't be alone out here."

Mark was living out here for years before Liam came back. But it was no use calling his brother out on his bullshit.

"Mum and Dad would roll over in their graves if their land was turned into cul-de-sacs."

"That's a bit much, Piglet."

"Can you please call me Liam?"

"So touchy." Liam knew it was no use, but at least he tried. "Mum and Dad would be proud of you for being entrepreneurial and taking advantage of a prime opportunity rather than playing farmer."

"I'm not playing farmer. I have almost forty sheep, and I'm going to have more soon."

"And very soon, you're going to be in over your head. Let's be real here. Brother to brother. You wanted to live life off the grid for a bit, go retro with farming and growing your mountain man beard. But do you expect to do this for the rest of your life?" Callum chuckled to himself. "I love you, Liam, but you are no farmer."

Liam heard the faint baaa's of his sheep. He tried focusing on their sounds rather than the words of his own brother.

"Think about it, Piglet."

Nathan

While Liam was talking on the phone, Nathan's own phone buzzed unexpectedly. Most of the field was a dead zone, but there were tiny pockets of good reception that Nathan happened to stumble into by accident.

Just got home from Hawaii. Are you still on holiday?

Nathan and his parents treated their apartment like they were all guests in a hotel who came and went as they pleased. Nathan would go out partying for a weekend and come back two days with nary a peep from his dad or stepmum. It surprised him that his dad considered his whereabouts.

But Nathan didn't dare tell him the truth.

I'm visiting friends in Lisbon. Hope you had a nice trip.

He thought that was the end of things, but the three text bubbles jiggled at the bottom of his screen.

When will you be back?

"What the hell is going on?" Nathan said to the screen. Did his dad get hypnotized at a luau?

I don't know. Is everything okay?

Yes. I wanted to make sure you were doing all right and staying "on the wagon."

Nathan rolled his eyes at the quotation marks around that phrase, but he couldn't deny a weird emotion blooming in his chest.

I've been thinking about you. Maybe when you get home, we could talk, his dad texted.

It was most alarming to Nathan, and if anything, it made him extra grateful to be a few oceans away from his father. Nathan had watched cute father/son scenes in television shows. He didn't need them in his real life. *And what made him start thinking about me now?* he thought.

Sure, Nathan texted. He wanted things as vague as possible.

See you in a few days?

Probably a few weeks.

Liam returned to the hoof house, and Nathan welcomed the distraction and the dead zone.

"Everything good?" Nathan asked him.

"Yeah. That was..." Liam nodded behind him at the house. "That was nothing. Someone trying to sell me something I didn't need. You good?"

Nathan tucked his phone back in his pocket. "Couldn't be better."

Chapter 14

NATHAN

The next morning, Nathan was up early. He beat his alarm clock by fifteen minutes. And it wasn't because he was hung over or going through withdrawal or some other type of turmoil. His biological clock had shifted back a few hours. He might never wake up after nine again. *What have I become?*

He went to the barn and checked on Tilly. A thought had sat on his mind all night and he had to get it out. Fortunately, Tilly was always in the same spot. Like any quality therapist, she was always available. No absconding to Brighton for a beach vacation without telling her clients.

"Tilly, y'alright?" Tilly lay on her side. She only acknowledged Nathan with a head turn. "You're trying to conserve your energy. I get it."

Nathan put a fresh clump of hay under her head. "I'm glad I didn't wake you. Can we chat?"

She let out a baaaa then turned her head to look at the wall. Nathan figured that was a green light. He petted her wool softly, letting it bristle through his fingers.

"I am here on a mission. I am here to find out about my mum and who she was and to get to know my new family, even if they don't know we're family. I am not here to have sex with anyone. Especially Liam. Even if I want to." Nathan squatted beside her. "This conversation is confidential, correct? I understand there's a conflict of interest since you depend on Liam for food, water, and shelter."

Nathan got up. He had to pace. He hadn't felt this way in a long time, not since his last boyfriend Eamonn. And that relationship imploded thanks to Nathan.

"Am I crazy for liking him? If he found out the truth about me and what I'm doing here, none of them would ever talk to me again. I have to resist until I figure out how to best tell them." He kicked pieces of hay aside. "He's probably not interested in me. I'm a liar and a bad influence."

Tilly emitted a loud bleat.

"Thanks, Tilly. I'm glad you like me."

She emitted another louder, and longer, bleat that echoed in the barn. Nathan wanted to cover his ears. Tilly wiggled in the hay and kept making noises.

"Till?"

She wouldn't stop. Nathan got on his knees and looked into her crotched area. He hadn't observed many vaginas up close, but he knew right away what he was looking at.

"Fuck."

LIAM

It was time. He blinked awake as soon as he heard Tilly's familiar bleats of labor. There was no turning back. Lambing season had arrived. He put on his clothes and raced to the barn with a bucket of water.

Nathan had beat him to it. He knelt beside Tilly and cleared away the area beside her for delivery.

"Liam!" He stood up, all business. "She's past the first phase of labor. She discharged the amniotic fluid a few minutes ago."

"How do you know about that?" He pulled a box of plastic gloves from his bag.

"I read about it online." Nathan held up his phone. "I think she's about ready to blow. You know what I mean."

The guy had done better than Liam expected. He knelt beside Tilly and checked out how dilated she was. Nathan was right. She was ready to deliver. Liam prepped the area, while Tilly wailed away.

"Do they make epidurals for sheep?" Nathan asked. He had rolled up his sleeves and put on a pair of gloves.

"No."

"So what do we do?"

"We supervise," Liam said.

"So we're just going to watch HOLY BLOODY FUCK!" Nathan stumbled back. Tilly's first lamb breached the surface still encased in the amniotic sac. "I feel like Sigourney Weaver in *Alien*!"

"Okay Tilly. I need one more good push from you," Liam told her. He liked to think she sort of understand that and appreciated the encouragement. It wasn't as if any of the rams who impregnated these ewes were helping. They hung out in a separate shed.

The lamb broke free of its amniotic confines, causing Nathan to jolt back again. It amazed Liam how in an hour or two, the lamb would be walking around, while it took humans years.

"It's beautiful," Liam said.

"It's a bit graphic."

"If you're going to vomit, please do it outside."

Nathan held his hand over his mouth. "I think I'm going to be all right."

"Great. Because we got one more coming."

"Twins?"

"Her breed can birth up to three lambs per litter."

Nathan knelt beside Tilly and patted her head. "And here I thought you were just super bloated."

Groans and loud bleats from the far end of barn made their way to Liam and Nathan. Just like with last year, Tilly was the catalyst that started the chain reaction.

"I hope you like this," Liam said. "This is going to be our life for the next few weeks."

"This?" Nathan pointed at Tilly, who was thrashing around on the hay, bleating for all to hear.

"Over and over again."

"Can I go back to shoveling shit?"

Liam laughed and was about to slap Nathan on the back, but remembered what was on his hands. He gave Nathan instructions for observing Tilly, then jogged to the far end of the barn where another ewe lay on her side. Her bleating sounded more desperate. Liam watched her carefully and checked her out, but fortunately, everything seemed to be going fine.

"It's your first time as a mum. Excited?" Liam wondered aloud. He had only been sheep farming on his own, but all of his memories from working with his mum and dad during lambing season rushed back to him. He found himself missing them so much in this moment, wishing they could see him.

The ewe groaned and bleated with desperation as she pushed out her lamb. Liam once thought he would be in this position with Kelly in a few years. They both very much wanted children, and Liam prepared to attend lamaze classes and be one of those hands-on fathers. He still wanted that, no matter which gender he wound up with.

He shook out of his thoughts when he heard his name being screamed from the other end of the barn.

Chapter 15

NATHAN

"There's a problem. Something's wrong," Nathan said as soon as Liam came over. Panic and concern took over Liam's face. "She started making these noises, not the ones she had been making."

Tilly emitted a groan of pain that sounded almost humanlike.

"Like that?" Liam asked.

Nathan nodded yes. "I peeked inside and it didn't look right. Like the lamb was stuck or something."

"Is it breech?"

"No. I see the head. It's not coming out." Nathan's first thought was that he screwed something up. Maybe instead of chatting with Tilly, he should've been checking on her more, perhaps massaging her stomach to make sure all the lambs just slid out like her womb was a laundry chute.

"Let's take a look." If Liam was scared, he didn't show it. He knelt down and examined Tilly, all while petting her to keep her calm.

"What do you see?" Nathan paced behind him. Tilly

caught his eye and held contact. He saw the pain and worry reflected back at him, which might have been his own reflection. He put on a hopeful smile, like a parent does for a kid about to go into surgery, but inside the scene tore him up more than he expected. Nathan was not one for emotions, except the fun ones like anger and jealousy.

"The lamb's shoulder is out. It's too wide for the opening. The lamb is like this." Liam demonstrated by sticking his elbows out like a chicken. "We need it like this." He held his arms at his sides.

"Can we tell it that?"

"Nah yeah. A newborn lamb speaks fluent English."

Nathan shot him a look. Desperate bleats came from the far end of the barn.

"Shit. That's my other ewe who's in labor. I need you to check on her," Liam said.

"No." Nathan said it without thinking. It was compulsory. "I'm not leaving Tilly."

"Nathan, this is serious."

"I know." Nathan didn't budge. His heart was telling him to stay.

"Fine. Then you need to do this." Liam looked over his shoulder, to the sounds of the other lamb bleating in labor.

"By myself?" Nathan said.

"Yes."

What had Nathan gotten himself into? The only thing he'd ever delivered was dialogue. Fear seized his body, but the confident smolder of Liam gave him hope. It shook sense into him.

"All right," Nathan said.

Liam gave him a sturdy head nod. "You have to reach inside Tilly and push the lamb's shoulders in." Liam demonstrated with his hands at his sides. "Once you do that, the lamb should come right out."

Fear ripped through Nathan. "I—can I practice on you?"

Liam tipped his head to the side like seriously.

"Just once."

Liam held his elbows out chicken-style. Nathan tried to push them down, but Liam flexed those arm muscles to make this more of a challenge. Now was so not the time to admire those muscles. Nathan managed to shove them down.

"The sheep won't put up nearly the resistance." Liam put his hands on Nathan's shoulders. Those dark eyes penetrated the most scared parts of him. "You can do this, Nathan. I trust you. Tilly trusts you."

Nathan thought of the lamb and the mother who needed his help, and that need overrode his trepidation.

"I can do this," Nathan said.

Liam nodded and ran off to tend to the other sheep.

Tilly wailed.

"You can do this," Nathan said to himself. "I mean, we can do this, Tilly."

All I have to do is push its shoulders in. He took a huge, deep breath and squatted down. Adrenaline shoved aside his squeamishness.

I'm doing this. I'm doing this. This is really happening. His fingers and hands squished through until he felt something firm. A head. A lamb head. He could feel it pulse and breathe.

"There you are." His fingers traveled down the head and yes! The shoulders. Tilly wailed in pain and kicked her legs out. He bet this was unpleasant for her. A lover had tried to fist Nathan once; he did not like it either.

Tilly's bleats hit a fever pitch.

"We're almost done!"

He counted to three and pushed the lamb's shoulders down. He held them down for a second to make sure they wouldn't pop up again, but the lamb did not put up a fight.

"How's it going?" Liam yelled to him from across the barn.

"I think..." Nathan gave the lamb a slight nudge before he removed his hands. He checked inside, and the lamb inched closer to the outside. "I think it's working!"

Tilly let out another groan. The lamb's head came closer and closer to the world.

"Holy shit, Tilly. You're giving birth." It was a duh statement, but it hit Nathan so profoundly. *This is that miracle of life shit parents were always talking about.*

The lamb slid out. Its legs touched the floor. Nathan's shirt and pants were covered with fluid he didn't want to think about.

Liam ran over. "Did it work?"

But his question didn't need to be answered.

"You did it."

"I..." Nathan was a storm of emotions. He wasn't the one who gave birth, so he didn't know why he had trouble speaking.

"Sweet as," Liam said in a whisper, in just as much as awe as Nathan.

Tilly got up, went to Nathan, and began eating what just came out of her like she was a sheep zombie.

"What the hell is she doing?" Nathan asked.

"She's eating her placenta. It's instinct. She does that to remove any extra evidence of her birth so that predators don't find her lambs. She doesn't think it's gross. Right now, all she's thinking about is keeping her babies safe."

Nathan and Liam gave her space. Her lambs worked on

walking. They stumbled around the barn, and Tilly watched them with a trained eye, like she was a helicopter parent with her kids at the playground.

She lay back down, and the lambs nuzzled up to her for their first feeding. Lambs didn't smile, but she seemed at absolute peace with her children. Nathan had trouble breathing. His lungs were clogged with some type of emotion he couldn't decipher, but it felt like jealousy. And not the fun kind. The sad type of envy when you know someone has something you never will have.

"This is so important right now," Liam said. "This is when mother and lambs bond."

"Excuse me. I need...fresh air." Nathan left the barn. It had begun to rain, but he didn't care about getting wet. Raindrops thwacked against his clothes, quickly soaking through his shirt. Water cascaded over his hair strands and onto his face. They hid the tears that sprung from his eyes. He thought of Tilly feeding her lambs, Tilly nuzzling them to sleep, Tilly protecting them from potential threats, Tilly licking dirt off their wool—those precious, intimate moments that mothers had with their children, the ones that made people feel safe even as adults. Tilly and her lambs, and every ewe in this hoof house, would have a bond Nathan never had. There was no nuzzling, no protective instinct for him. His mother dumped him as soon as he was born. How could a person ever recover from not having that bonding time? It left him with a missing piece that he would never replace. He was damaged goods, permanently.

Nathan gasped for air, the sobs coming fast and hot from his throat, tears spilling down his cheeks. He cried for every moment he never got to have. He cried because he only heard Mariel's voice through a screen, because he never knew what she smelled like, because he never knew how she hugged. He was a soaking wet shell of a person.

Then, the warmth came. Strong arms wrapping tight around his chest, pulling him close, nuzzling his neck. But it wasn't his mother and it wasn't a dream. It was Liam, holding him against his body, sealing him off from the cold rain, rocking him back and forth, pressing his lips to Nathan's head.

Nathan turned around and tilted his head up. Those milky blue eyes were their own nuzzling hug, promising to keep him safe. Their lips met in a kiss that started tenderly but in an instant tore through Nathan's body with unrelenting passion. The jumble of feelings and release of tension from Tilly's ordeal shot out of them. Nathan didn't want to think about his mother or his past. He only wanted this moment. He was hungry for life.

Chapter 16

NATHAN

Liam's lips infused Nathan with electricity. His mouth was the warmth that saved him from their cold surroundings. Soon, Liam's tongue was prying his lips apart and slipping inside.

"I reckon I really like kissing guys," Liam said.

Nathan held onto his tree trunk-like neck, breathing in his manly scent, feeling the straggly hairs brushing against his fingertips, as their tongues swashbuckled. His mind was a blur of need.

But then it began to unscramble.

What am I doing? Nathan asked himself. There was one giant secret between them. Underneath all the lies Nathan had told, there was the truth, trying to claw its way to the surface.

"Liam." Nathan pulled away, catching his breath. He thought about how to tell him, how to begin, what to say.

But the lust blazing on Liam's chiseled face overpowered him, as did the swollen cock pressing against Nathan's thigh. He could tell Liam needed this as badly as he did.

"What is it?" Liam asked.

"I want you so fucking bad." It wasn't a line. It was practically a medical diagnosis.

Liam pulled him hard against his chest, locking him into place with his strength. His thick beard rubbed against Nathan's cheeks as his forceful kisses sent waves of lust and need down Nathan's spine. His muscles flexed around Nathan's frame. Rain cascaded down their faces.

Liam tugged on Nathan's hair, yanking his head back at an angle to go in for a deeper kiss. The sounds of their lips and tongues smacking together sent blood rushing to Nathan's crotch and his heartbeat vibrated against his chest.

Nathan pushed him back against the barn. He ran his hands down Liam's rain-soaked shirt, which clung to his jacked physique. He grabbed Liam's tight ass and their hard cocks grinded against each other through layers of denim. He wanted to devour and be devoured by Liam's broad, firm body.

He slipped his fingers under Liam's shirt, which proved difficult when the rain made it stick to his skin. His fingers grazed his furry abs and traveled up to his hairy chest. His body was all man. Nathan couldn't stop himself. He had looked, and now all he wanted to do was touch. He pushed Liam's shirt up, and Liam whipped it the rest of the way off. Nathan kissed along the muscles in his shoulders and the curve of the pecs. Raindrops clung to the tips of his hair and his eyelashes. Nathan realized how badly he needed Liam close, how badly he needed this connection.

Their mouths met again in a ferocious round of making out. Liam kissed along Nathan's neck, making his arms and legs shut down. Nathan had been with plenty of men, but holy fuck this was on some other level. Want and lust coursed through his veins.

Liam shoved him against the barn. He grabbed hold of Nathan's shirt in his fists and tore it apart. The fabric ripped asunder.

"That was a Marc Jacobs shirt."

"And now it's junk," Liam said with a mischievous smile that went straight to Nathan's cock. He yanked the destroyed shirt off Nathan's lean frame. Farming had given him more definition that Liam eyed with desire. Sheets of rain slicked his smooth muscles and abs. Their soaked chests mashed together.

Nathan grabbed onto the waistband of Liam's jeans like he was hanging onto the side of a mountain. He flicked his fingers inside and brushed against that bush he'd glimpsed the other night. He liked that Liam told male beauty standards to fuck off. He moved further south, and Liam let out a moan when he took hold of his meaty cock. The thing was a fucking mallet, and Nathan wanted it thrust in every eligible hole of his.

Liam groaned into Nathan's mouth as he stroked his thick cock inside his rain-soaked jeans. He reached into Nathan's jeans and stroked him back.

"So smooth," Liam said between kisses. "Sweet as."

"I reckon every time you say that on the farm, I think you're checking me out."

"Maybe I am." He squeezed Nathan's ass. "So, you think I should clean up down there?"

"Don't you fucking dare," Nathan said, brushing his fingertips through the manly thicket of hair that circled his cock. He jerked him off faster, then realized the pants needed to come the fuck off.

He shoved Liam's jeans to his knees. His dick sprung out, and Nathan had no choice but to get onto his knees as well.

He knelt in a puddle of mud, but could care less. The dirtiness somehow made it hotter.

Nathan licked the tip of his uncut cock, which was slick with excitement. He was also excited, and he deep-throated Liam's dick right away, taking him to the base. Or the bush, in his case.

"Aye, you don't mess around," Liam said.

"No, I fucking don't."

"Now I know the best way to shut you up. Shove a cock in there." He leaned against the barn and let out a loud, unguarded moan that was like heroin to Nathan.

Nathan sucked him off real good, licking and stroking that delicious cock until the fucker shined. He felt its thick warmth filling him up, tasting the musk mixed with hot pre-cum. Liam threaded his fingers through Nathan's hair and shoved his cock deep inside. Nathan groaned with delight as Liam fucked his mouth. As befitting someone with as much self-loathing as Nathan, it should come as no surprise that he liked it rough.

He tongued Liam's balls, which tasted of sweat and rain. His tongue traveled further south and flicked against his hole. Liam jolted back.

"Too much?" Nathan asked.

Liam hesitated. "It feels different."

"Something you missed out on in your threesome?" Nathan massaged a finger back and forth over his tight hole. Liam shivered underneath his touch. "It's one of the best parts of being bi."

Liam bit his lip and nodded. He emitted more unguarded moans that broke through his rigid exterior. "Yes, baby."

He kicked off his shoes and used his feet to tug off his jeans. Except for his hat, Liam was now completely naked, an image Nathan had fantasized about for weeks come to life. And in 3-D. Nathan overturned a bucket for Liam to lift a leg onto, giving him better access to the Kiwi's tight opening. Nathan slipped a finger inside, finding a surge of warmth on this cold, cold field.

"Yes," Liam heaved out. "Feels so good."

Nathan flicked his tongue on his opening, loving the heat coming off his rancher. He shuttled between licking his ass and sucking his cock, tasting the mix of salty sweat and pre-come. Liam's moans and panting were a world-class symphony to his ears. Nathan unbuttoned his own jeans and stroked himself.

"I…I have…"

Nathan stopped. *Please don't say an STD or a secret boyfriend.*

"Lube." Liam rested his head against the barn. "I bought it before the threesome…but we never used it…"

"So you're saying you want to have sex?" Nathan asked.

"Yes."

"Why didn't you say so?"

LIAM

That could've been smoother, Liam thought as they entered his house. But Nathan didn't seem to mind. His cock remained fully hard, as did Liam's.

Liam couldn't stop himself. When he saw Nathan outside crying, so wounded and raw, he wanted to be with him. He wanted to hold him and protect him.

And now he wanted to fuck him.

Liam blushed when he saw his reflection in the window, entering his shed in his birthday suit. Nathan soon took his pants and shoes, giving Liam a glimpse of a body he had dreamt about for weeks.

"Eyes up here," Nathan said with a wink.

Liam couldn't stop admiring his body. He wasn't bulky like Liam, but there was hidden strength in those sharply defined muscles. He'd gotten a taste of it by the barn. And naturally, his eyes immediately flicked to his manscaped area. It made his cock more pronounced. He wondered if he should clean himself up similarly.

"I know what you're thinking, and don't you fucking dare," Nathan said. His eyes raked over Liam's hairy chest and cock, making Liam even harder.

"I used to. Kelly wanted me to."

"Fuck her." Nathan walked up to him, threw his arms around his shoulders, and kissed him. "On second thought, fuck me instead."

Liam picked him up. Nathan wrapped his legs around his waist as they stumbled to the bed. He held them in this position for a little bit and continued making out. He loved the feel of Nathan's hard lips on his mouth and how his cock pushed against his abs. And his own cock brushed against Nathan's opening, a tease for both of them.

God, I could fuck you right now.

"I think you should fuck me right now," Nathan said. Great minds thought alike.

"Just so you know, I've never been...on bottom before," Liam said.

"That makes sense since you've never been with a guy. Did you want to switch positions?"

Liam thought about it, but his hands wouldn't let go of Nathan. His cock strained to get closer to that tight ass.

"Maybe next time."

"Good because I want you to fuck my brains out."

"You're as lazy at sex as you are at farm work," Liam said with a smile.

"Oh trust me, you're about to see how untrue that statement is. Now suit up."

Liam kept Nathan in his arms as he shuffled to his nightstand drawer for the lube and a condom. They tried to make this work, but Liam wasn't that coordinated. He threw Nathan on the bed.

As he opened his nightstand drawer and took out supplies, Nathan fingered himself and stared right at him.

"As you like to say, sweet ass, right?" Nathan winked at him.

Fuck.

Liam tried to join in, but Nathan's foot pushed him back.

"You need to get yourself ready," he said with a teasing grin that made more blood pump south.

"I can't wait to fuck that grin right off your face."

Liam watched Nathan pleasure himself with two fingers while he rolled on his condom and lubed up his cock. He pictured himself minutes in the future pounding the shit out of that polished man. Nathan's moans echoed in the house. Liam shoved Nathan's hand away and replaced it with his tongue.

Liam had never rimmed anyone before, let alone a guy, but Nathan's hole looked too fucking good to pass up. He had to have it. The Brit tasted amazing, all rough and manly. Liam couldn't wait to pummel his tight little ass. Nathan shoved his head closer.

"Eat that hole, farm boy."

"That's Farm Man. Or Farm Boss in your case." Liam spread his ass wider and fucked his hole with his tongue. Nathan let out a scream that Liam worried his family would hear across the field.

Nathan yanked Liam back by the hair. "You need to fuck me now."

"So bossy."

"I told you I'm not a lazy bottom."

Liam lubed up Nathan's hole and slid in slowly. Nathan pushed back when he went too fast.

"It's been a while since I had a cock this big. The guys in rehab were nothing special."

Liam pushed all the way in.

"Yes!" Nathan yelled.

He watched his cock disappear inside Nathan's warm, tight hole, and he nearly came that second. Nathan rocked his hips into Liam as he thrust, like waves crashing into the shore, making him plunge deeper inside his ass. Liam leaned over Nathan and kissed him, remembering how amazing that kiss outside the barn was, how Nathan's lips sparked new life within him. He clamped his hand on Nathan's neck and brought his mouth closer. Nathan dug his fingers into his back muscles.

"Pick me up," Nathan whispered against his lips.

"Right." He lifted him in one smooth motion, and they were back to their original position, Nathan wrapped around Liam's muscular, firm body.

Liam impaled that posh ass on his cock, slamming in with lust and need, something he'd been wanting to do for a while. Each time he watched Nathan laboring on the farm, or spitting out a snarky comment, it was like another pull of a magnet, dragging him closer to the inevitable. Nathan threaded his fingers through his chest hair, then up to his beard.

"Fuck me harder, like you've probably done to your sheep."

"Fuck you, Posh Spice." Liam shoved Nathan against his

refrigerator and shagged the living daylights out of him, his tension and anger about the past getting exorcised out of him. But this was also...fun. He and Nathan were opponents in a game, trying to one-up each other. They were each trying to win, even though there would be no losers in this game. The fridge rocked back and forth with each hump. Liam's hips slapped against his cheeks. He wanted to tear him up, fuck Nathan so hard that he split in half. Liam hadn't had sex since Kelly. To say it had been a while was a severe understatement. The fridge sounded as if it were going to tip over.

Shit. Nathan tightened around Liam. Even though it was his first time fucking a guy, he knew what that meant.

"I think you're going to come," Liam said. "I didn't expect you to come first."

"I'm not going to come first. You are," Nathan said through pinched lips.

"I think you are. I think you're right on the edge."

"Fuck you."

"You already are." Liam moved them from the fridge to the kitchen counter, clotheslining it clear. Cups and mugs and plates crashed to the floor. Nathan held onto the cabinet door handle behind him. Liam grabbed his engorged cock and stroked away. Nathan tried to swat him back, but Liam held it tight. It was drenched in lube and pre-come. The pained look on Nathan's face hurtled Liam to the edge, too.

Liam fucked him in short, jackhammer bursts.

"You're going to watch me come?" Nathan asked. "Going to watch my cock shoot all over my stomach and my chest? Going to watch me lose total control as your fucking cock destroys my body?"

Just picturing that made Liam about to come.

Nathan slammed his head into the cabinet door. “Holy shit, Liam. You’re going to make me come. Fuck. Don’t stop.”

Liam didn’t want him to stop. It went to his head and caused his body to melt down. Liam’s balls tightened up. He screamed and unloaded into his condom.

He opened his eyes on a smiling Nathan who still had not come.

“Worked like a charm.”

Liam wiped away sweat from Nathan’s face and kissed him. “Fuck you.”

With the last remaining moments of his erection, Liam fucked Nathan to completion. Liam dragged a finger through the come on Nathan’s stomach and tasted it.

Bitter, salty, but still delicious. Just like Nathan.

Chapter 17

NATHAN

What just happened? Nathan stared up at the ceiling – from Liam's bed – contemplating that very question.

Sex, Nathan. You just shagged the one person you said you wouldn't. Sex led to awkwardness, and if things got awkward with Liam, they would be awkward with Mark and the kids by extension.

He sat up and looked around at the horror their sex tornado had caused. Cabinets flailed open and clothes thrown every which way and the coffeemaker askew with the plug saving it from falling into the sink. They had really strange, but really good sex. Nathan rubbed his head, expecting a hangover, but there was none. His mind was clearer than it'd been in a long time, even as it wrestled with the inevitable fallout.

He watched Liam's chest move up and down with the contented breaths of post-sex napping. The bed sheet rested just below his waist, blatantly teasing Nathan. Liam was all hot ruggedness on the outside and sweetness on the inside. He was a good guy, and he deserved better than some wild fling. He was not built for one-night stands. Which was going to make the rest of today very uncomfortable.

"Where are you going?" Liam asked in a scratchy voice, a foot still in his dream world.

Nathan put on his pants. "I should check on the ewes. See if any more of them are popping out lambs. Like you said, it's a chain reaction."

He found his shirt stuck under the nightstand, curious as to the aerodynamics that led it to that spot. This was what Nathan did best. He knew how to beat a quick retreat, even if this time, he wanted to get back in bed and rest his head against Liam's chest.

"Nathan." Liam grabbed hold of his hand. His milky blue eyes fixed him in place, but Nathan had to be stronger. "The sheep will be fine for a few more minutes."

Liam held his hand like he had held Nathan a little while ago: with confidence and surety.

"I suppose there's some policy in place against the boss shagging his farmhand."

"I'll have to check with human resources."

Nathan reached for one of his shoes, but Liam gave his hand a little tug.

"You don't have to run out so fast."

"We both know this can't happen again." Nathan made sure there was levity in his voice.

"Nah yeah, I wasn't even planning for it to happen at all."

"Same."

"And you're leaving soon anyway." Liam said it with a matter-of-factness that startled Nathan. He wasn't wrong, but it didn't sound right either. "When does your movie start shooting?"

The movie. Fucking Babe the fucking pig. The lie was like a virus, spreading and growing.

"Soon." There was no use getting attached to Liam, to anyone. They could ditch you on a doorstep at any moment.

"I hope you'll stay through lambing season. I can't get it through it without you."

The words hit Nathan right in the gut. Before he could stop himself, he returned into the warm bed and let Liam's arms curl around his body.

"I'll be here," Nathan said.

ONE MORE EWE gave birth during the day. It was just as amazing as it had been yesterday. The lambs came out and were walking and bleating within hours. It was a miracle, Nathan thought. And again when the ewe took care of her newborn lambs, the scene tugged at Nathan's heartstrings. He couldn't imagine an ewe abandoning one of her lambs, just pretending it never existed. How could humans do that? It didn't make sense to him, and he liked to hope that his mum thought about him even after she gave him up.

That night, he and Liam went to dinner at Mark's. As soon as they opened the door, Franny ran up to Nathan and enveloped him in a hug.

"And a good evening to you," he said.

She pulled back. Her face was bright and eager. "I'm Cinderella!"

"In the play?"

She nodded over and over like she was a bobblehead. "I'm Cinderella in *Into the Woods*! I can't believe it."

"Franny, that's wonderful!" Liam gave her a hug.

"You're barely going to see me these next few weeks," she

said. "I'm going to be busy with rehearsals. The show goes up in five weeks!"

"And you will stay busy with rehearsal so long as this doesn't negatively impact your schoolwork." Mark came out of the kitchen and put a casserole dish on the dining table. He pointed at his daughter with his oven-mitted hand. "I mean it, Franny."

"Dad." She sighed, embarrassed. "I know."

"I'm just reiterating so you don't forget." Mark came over and kissed her on the head. She pulled away with embarrassment in a way that Nathan remembers from seeing his boarding school classmates squirm from the public displays of affection they received when their parents came to visit. With his free hand, Mark patted Walt, who was sitting on the couch, looking at his mobile, presumably already up to speed on Franny's news.

"It's exciting," Nathan said to Mark.

"When this playhouse put on *Into the Woods* years ago, Mariel played the witch."

"We should watch the performance tonight after dinner," Franny said.

"For pointers?" Nathan joked, though inside he was already excited about watching more video of his mum.

"Thank you so much, Nathan. I never thought I could do this, that I could even sing. I wouldn't have been able to audition without your help and telling me I could do it."

"You could do it." Nathan found himself overcome with emotion, but kept it restrained. However, Liam seemed to notice. "It was a whirlwind week of practice, but you did it."

A few minutes later, Mark announced dinner was ready. Nathan noticed that his folding chair was missing. He looked at Mark and pointed at the empty space where his chair should have gone. Mark exchanged glances with Liam,

Franny, and Walt. Nathan was the monkey in the middle of his telepathic moment.

"We decided to put the folding chair away," Mark said.

He gestured to Mariel's empty chair.

Nathan was about to say something, but his voice stopped working. His eyes fell on his mum's chair. The light hit it in a special way and give it an ethereal glow.

Liam pulled the chair out for him. Around the table, he was greeted with the warmest looks, the looks that the ewes gave their newborn sheep.

This time, Nathan couldn't restrain the emotion. He cleared his throat to say something, but was at a loss for words.

He sunk into the firm cushion of the seat and felt the wood against his back. He was extra careful pulling the chair in, making sure to hold it gently and not drag it across the carpet.

"Much better," Franny said.

"I'll say the prayer tonight." Mark bowed his head.

They held hands. A spark of electricity hit Nathan's palm when it made contact with Liam's.

"Dear Lord, thank you for your bounty, for filling our bellies, for filling our hearts. Thank you for bringing this unique web of family into our lives."

"Amen," Nathan whispered.

He didn't let go of Liam's hand when the prayer was over. Quite the contrary. He squeezed it tight. And Liam squeezed back with equal tenderness.

Chapter 18

NATHAN

Over the next two weeks, Nathan and Liam's life consisted solely of birthing lambs and fucking each other's brains out. Nathan soon learned how all-consuming lambing season was, and sex was the perfect antidote to get through the stress. Ewes would go into labor at any time of day or night. It seemed like as soon as one finished giving birth, another one would start up, the familiar painful bleats emanating from another corner of the pen. No matter how used Nathan got to some of the more graphic parts of the birthing process, the sight of a ewe with her newborns hit him in the gut each and every time. Liam taught Nathan how to tail dock. They had to put a special rubber band around the lambs' tails so they would fall off. Liam assured him it was humane and safe because bacteria frequently built up in tails.

The farm was like a department store during the height of the holiday season, or an emergency room after a natural disaster. And yet no matter how busy Liam and Nathan were, they found time to fool around. After a particularly trying lamb birth, Liam would pull Nathan behind the hoof house, and they would make out and suck each other off. Or Nathan would surprise Liam in the outdoor shower. Even eating breakfast together somehow led to sex.

Day after day of watching Liam in action, of him taking charge running the farm and being tender with the animals, made Nathan perpetually stiff in the pants. Farm work was its own form of unending foreplay. The guys didn't sleep; they got by on wisps of naps throughout the day. The exhaustion became its own aphrodisiac, tearing away their inhibitions. It reminded Nathan of the time he had sex while on Ambien, only this time he remembered everything clearly. He remembered Liam's calloused, rough hands peeling off his clothes and exploring his body, the storm of passion glowing in his blue eyes as he grunted with orgasm, the moans of pleasure that wafted through their tiny abode, the way his own long cock slid into Liam's thick ass.

When they weren't birthing lambs, or fucking, they were building a new pen for their expanding brood. Nathan had never built anything before in his life, save for primary school arts and crafts projects. Mark and the kids would come over to help them out when they could.

Liam and Nathan had to keep track of the lambs being born, make sure their farm's new additions had food, water, and a place to sleep. That meant more fresh hay, more feeding rounds, and of course, more manure to shovel.

So much manure to shovel.

Lambing season was so all-consuming that after the first week, Nathan stopped sleeping at Mark's house. Mark set up a cot for Nathan in Liam's living room, which he used for only the first two nights before he wound up sleeping with Liam. At first, it happened naturally after a bout of night-time sex. Nathan was so exhausted that he literally couldn't fathom stumbling to his cot. He woke up in Liam's arms from what was probably the best sleep of his life. There was something about Liam's arms and his warm chest that dipped Nathan right to sleep. Everything felt strangely natural, as if they'd been sleeping like this for years, though Nathan chalked that up to the fog of sex. Each morning, Nathan purposely mussed the blankets on his cot in case Mark dropped by.

"You don't have to do that," Liam said while sipping his coffee. He watched from the kitchen area as Nathan balled up portions of his cot's top sheet in his fist to create creases.

"Your family will wonder why I don't seem to move when I rest."

"If only." Liam laughed and handed Nathan a piping-hot mug of his new favorite beverage. "You play tug-of-war with the blankets in your sleep."

"I do?"

"Even in a REM cycle, you're still a prick." Liam kissed his neck, sending a rush of heat through his body. "Are you still up for dinner tonight at the house?"

"Absolutely." Mark had convinced them to come out of lambing hibernation for a family dinner. He'd been nice enough to bring over home-cooked meals. Nathan looked forward to other human contact.

"We'll just remind the ewes not to pop out any lambs after four o'clock." Liam leaned against the kitchen counter, mug in hand, his shirt half-unbuttoned, glancing out the window at the livestock.

Nathan was hard in seconds.

"Are you getting good research for your film role?" Liam asked.

And then he wasn't. Nathan had drafted a synopsis of the gritty *Babe* reboot to show to Liam, more proof of his alibi (and his shoddy writing skills). The guilt over lying to Liam and his family lingered in the back of his mind everyday. He wondered how much longer he could keep the truth locked away inside him.

"I'm getting really good material to use, yeah," Nathan said. "I'll make sure you get acknowledged in the credits."

"I have to admit, I love seeing my name in the credits. This time, I won't be mentioned alongside a hundred other visual effects artists."

"Is this your family?" Looking for a change of subject, Nathan picked up a framed picture partially hidden on the corner of Liam's desk, one of those awkward family photos destined for internet mockery.

"Nah yeah, it is."

Nathan pointed to the youngest child on his father's lap. The boy was giving the camera a pouty sneer, one that had been given to Nathan several times when he first started on the farm.

"That's me."

"You have a big family." Nathan felt a twinge of jealousy.

Liam came over and wrapped Nathan in a hug from behind as he looked over his shoulders. "I have four older brothers."

"That's hot."

"Why is that hot?"

"I don't know. Five brothers is just hot."

"You think we sat around giving each other hand jobs?"

Nathan pictured being in the middle of it. Liam yanked the picture away.

"It was not fun being the youngest."

"Aw, you got teased?"

"Yeah." Liam's voice got heavy. "Mark's great, but Callum, James, and Oliver were...they loved to torment me, beat me up. They called it roughhousing so Mum and Dad wouldn't punish them. They knew where to hit me so our parents wouldn't see the bruises."

"Punches in the thigh because they left the biggest marks," Nathan said with familiarity. The phantom pain tingled in his leg. "But you're all adults now."

"You might want to remind them." Liam stared at the family picture with a mix of sadness and disgust. "By being the youngest, I was the black sheep without even trying."

"I'm the ginger sheep," Nathan said. "Only there's nothing lighthearted and playful about my family's hatred of me."

"The ginger sheep?" Liam replaced the picture on the table. "Cause of your hair?"

"My oldest cousin, Damian, called me that and it stuck. He was named after the demonic child in *The Omen*, which seemed to be appropriate foreshadowing."

Liam cheeks bunched up in that cheeky smile that was familiar to Nathan, one he had on while throwing teasing comments at each other during sex or even when he was microwaving dinner for them.

It was a smile Nathan didn't want to forget.

"You're the coolest ginger sheep." Liam put his arms around Nathan and pulled him in for a soft kiss.

Nathan kissed him back, although inside, he flinched at something in the moment. He didn't like talking about his family, especially such personal moments like those. It was too easy to drop his guard around Liam, and that was dangerous.

"Mark kind of feels that way with his own family of redheads. He's the black haired sheep. You'd fit in perfectly with him."

Nathan bit his tongue and gulped back the awkwardness. The truth rattled in its locked cage deep down inside him.

You have no idea.

Nathan let out a sigh.

Yet.

Chapter 19

NATHAN

Nathan recognized a new car in Mark's driveway when they walked over for dinner. Had he been ensconced so much in lambing and sexing season that he didn't know Mark got a new car? Hanging from the rearview mirror was a gold cross that caught the moonlight in its clutches.

"Did Mark find religion recently?" Nathan asked.

"Shit," Liam said when he saw it. "That's Pastor and Mrs. Fry. Mariel's parents."

"Mariel's parents?" Nathan repeated. *Mariel's parents equals my grandparents!* Nathan hadn't thought about having grandparents. He thought that since Mariel had passed, so had her parents. They must have been ravaged by losing her, so hopefully finding out they had another grandson might cheer them up.

But the spring in his step vanished by the time he reached the front door. How could he tell them the truth and not Mark and Liam?

Liam let out a sigh and turned to him. "Just so you know, you might be the first openly gay person they've ever met."

"That they know of."

Liam raised an eyebrow, somewhat agreeing with him. He opened the door.

And there they were. Nathan's grandparents. They sat on the couch with Walt as he showed them something on his phone. They had to be in their late sixties, but they looked like a pair of those active senior citizens who play golf and tennis. The Pastor was a tall man with a full head of unabashedly white hair and a bulbous nose that Nathan remembered from his pre-nose job days. (Fortunately, Damian hit him in the face with a ball once. It was the nicest thing the kid ever did.) He hoped he held onto his hair like the Pastor had. His grandmother was shorter and had a plumper frame. She wore an ankle-length skirt and very little makeup.

"Hiya Pastor Fry. Hi Brenda," Liam said with reluctance. Nathan's grandparents stood up. Pastor Fry shook Liam's hand, while Liam went in and kissed Brenda on the cheek. "Good to see you. This is Nathan."

Liam stepped aside and let the grandparents have a good look at their grandson. Nathan found himself straightening his back and smoothing down his hair.

Nathan found himself getting emotional instantly, the same way when he'd first seen Franny and Walt. This was his *family*. His grandparents back in London had favorites, and Nathan was not one of them. They went three years without acknowledging his birthday, and gave a shrug when he was cast in a movie.

Pastor Fry looked him over for a lengthy moment, and Nathan wondered if he knew. Oh, how he wanted to ask, but now was not the time. He would charm them at the dinner table and let them fall in love with him like his half-siblings had.

"Pleasure to meet you." Nathan shook both of their hands.

"Likewise," Pastor Fry said. Brenda gave a polite smile.

"I'm working on Liam's farm during lambing season. It's been quite an experience."

"Busy, eh?" the Pastor asked.

"You have no idea. Lots of lambs. We had to build a whole extra pen to house them. But it's part of Liam's grand plan to expand this operation." Nathan couldn't stop himself from speaking. He was like a little kid wanting to impress his grandparents with all the cool, new facts he learned in school.

"Nathan!" Franny ran down the stairs. She wore the baby blue dress Nathan had bought for her and still looked like a million bucks. "And Grandma and Grandpa!" She hugged them, too, though with less enthusiasm.

"When is your show, dear?" Brenda asked.

"Three weeks away! We're in the thick of rehearsals."

It turned out Franny had quite a voice, and with each practice, she was sounding more and more like their mother, according to the videos Nathan had watched.

"You're going to be great," Nathan said. "I've been helping her practice her singing and getting down her lines. I've dabbled in acting."

"Very nice!" Brenda said with an exaggerated nod.

"Well, more than dabbled. I've acted in theater and movies." Judging by their impressed head nods, he believed he was quickly getting on their good side.

"I just had a fitting for my costume," Franny said.

"It seems like only yesterday we were going to watch Mariel in her performances at that playhouse," Brenda said.

"Well, the performances that were appropriate," Pastor

Fry added. “Some of those shows were not right for a family-friendly community theater.”

She turned to Nathan. “Our daughter used to be an actress.”

“I’ve heard.” Nathan played along.

Brenda stared into his eyes for an extended second, as if she recognized him. The world seemed to stop turning. Nathan thought he was going to explode from nerves.

“Is everyone ready for dinner?” Mark asked from the dining room, breaking their staring contest. “The food is ready.”

They made their way to the table. Brenda sat down first.

“Franny,” Pastor Fry said. He stopped at the foot of the couch.

“Yes, Grandpa?”

Nathan turned to listen from the dining room, as did Liam.

“Is that dress new?” he asked.

“I got it a few weeks ago. Isn’t it nice?”

“It’s a bit short, don’t you think? I can see above your knees. It’s too revealing. You’re a young lady, Franny.”

“It’s the style, Grandpa.”

“What have we talked about? There are many things in our culture that may be popular, but are not acceptable. I think you should go upstairs and change into something more suitable for dinner.”

“But Grandpa, I like it.”

“Don’t talk back.” Pastor Fry didn’t raise his voice, but that didn’t make it any less intimidating. “Upstairs and change now.”

Nathan looked down at his empty plate, hating that he caused this drama. He had seen revealing dresses in London, outfits that would give Pastor Fry a real heart attack. Franny's dress was fun, but not reckless. Liam seemed to sense his guilt and gave him a supportive knee squeeze.

Mark rushed past him. "Is there a problem?"

"Mark, how could you let your daughter wear something like this?"

"What? It's a lovely dress. I don't see a problem with it."

Nathan did a silent cheer for Mark.

"It's okay, Dad. I'm going to change," Franny said with a flatness that made Nathan believe this was a regular occurrence. It was like when Nathan's paternal grandparents made racist remarks and Nathan just rolled his eyes because there was no use trying to have a real discussion with them about it. She ran upstairs before anyone could say another word on the subject.

"Sorry," Nathan mouthed to Mark when he came back into the dining room. Mark emphatically shook his head no, like he had nothing to apologize for.

Once Franny came back down wearing jeans and cotton sweater, everyone took their seats. Nathan sat in Mariel's chair, and his grandparents sat across the table in Franny and Walt's seats. The kids used folding chairs.

Mark brought a water pitcher to the table. "I'm glad that Grandma and Grandpa could join us this evening. It's always a pleasure when they drop in."

"We miss seeing you at weekly services," Pastor Fry said. "You should come back to a real church, not that naff place you take the kids."

"We'll take it under consideration. Would you care to say the prayer tonight?" Mark asked.

Pastor Fry proceeded to recite a traditional, bland version of grace. There was no flair, no personality like there had been with the rest of the family. Liam liked to incorporate lyrics into his grace, while Walt always made sure his rhymed. Pastor Fry had the authoritative, booming church voice that made Nathan feel like he was stuck in a pew for midnight mass.

"Amen!" Brenda said, with the others following shortly thereafter.

They dug into steak and potatoes with a side of vegetables. It was the plainest meal Mark had ever cooked, though still tasty.

"Mark, you should try cooking mutton. It is so tender and juicy," the Pastor said.

"We don't eat lamb," Mark said. "We raise them."

"Our parents only raised sheep for wool, never for meat," Liam added.

"Well, that's ridiculous. You are missing out."

Liam plunged his fork into his potatoes extra hard. Nathan gave his leg a stealth squeeze under the table.

"Nathan, I can't help noticing your accent. You're not from around here," Brenda said with a teasing smile. "Do we have a Brit in our midst?"

"We do," he said. "I am doing some traveling and have stopped in New Zealand."

"And decided to work on a farm?" Pastor Fry shoved a forkful of meat in his mouth.

"Nathan's preparing for a movie role," Walt said.

"Yes! A small, independent film." This was the type of smalltalk that Nathan could never do without being completely smashed. "It's very different from my prior acting work back in London, but I'm excited about the challenge."

"You're from London?" Pastor Fry asked.

"Born and raised."

"You were born there?"

"Correct."

"Are you at university?"

Pastor Fry shot out questions rapid fire. Nathan got the feeling that was how he was with everyone.

"I am not. I took some time off to travel. I wanted to travel now when I'm young."

"Lovely," Brenda said. There was a quiet current under her words, not as bubbly as she was on the couch. "I wish we'd done more traveling when we were your age."

"How old are you, Nathan?" Walt asked, one of those random questions kids didn't know to hold back.

"I turned twenty-two back in May." Nathan checked across the table to see if that rang any bells for his grandparents. The moment got so quiet he could've heard a pin drop.

"Happy belated birthday then," Pastor Fry said with a polite smile. He and his wife turned their attention back to their food, Walt regaled the table with a story about a spider in his room, and it was like whatever moment Nathan thought he felt never happened.

"Really great dinner, Mark!" Pastor Fry said.

LIAM

"You have the patience of a saint." Liam pulled a freshly-scrubbed plate from the sink and handed it over to Mark to dry. He looked over his shoulder to make sure nobody else was in earshot. "If they were my in-laws, I would move and not give them my new address."

"They are the grandparents to my children."

"That's only a fluke of genetics. Did you hear what he was saying about Franny's dress?" Liam wished Pastor Fry and Brenda had seen when Franny first showed it off to them, how new levels of confidence radiated out of her.

Watching his niece deflate in front of his eyes because of their words infuriated him. He added it to the long list of things he couldn't stand about the Pastor.

"They're just from a different time," Mark said, forever the mediator.

"A different century. Whenever they come over, they always criticize your parenting or complain about something."

"So do you," Mark said with a teasing smile. Liam made sure there was dishwater in the spoon he handed to Mark.

"Oops."

"That's what in-laws do. It's because they care."

"Mariel didn't seem to think so." Liam wanted to take back his words, but he knew that his late sister-in-law would agree with him. She always seemed to have this look of barely concealed frustration, even hatred, whenever Liam saw her and the Pastor together. "She was the one who decided that you and the kids should stop going to their church. And remember those stories you used to tell me about what a rebel she was in high school, changing into dresses in the parking lot that were a lot more revealing than what your daughter had on."

That was before Liam was born, but Mariel had showed him pictures of her teen years, and she totally would've tried to get him to smoke cigarettes with her behind the school. In a way, she kind of reminded him of Nathan. They had the same hint of mischief in their eyes. They even held their cigarettes in a similar fashion. Although if Liam's father had been a conservative preacher, maybe he would've tried to rebel, too.

Mark balanced the final serving dish on the drying rack. "Mariel's relationship with her parents was complicated, but they loved her deeply, and they love those kids just as deeply. They just want the best for them. We all do."

"I think their version of best and our version of best are not the same."

Mark put down his dishtowel and heaved out a breath. Having saint-like patience was not for the weak.

"I'm sorry. I'll shut up."

"Nathan seemed to like them," Mark said.

"He did." Liam thought about all the questions he asked the Pastor and how eager and friendly he seemed when chatting with Brenda. It was cute.

"Things seem to be going well with you boys."

"What?" Liam dropped his sponge in the sink. It splashed a few droplets in his face. "What do you mean?"

"With lambing."

"Oh, right. Good as gold. Listen, Mark. There's something I need to tell you. Or rather, that I want to tell you."

Mark turned to him, his face switching to concern in a blink. "What is it?"

Liam had been both looking forward to and dreading this moment. He didn't like keeping secrets from his brother. "I'm—I'm bi."

"You mean bisexual?"

Liam nodded yes. Mark nodded as well.

"I think it's been something that's always been there. And Nathan's helped me...discover it."

Mark nodded again. His apparent stoicism was burning a hole in Liam.

"Well, out with it," Liam said.

"Do I say congratulations?"

"If you want to."

"Congratulations, then." The smile that broke out on

Mark's face made Liam exhale a massive sigh of relief. "Wonderful news."

They hugged, getting dishwater stains on each other's clothes but not caring in the slightest.

"I know it's a surprise," Liam said.

"It's not."

"It's not?"

"I could tell something was percolating with you and Nathan."

"You could?" Liam felt his ears get red. Maybe they weren't as careful as he thought.

"I've noticed how you look at him, like you're constantly pinching yourself that you get to spend time with this person. I don't care what gender the person is who's able to make you feel that way. I haven't seen you this happy in a long time."

"Since Kelly?"

Mark flicked a stray soap bubble off Liam's beard. "Happier."

Chapter 20

NATHAN

At three the next morning, two ewes went into labor at the same time. It was almost as if they were competing with each other for who could have the loudest, most painful delivery. Liam even shushed the ewes at one point, worried they would wake up his family. Nathan had gotten over any kind of squeamishness he might have had about the lambing process. The ewe this morning had one breech birth, and Nathan didn't blink when it came time to turn the lamb around inside the uterus.

After the early morning births, he and Liam took turns napping during the day. He didn't know how Liam was able to handle lambing season on his own last year. Nathan watched him sleep peacefully, sprawled out cold against a bale of hay, his chest rising and falling with breath. He would have moments like these on the farm, times when he caught himself looking at Liam for no reason and feeling a pang of tenderness in his chest at whatever he saw. It wasn't as if Liam was bent over or shirtless, although those were wonderful moments, too.

Liam would be writing out a grocery list at the kitchen table or giving one of the lambs a checkup and Nathan would feel a bolt of heat feeling rush through him. And then when Liam would look up and cock an eyebrow at him? Damn.

Rather than question them, he savored these moments, even though they were followed by his brain reminding him that this connection was built on lies. It was like the housing development in *Poltergeist* that was built on a Native American burial ground. That did not end well.

Later in the afternoon, post-nap and post-impromptu literal roll in the hay with Liam, Nathan headed over to the house to run lines with Franny and give her notes on her performance. Each time they met, he had less feedback for her. She was taking to acting like a fish to water, turning the living room into the Globe Theater. Nathan couldn't help but think that her talent was genetic. It was something else that connected them.

"You want to be serious when you say this line. It'll get a big laugh," Nathan said. "You don't want to hint that you're in on the joke at all. That takes away from the humor. I need to believe that you are convinced that you will marry the prince. Make me believe, Franny."

Franny nodded with her big eyes taking in every syllable of feedback.

"I can't believe I'm being coached by a real, professional actor. When will we get to see you on the big screen?"

"It takes forever for movies to get released. They have to edit, put in sound effects, dub in any muddled dialogue, and then the studio decides when the most advantageous time to release it will be, which could be a year or two from now. And my part might get cut completely."

"Like Coco the housekeeper in *The Golden Girls*."

"Precisely. Where did he go after the first episode?"

Nathan shrugged. "It's the nature of show business."

"My mum once told me about how she was an understudy in a production of *My Fair Lady*, and when Eliza got sick the day before opening night, Mum had to take her place, and she received such great notices that they kept her in the part."

Our mum was a total badass, he thought.

"I think she even has the reviews clipped out in one of her scrapbooks."

"She kept a scrapbook? That's adorable," Nathan said. He had started one for his early performances, but his stepmum threw it out during one of her spring cleaning purges. The only thing she hated more than tasteful décor was clutter.

"Not a scrapbook. Several. Mum was a complete pack rat. She saved everything." Franny laughed to herself. Nathan gave a stage laugh while other thoughts circulated in his mind.

Mariel kept everything. Including the photograph from the Oasis concert. Who kept a random picture of a random mate she shagged at a random concert? If she was such a packrat, Nathan wondered what else she kept from that time in her life.

"Did she save receipts going back ten years and craziness like that?"

"Probably. There's so much junk in the basement. We tried keeping it in the attic, but Dad was afraid the ceiling would cave in."

The basement. Nathan remembered it'd been mentioned once before over dinner, but he didn't realize it contained treasure troves of Mariel's stuff. He had passed a door by his bedroom and always assumed it was a closet.

His mind spun with what could be down here, the truth about what happened waiting to be found. Even if he had the basic facts—she cheated on her boyfriend and left the evidence back in London—Nathan still wanted to know why. Why was she such a wonderful parent to Franny and Walt yet couldn't be bothered to check in once with Nathan? Why was he so unlovable?

"Honestly, we tried going through her stuff but there was so much and…" Franny got quiet, a spell of grief overtaking her like storm clouds rolling in. She pulled her knees up to her stomach.

"It was too painful," Nathan said.

"I started bawling at the first box. It was old birthday cards Walt and I had drawn for her. She saved every single one."

"She sounds like a great mum."

Franny wiped away an errant tear. "What was your mum like?"

Nathan could've given her an easy answer, another story to spin, but the words got caught in his throat. His own grief spell snuck up on him. Could you miss someone you never knew? Franny's face shifted slightly, sensing the difficulty he was having. They spent a moment in joint silence that brought them closer.

"Eventually we'll go down there and sort things out," Franny said. "But not today."

"When you're ready," Nathan said, looking at a family picture hanging on the opposite wall, wishing he could tell her that he'd been waiting his entire life and he was ready now.

Franny rested her head on his shoulder. "I'm glad you're here, Nathan."

. . .

Liam

Liam had finished his farm chores early and was taking advantage of the alone time to work on one of his freelance graphic design projects. The farm was at peace, which would not last long. But disruption didn't come from one of the sheep.

Callum did the knock-and-twist and didn't wait for Liam to let him in. That was only charming when Nathan did it.

He barged through the door flanked by their two brothers Oliver and James. Oliver had a beer gut and a perpetually sweaty complexion, while James had unkempt black hair, a double-chin, and a mustache stolen from a 1970s porn star. Did Nathan really want this brother gang-bang scenario?

"Piglet, how's it going?" Callum clapped him on the shoulder.

"Nice place, here." Oliver ground his fists into Liam's shoulders, sending jabs of pain down his back, just as he had done since they were boys.

"This is a pleasant surprise," Liam said. He drank the last drops of coffee from his mug. He would not be offering them any of his special locally roasted coffee.

A fourth man in a suit pants and a dress shirt with rolled-up sleeves followed behind them.

"I realize we haven't seen your new abode," James said. He was shaped like a match, one long skinny frame with wild finger-in-socket hair on top. He looked around the premises. "Nice. Small."

"In real estate parlance, we'd call it cozy," Callum said.

"I reckon Piglet doesn't need much room." Oliver rubbed his fist in Liam's head, potentially causing cranial bleeding.

Liam couldn't stop looking at the fourth man here with

the rolled-up sleeves, like he was running for office. The man gazed out the front window at the field.

"I'm Liam." Liam stuck his hand in the man's face for a shake. "Nice to meet you."

"Harold Grates." The man shook it back. "This is a gorgeous piece of land you have. The view of the mountains in the distance is breathtaking."

His whole demeanor, whether he meant for it or not, chilled Liam to the bone.

"Harold is the real estate developer I was telling you about," Callum said. "He wants to turn all of this into a beautiful neighborhood. I brought him here to tell you more about his plan."

Callum had the type of restrained excitement that teenagers had at Christmas. They were just as eager as little kids for gifts, but did everything they could not to show such blatant excitement. Callum needed specially made contact lenses so he could have literal dollar signs in his eyes.

Harold took an iPad from his briefcase. "I have some wonderful ideas for how I see this place. As you know, housing in Wellington is getting scarcer, and more families are angling to move out of the city into clean, safe neighborhoods."

Liam's brothers moved aside so he could sit on his couch. Growing up, he'd always had to sit on the floor since there was never enough room for all the brothers on their family's couch. Couch space was reserved for seniority, though Mark would let Liam take his spot.

Harold put the iPad on the coffee table. It had one of those covers that also doubled as an easel. He played a simulation video of what the development would look like: kids biking down sidewalks, freshly-washed cars pulling into garages. The whole footage reminded Liam of a horror film, with its opening shots of a perfect suburbia that was about to be attacked by an unknown terror.

"The town needs a development like this," James said. "It'll bring more families and get the schools in better condition. Maybe I should move Elise and the kids here."

"Us first!" Callum said. They laughed.

The video went into a 3-D simulation of what the development would look like. His parents' farm would be its own village, the earth his dad tilled would be pristine blocks and cul-de-sacs. It was nauseating.

"And the best part," Harold said, as he folded up his iPad. "is how much money you're going to make off this sale."

"More than we could ever make from renting it," Callum said.

"We are going to be a couple of rich arseholes!" Oliver punched Liam's back in celebration. He was the rugby player who never left the field.

"What do you think, Liam?" Callum asked. "It's a phenomenal opportunity."

"Our family's been on this land for over fifty years," Liam said.

"So?" James asked.

"This is what our parents left us."

"Harold, mind if we have a minute?" Callum asked.

"There's no pressure to decide right this instant," Harold said, the only sane voice in this room, shockingly. He handed Liam his card. "Talk it over with your family. Think about it. I'll need an answer by next week though, in case I need to move forward with other prospects."

"Thank you." Liam nodded his head, and Harold left to return to his car. The second the screen door shut, Liam wished he had stayed. He was the only thing keeping his brothers in check.

"Piglet, are you serious right now?" Oliver asked, his face mashing like lumps of clay into a grimace.

Callum got in front of Oliver and James before they did anything stupid. "Mum and Dad wanted us to be financially secure. Dad worked day in and day out for decades. Don't romanticize it, Liam. He hated it. If he was given this payday, he would take it."

Liam didn't believe that, though. Their dad talked about how he saved up for years to buy this initial plot of land. He would carry Liam through the fields in his wheelbarrow, gazing out on his flock with immense pride. Liam knew there were hard times. He had experienced them, too. But it was satisfying in a way he'd never experienced as a visual effects artist.

"Dad could've sold or rented the land anytime he wanted. He stayed. This is what he wanted."

"And we're supposed to want it?" James asked. "You have a very different idea of what Mum and Dad were like. You got them at the tail end. You were the baby. They didn't treat you like free labor. They doted on you. And they treated Mark like a prince. That left us in the middle, fighting for scraps."

James stepped away and took a beat to cool off in the kitchen. Liam looked out at his field. The thought of getting rich off land his parents gave their lives to didn't sit right with him, not when he was finally getting the hang of running his own farm.

"What if I bought the land from you?" Liam asked. The idea caught fire in his mind. "I just built a second pen for the lambs. It's only going to grow."

James laughed out loud. "Are you fucking serious,

Piglet? You still think you can make a living out of being a sheep farmer?"

"Yes." Liam didn't say that with as much confidence as he hoped. He was still convincing himself.

Callum tapped his computer screen. "You're still doing freelance jobs. This farm isn't even profitable for you."

"It will be."

"No, it won't," Callum said. "We've known you your entire life, Piglet. We've seen you screw up your fair share of shit. That time you saved up for a car, then got in an accident the first week. Or when you fell into that pyramid scheme at university and were on the hook for six hundred dollars."

"We say this with love, but you are in over your head," James said. Liam hated the sound of his voice. It was pure snivel, and it pricked at him even more now. "It's a miracle that you haven't killed all your sheep at this point. I know you needed a change when you got dumped, but it's time to end this quarter-life crisis, bro. Get out now while you can. Don't drag us down with you."

Liam had no counter-argument. Maybe they were right. But mostly, he just wanted them gone. "I'll think about it."

"I'll have Harold send you that presentation," Callum said. "We'll talk in a few days."

Chapter 21

<u>LIAM</u>

That night, Liam washed off the day—the lambing, the farm work, his asshole brothers—in the outdoor shower. The moon was in full force and was all the light he needed. The warm rivulets of water cascaded down his chest and back, soothing his tired muscles. It streamed down his shaggy hair into his beard, releasing tension he held onto in his jaw.

"Mind if I join you?"

Nathan stood at the entrance to the shower, sneaky smile on his face.

"You're a bit overdressed," Liam said.

"I think I'll enjoy the view for a bit more." Nathan leaned against the slats of wood that walled in the shower.

Fucker.

Well, if he wanted a show...

Liam slid a hand to his hardening cock and stroked himself under the water for Nathan to see. He liked being on display, giving a one-man show for one man. He ran his free hand over his chest and abs. Nathan didn't blink. Liam turned around and let the water slip down his back over his round ass. He never felt so sexy, so wanted. His body sparked with raging desire.

He heard Nathan take a step closer, then stop. A buzzing sound cut through the pheromones. When Liam turned around, Nathan was slipping his phone back into his pocket.

"Is a third person joining us?"

"They wish," Nathan said. Liam sensed hesitation catching in his voice.

"Who was it?"

"I didn't recognize the number. Telemarketer, probably."

Liam wasn't sure he believed him. Unknown numbers don't make people go quiet. But before he could turn it over in his mind, Nathan's shirt was off and in his face.

"Shouldn't you be showing off that amazing arse of yours?" Nathan spun his finger to signal Liam to turn back around. He unzipped his trousers. They fell to the ground, and the wood sprouting in his underwear pointed right at Liam. Nathan tossed his pants outside the shower. His pants which held his phone.

Liam shook the thought out of his head and turned around as requested. He slid a hand over his firm cheeks down to his hole. He rubbed a finger against his opening. The water trickling over his puckered area made it extra sensitive, sending shivers over his skin. Suddenly, Nathan's arms were around him, fingers threading through his chest hair, hard cock pressing against his hole. Liam let out a deep moan of pleasure, wanting what came next but wanting to live in this moment, too.

Nathan kissed his neck. His tight, wet muscles pressed against Liam's back. His rubbed Liam's nipple with one hand while the other traveled down south, cutting a path through his bush to his rock hard cock.

"You are so fucking sexy, Liam," he whispered on his neck. "I want you so fucking bad."

Liam spread his legs apart, his body begging to be taken over by Nathan. Nathan spanked his ass hard. Liam could feel the handprint forming. He let out a low growl, desperate for Nathan to free him from the pain and stress. Nathan jerked his cock faster. He pulled Liam back by the neck and nibbled at his ear. Liam's legs quaked to keep him upright. He reached out a hand to the wall to hold himself steady. Nathan's cock teasingly brushed against his hole.

His mouth kissed down Liam's spine and made its way to his ass.

"God, yes." Liam's bottom lip quivered with lust. He wiped water out of his eyes.

Nathan spread his cheeks apart and flicked a tongue on his puckered opening. Liam groaned with approval. Nathan's hot breath on him sent shivers racing up his spine. He felt Nathan's tongue open him up, slipping in and out of his hole, stoking an unquenchable need building inside him. He grabbed Nathan by the hair and pushed him deeper inside.

"Easy, mate. You don't want me to asphyxiate," Nathan said.

Liam let go and wrapped his hand around his aching cock, desperate to release a hot load of come. But not yet. "I fucking love what you're doing to my arse."

"Just you wait."

Nathan rubbed his thumb on his hole and pushed inside. Liam put a foot up on a wooden slat, sticking his ass out to give Nathan better leverage. He plunged his thumb deeper, using his free fingers to play with Liam's balls. The water couldn't cool him down. When Liam and Kelly had had shower sex, he'd sometimes secretly wish he could be on bottom, a fleeting desire that he shoved down instantly. But now it could be unleashed. Now he could fulfill that desire with a man, a man he couldn't stop thinking about, a man he got to wake up with and go to sleep with.

Nathan gave his ass a final slap and stood up. He turned Liam around and pulled him into a heat-killed kiss. Their mouths collided in an explosion of passion, but there was caring, too. Nathan cradled his cheek, and the connection between them outshined the moon. Liam tasted the mix of himself on Nathan's lips. Water gushed between their slicked-up chests as their cocks dueled below.

"You are wonderful," Nathan said.

"You are, too." Liam pecked his soft lips. He looked into Nathan's blazing green eyes, stormy with lust, just like his were. "Now fuck me."

"Ask nicely."

"Now please fuck me."

"As you fucking wish." Nathan kissed him once more and bit at his lower lip. He had Liam face the wall, gave his hole a quick spit shine, and pressed his cock inside him.

"God, yes," Liam cried out.

"Don't wake the sheep."

"Fuck," was all Liam could respond with to Nathan. It felt so good that words failed him. Nathan pegged his tight hole and nuzzled his face into Liam's strong back. Each thrust was another bolt of ecstasy that made every nerve fizzle with pleasure. Nathan rubbed this thumb over Liam's nipple, the same thumb that had just been inside him. Liam loved the sound of Nathan's abs slapping into his firm cheeks. His body became extra sensitive to the water dripping down his body, to the chirp of crickets outside, to Nathan's hot moaning on his back.

"You're so tight, baby. God, you feel so good," Nathan said.

Liam held himself up against the wall of the shower. He jerked his cock slowly and methodically. He'd been on the verge of coming for a while, but he wanted them to finish together. He wanted to feel Nathan release inside him. By the pained groans leaving Nathan's mouth, the Brit was awfully close.

A familiar buzzing sound cut into their hot moment. On the other side of the shower wall, Nathan's phone buzzed. Another telemarketer?

It's nobody. It's nothing, Liam told himself. *People are allowed to receive phone calls.*

He was over-reacting. But he couldn't help think about all the times Kelly had to sneak away to take a call.

"Fuck, I'm going to come, mate." A deep moan ripped out of Nathan. He took hold of Liam's ass with both hands and fucked him fast and hard. He fucked the worry out of Liam's head, until all his mind could think about was shooting their loads.

"I want you to come inside me," Liam said. "I want to bloody feel it."

"Dirty bastard," Nathan sneered through muffled, heated breaths, choked with impending orgasm.

"Don't...stop."

The world went white as Nathan let out a groan and emptied himself into Liam's ass. Liam sprayed the shower wall with his seed. He felt a trail of Nathan's come sliding down his leg, making him stiff all over again.

"I can't get enough of you." Nathan kissed his ear.

Liam kissed him right back, tasting his hot, salty breath, savoring the sweaty smell of sex between them. He gazed into Nathan's eyes, then realized he was studying them.

"Best part of shower sex. Easy cleanup," Nathan said. He washed himself off in the water. Liam kept watching him, a sense of uncertainty creeping into his mind. He joined Nathan under the shower head.

"By the way, your phone rang again," he said to Nathan.

"Oh."

"Damn telemarketers, right?"

NATHAN

The next day, Liam collapsed on the bed for an afternoon nap after an especially busy morning constructing the new lambing pens. Each ewe and her young needed their own pen so as to prevent mismothering.

"Lambs could easily wind up with the wrong ewe. Imagine if that happened with humans," Liam had said.

"Imagine," Nathan deadpanned. *Imagine being purposely mismothered.*

Nathan told Liam he would watch the sheep while he rested. None of the ewes were on the verge of popping out babies. The new mothers were content in their pens nursing their newborns, while the mothers-to-be rested in the hoof house. On the human side, Mark was still at work, Walt was at school, and Franny was at play practice. Nathan could easily sneak off to the house and explore in the basement for a few minutes. Liam wouldn't even know he was gone. The man napped hard.

It's not wrong, is it? I have a right to know who my mother was.

He was running out of time to find answers. Lambing season was winding down, and he would have to leave for his movie shoot soon. Plus, the outside world kept trying to pop this bubble he enjoyed living in, such as having his very-much-alive father call him whilst enraptured in unbelievable outdoor shower sex.

He looked at Tilly for support. She seemed to give him the stink eye, but she also had a lamb pulling at her udder.

"I'm not looking for anything scandalous. I'm not trying to crack their safe and steal priceless heirlooms," he said to her. "I just want answers."

Tilly tended to her lambs. She wasn't getting involved.

THE HOUSE WAS empty and still, but Nathan made sure to be quiet nevertheless. He figured the basement stairs would be creaky. Weren't they all? He took them one at a time, resting each foot softly on each step.

The basement was even worse than Franny had described. Stacks of worn, sinking in boxes stood against every available wall. Each stack looked about to collapse, the cardboard fighting from giving in to time and gravity. Around the boxes were shoeboxes, plastic bags, and old dusty suitcases filled with more of Mariel's stuff. Nathan figured the basement was like this when she was alive, a dirty hoarding secret she hid from the world.

Nathan didn't know where to start. None of the boxes were labeled.

"Jump in anywhere," he muttered to himself.

He opened the box closest to him. Inside were old clothes of hers, black choker necklaces from the '90s and black cardigans. Mum was a total goth chick, he thought. That probably did not go over well with Pastor Fry. He found one of those tiny knapsacks girls carried instead of purses back then. Inside was an old student ID and an empty bag of tobacco. They could've rolled cigarettes together. Nathan realized he hadn't smoked since lambing season started. Sheer exhaustion and rowdy sex had supplanted his vices apparently.

The boxes weren't organized. Nathan was like an archaeologist peeling back layers of the earth to reveal different historical eras. Underneath the goth outfits were old photos of mum in high school. Nathan pulled out a pocket bible. Inside, she wrote her name in curly cursive. Under the stamp with the church's logo, Mariel doodled a penis. Nathan laughed to himself.

"Nice one, Mum."

His eyes lit up at the next artifact he found. A diary. Nay, journal. His mum seemed like the kind of gal who preferred to call it a journal. Nathan felt the weight of her most private words in his hands. The spine cracked when he lifted open the cover.

Mark wants to see Jurassic Park AGAIN. The dinosaurs are awesome, but they're still fake, so I don't see the big deal. It's nothing like actors performing live on stage. That's thrilling.

Nathan smiled to himself reading the old entry. Judging by the date, she was about seventeen. He wondered if she kept a journal while she was in London and after.

He searched through the box for more journals, but he stopped when he felt a sick feeling creeping down his throat, the kind of feeling that comes when he knew he was being watched.

Walt stared at him from the bottom of the stairs.

"Nathan, what are you doing?"

Chapter 22

NATHAN

Nathan froze at the voice. He looked up slowly, calculating excuses in his head. "Hiya Walt."

Confusion creased his little forehead, as if he woke up and bumped into Santa on Christmas Eve.

"I was just looking for something," Nathan said.

"What?"

"An extra blanket." *Good save.* Nathan considered this the improv exercise of his life. "I've been a little chilly at night, and I thought there might be an extra blanket down here."

"Doesn't Uncle Liam have extra blankets at his house?"

"He does not, if you can believe it."

Walt nodded, and Nathan thought he was safe, until:

"Why were you looking through my mum's old stuff? Extra blankets are in the linen closet upstairs."

"Oh, they are?" Nathan glanced at the boxes of his mother's stuff, like he had no idea he was in the lair of a hoarder. "Thank you, Walt."

Walt kept a watchful eye on him. He was ten. He wasn't a guileless child.

"What were you reading?" he asked.

"Reading?" Sweat percolated on Nathan's palms.

Walt pointed to the open journal on top of the box.

"I was looking for blankets, like I said, then I stumbled onto old theater programs." Nathan found a program for *Cats* (*Really, Mum?* Cats?) shoved inside the open box. "They caught my eye like the ones in your dad's bedroom."

"Why were you in my dad's bedroom?" Walt shot back immediately. He would grow up to be an ace detective.

"Just the theater nerd in me, I reckon." Nathan showed Walt the program.

"Dad said when I was little, I saw her dressed as the Wicked Witch in *The Wizard of Oz* and I started crying."

"She scared me, too. Being scared of the Wicked Witch is like a rite of passage for children."

Walt peeked inside the box. Nathan stepped back to let him look, but he was hesitant to dig in.

"Dad doesn't want us down here," Walt said.

"I didn't know that."

"He doesn't want us messing things up or getting injured."

Things appeared extremely messed up already, Nathan thought.

Walt gave the box one last peek before closing it shut. "I'll have my Dad get you an extra blanket for tonight."

"Walt," Nathan said quickly, his nerves threatening to spill over. "Don't worry about it. I'll be fine."

"Are you sure?"

"Absolutely." They walked to the basement door, and even though Walt didn't seem suspicious anymore, Nathan's nerves refused to subside. "Walt, can we keep this between us? Being in the basement and all."

"Like a secret?"

"Right." Nathan's stomach twisted into a knot. "We shouldn't tell anyone, especially not your dad and Uncle Liam."

"Why not?"

"I don't want to get in trouble. Uncle Liam could boot me off the farm for looking around down here."

"I don't think he'd do that," Walt said with a smile.

Right. Because we're a couple...or something like that. Nathan got desperate.

"Well, I don't want you to get in trouble."

"I would get in trouble?" Walt's eyes opened wide. They threatened to crush Nathan.

"Your dad said not to be down here."

"You were just looking for a blanket."

Nathan's palms were so sweaty they could've ended a drought. "I'll ask Uncle Liam for one, like you said." *Nobody has to know I was down here poking through Mariel's belongings.*

"What if my dad sees the box had been opened?" He pointed to the ripped-open tape. Nathan had tried to be careful when opening, but it was obvious that it'd been tampered with. He didn't know how often Mark came down here, if it was his own little secret.

"Then you..." Nathan gripped the banister. He had to pull the words out from deep inside his black soul. "Then you just lie."

Nathan could feel the innocence being sucked out of Walt.

"You say you don't know what happened. And if your dad asks what you were up to today, you leave this part out. It's not really a lie, per se. It's a lie of omission, which is different."

I'm teaching my little brother to lie. I belong in hell.

"It's a secret, Walt. Let's shake on it." Nathan held out his hand. Walt's limp, soft hand met his for a deflated shake.

Nathan went back to his bedroom in Mark's house and sat on the bed, staring at the blank wall, hating himself. He realized this was why he was incapable of being loved, incapable of having a family. Because he always found a way to fuck it up royally.

IF THERE WAS EVER a need for a Jiminy Cricket to tell him what to do, it was now. Nathan walked across the field from Mark's house and stopped in a patch where he remembered getting reception previously.

"It's three o'clock in the bloody morning," Eamonn said when he picked up.

"You're getting an early start to the day. You're welcome. It's four in the afternoon where I am, because I am still in New Zealand, wreaking absolute havoc on a very nice family."

"What happened?" he asked, now wide awake. "Have you told them the truth?"

"Worse. I just convinced my ten-year-old half brother to lie for me." A pain lanced his heart as he pictured Walt reluctantly agreeing to keep a secret.

"What is going on? Are you still working on the farm?"

"Yes. And I've gotten quite good at it. I'm also buggering the farmer, who is the brother of the man whose son I just asked to lie." Nathan collapsed on the ground, not caring about the grass stains he was getting.

"Bleeding Christ, Nathan. You really know how to cock things up."

"Tell me about it." He stared at the clouds being carried

across the sky by some celestial conveyer belt. "My mother was amazing. She was the greatest performer I've ever seen. But she was also a badass bitch."

"Sounds like someone I know," Eamonn said. "You have to tell them the truth."

"But if I do, everything will change. They'll know I've been lying to them. For the first time, I feel like I'm part of a family. I'm afraid to lose that."

"They'll understand."

"Come on, E. I've been lying to them from the moment I stepped foot in their house, and even if I do come clean, that will just make me the illegitimate bastard son of their wonderful mother. That won't make me family." Nathan pictured their faces glaring at him, the same way his real family looked at him. "Liam will never talk to me again."

"The farmer?"

"He hates liars, and I can't stop. The other night, my dad called in the middle of some *really fantastic* shower sex—"

"TMI"

"—and I kept having to say it was a telemarketer."

"Why?"

"I told him both my parents were dead."

"Nathan!"

Nathan smacked a hand on his forehead and slid it down to cover his eyes. "I had a good reason in the moment."

Eamonn let out a sigh.

"And I've managed to cock everything up while being completely sober, so I deserve a little bit of credit."

"Really?" Eamonn asked.

"I haven't had a drink in weeks."

They both let that sink in. Nathan beamed with pride up at the clouds.

"That's wonderful, mate," Eamonn said. "But you have to come clean."

If only it were that easy. Some flashing alarm inside Nathan kept warning him that this would all blow up in his face. Because that was what Nathan did: he took good things and ruined them. This was why his dad kept his distance from him and his real family wanted nothing to do with them.

"They'll hate me. Liam will hate me," Nathan said.

"I thought you were just shagging."

"We..." Nathan thought about the way Liam smiled at him on the farm, and the way he spooned him in bed. Just the image of Liam's face in his mind caused his heart to pump a warm feeling throughout his body, followed by a surge of panic when he pictured losing him forever. "I have to go. Thanks for chatting, E."

Nathan tucked his phone in his pocket and looked at the rolling green hills against the cloudy sky, hoping that maybe they had a solution to get him out of this mess.

Chapter 23

LIAM

By the end of the next week, lambing season had finally wound down. The new family pens were built, mothers and lambs were sufficiently bonding. And Liam would not have been able to get through it without Nathan. He was grateful to Mark for putting up those flyers, for more reasons than one.

To celebrate the end of the season, Liam took Nathan out to dinner as colleagues. After not leaving the farm for a month, he figured they deserved a night on the town. Liam made a reservation at a restaurant overlooking the water. He wanted Nathan to get the full experience of the city.

On the drive into Wellington, Liam pointed out places he used to frequent. The café where he'd pick up his morning coffee. The street stuffed with dive bars where he and his co-workers would party after a long night. The old cinema where they would watch their finished product and clap for each other's names in the credits. It seemed like a whole lifetime ago.

"Do you miss it?" Nathan asked him. He was fashionably

dressed in a blazer and pressed jeans. Liam kept up with a similar outfit, although his blazer was more of a light jacket, and his jeans had a permanent crinkle in them from too much wear.

"Do I miss it?" Liam repeated as he looked out the window. Each location had a memory and a story, and unfortunately, many of those stories involved Kelly and Craig. "Miss is the wrong word. I liked my life then, and I like my life now."

"But your life now is better, right?" Nathan asked with a smirk.

With you in it? "Yeah."

Liam forwent valet parking in favor his special spot on a quiet side street about which few people knew. They arrived at the restaurant early, and the host suggested they could wait at the bar until their table was ready. Nathan and Liam traded a knowing look. That was a bad idea waiting for happen. Liam suggested instead they go for a stroll on Cuba Street, a promenade with shops and good people-watching that led to Lambton Harbour.

It was a clear night, and as Liam looked ahead to the water, he thought he could see to America.

"It's beautiful. It feels like I'm in this secret corner of the world," Nathan said.

"You Brits, thinking you're still the center of the planet. What if we're at the center, and England's in the corner?"

Cuba Street was alive with people gathering at pubs, filtering in and out of stores, and eating al fresco. Hints of the salty ocean breeze fluttered in the breeze. Liam liked being able to share this with Nathan.

"I'm glad you're here. I could not have gotten through lambing season alone."

"How'd you do it last year?"

"I had a smaller flock, and I leaned on Mark. A lot." He and his usually even-keeled brother had gotten into several screaming matches as Liam figured out what he was doing. Mark worked a full-time job, took care of the kids, and still made time to assist him. Having such a dependable, caring brother made up for having three shitty ones. "But all farmers have rough seasons in the beginning. I'm sure my mum and dad did, too."

"You'll be able to deliver lambs in your sleep next year."

Liam heaved out a breath. "If I'm still on the farm."

Nathan bobbed his head up. "What do you mean?"

He pulled up an electronic copy of the real estate agreement on his phone and showed it to Nathan.

"You're selling the land?"

"I don't know. Grates Realty is a very well-known company here. They know what they're doing."

His brothers each called him this week to find out what he was deciding. Callum messengered over a hard copy of the proposal to move things along, even though Liam said he was still deliberating.

"It's not with Grates. It's with Musket Development Group. I'm assuming they're a subsidiary," Nathan said, perusing the e-document.

"Nah yeah, probably," Liam said with complete uncertainty. He had perused the contract while on the toilet the other day. Not his most professional moment.

"Take it from someone who's had to read theatrical and representation contracts where the whole point is to screw over the actors: make sure you know what you're signing. If you wind up signing." Nathan handed back his phone.

Lambing season went well this year, but would it translate to better wool sales? Would he be able to do this next year if Nathan wasn't around?

"It's a very good offer," Liam said. "I could get a swanky condo in Wellington."

"You want to move back to the city?"

"I could also purchase a cottage in the country. I'll have options."

"Do you want options?"

Nathan was damn quick with the questions.

"I don't know."

They reached the harbor. Docked boats wobbled on the choppy water as others plowed into the sea. Liam looked to the water, hoping it could give him the answers.

"I think you do." Nathan's eyes beamed at him. "You have to get out of bed before dawn seven days a week for long slogs of manual labor. You're constantly corralling sheep and dealing with their shit, no pun intended. And you love every minute of it."

I love it even more when you're working beside me.

"I don't know if it'll ever be profitable. My family struggled our whole lives. I can understand why my brothers hate the farm. Being the youngest, I wasn't there for the really tough times. What if I can't hack it?"

Nathan grabbed both his arms and stared straight into Liam's eyes, making Liam swallow a nervous lump in his throat.

"You can. I've seen you out there. You work hard, and you care about the work you do. I reckon you can sell this land and make bank, but what will you do then? Will anything light a fire in you the same way sheep farming does? There are plenty of people with plenty of money who are miserable. They spend their days redecorating their apartment for the umpteenth time and wasting away at resorts and getting smashed at pubs because they don't have what you have. They don't have something that fills their soul.

"If you wanted a condo in Wellington, you would've stayed in visual effects. Even after what happened with Kelly, you could've gotten a job at another design firm. But something inside you called out for a different life. Your parents may have given you the farm, but you *chose* it."

Nathan turned on his heel and returned to Cuba Street, leaving Liam gobsmacked behind him.

AT THE RESTAURANT, thanks to Nathan charming the hostess, they got a table by the window. It wasn't worth coming to a place on the water if one could not see the water.

"Wellington faces east, so we don't get the best sunsets," Liam said of the view.

"I love it."

Flecks of waning sun still managed to dance on the water. There was no such thing as a bad sunset, Liam thought.

"I prefer sunrises," Nathan said. "It's like God giving us another chance. No matter what kind of shit we got ourselves into the day before, the sun wipes our slate clean. I was used to seeing them when I stayed up all night."

"Now you're beating them."

"The sunrises here are the most beautiful things I've ever seen. The light coming over the mountains, then across the fields. They literally take my breath away. Or that may be residual lung damage from my cigarettes."

Nathan hadn't smoked since lambing season begun, as far as Liam could tell. When he first started on the farm,

Liam had either caught him with a quick cigarette or found butts hidden in the trash.

"What's been your favorite ocean?"

"My favorite..." Nathan tapped his fingers against his scruff. "Right. Um...I'd have to go local and say Brighton, in England. There's no place like home. And there's tons of puffs there, so the *Wizard of Oz* reference is especially apt."

"I've never been to England. Mariel went years ago for this drama program, right around when I was born. This was back when she and Mark were still dating. I think they'd just gotten engaged."

"Oh? She must've loved it."

"She never said. She didn't like to talk about it. I remember I asked how it was years later, and all she said was 'It was all right.'" It struck him how taciturn she had gotten. It was as if he'd asked about a relative who was now dead and there was an awkward silence. "I think she didn't like it there. She really missed my brother. Mark didn't have the money for a plane ticket to visit her."

The waiter came by and took their drink order. Nathan eyed the drink menu, but didn't pick it up, even though the temptation burned on his face.

"I'm going to just have water," Liam said.

"The same," Nathan said quickly.

Liam handed the waiter the drink menu, and he went on his way.

"You can order yourself a beer," Nathan said. "I really don't mind."

"And neither do I."

"You and your brother haven't had a beer at dinner for over a month, and the liquor cabinet is empty. Yes, I checked in a moment of desperation." Nathan ran a hand through his hair. "You don't have to do this, upend your life for me."

"We're not." Liam squeezed Nathan's hand and rubbed his thumb over the calluses. "Do you miss it?"

"On some level, I always will. There is a fully-stocked bar in this establishment with top shelf liquor. But I sublimate all my cravings with rigorous farm work. And sex."

Liam felt his ears get red, something he had a feeling Nathan enjoyed.

"It's...it's nice knowing that someone else gives a shit about my sobriety. My father—I mean, if he were still alive, he wouldn't care. I always seemed like an annoyance to him, and that would make me want to drink more, because if I was going to be a nuisance, I might as well do it right, y'know?" He laughed it off, but Liam could tell there was real hurt. It was awful not being able to make amends with someone who passed away.

"You're not a nuisance." Liam didn't take details like Nathan had just shared lightly. The man was so walled off with sarcasm most of the time that he appreciated these rare glimpses into his life. "Listen, I know you're only working on the farm to research a film role, but you're welcome to stay longer. You have an open invitation any time."

Please stay. The words pressed against Liam's chest. They hadn't talked about when Nathan might be leaving. Liam had heard of movie shoots getting postponed. He hoped that was the case here.

The waiter returned with their waters. They went ahead and ordered entrees.

"I'm going to use the toilet." Liam got up and walked to the restroom. He stopped when he saw Kelly and Craig at a table on the opposite end of the restaurant.

Crap. I hope they don't see me. Liam tried to beeline to the bathroom without being seen, but he couldn't stop himself from seeing them. He hid behind a column and watched them. *What am I doing?* But curiosity got the better of him. He had stuck to Nathan's deal to avoid Facebook, and it had helped. He rarely thought of Kelly and Craig, but he would never forget what they did. The deceit, the lies. Those feelings came rushing back to him.

Craig caressed Kelly's hand over the table. He poured her a glass of wine. When she picked up her glass, her engagement ring sparkled in the light. It threatened to blind Liam.

"Watch out, sir!" A waiter with a huge tray overloaded with food swerved around him.

Kelly and Craig naturally looked over and found the former third wheel of their threesome gawking at them from behind a column.

She gave him a half-wave. She did not seem to know the proper protocol in this situation, and neither did Liam. He approached their table, nervously, like a boy in trouble who would rather face up to the punishment now than drag it out.

"Well, this is a coincidence," he said. He tried to play the whole thing off as a joke. Inside, he felt anger gushing through him all anew.

"Liam," Craig said. He still had his tanned glow. "How ya going?"

"Sweet as. And you."

"Kelly raved about this restaurant for the longest time," Craig said.

"I introduced her to it," Liam said through a tight-lipped smile. That got them quiet. It amazed him how fresh the wounds could still feel.

"How are things on the farm?" Kelly asked. "Did you finish with lambing season?"

"How do you know about lambing season?" Liam asked.

"I have some family members who used to be sheep farmers."

"That sounds like every person in New Zealand," Craig said. The three of them laughed, and it was just as awkward as Liam expected.

"The season just ended. I'm celebrating," Liam said.

"Things on the farm are going well?" Kelly asked. He liked that she still cared. She was always polite and kind. She remembered details and seemed genuinely interested in answers. That was why what she did hurt so much. Never in a million years did he expect Kelly to betray him.

"They're going great. Lamb central. I'm grateful for the night off. It's not like it was at WETA with weekends off."

"You got weekends off?" Craig interjected, and they shared a genuine laugh. Liam did not miss those sixteen-hour days when they were on deadline, finishing up effects shots for a film releasing in mere weeks. They seemed more grueling than his farm work.

"Speaking of WETA, Craig was recently promoted. He's going to be supervising the effects work on Peter Jackson's next film."

"Mean!" Liam said with forced enthusiasm. That was the dream for every computer animation artist at WETA, to work directly with Peter Jackson, the founder of the company. The man had directed *The Lord of the Rings* and *The Hobbit*. That was a name everyone wanted on his or her resume.

And now it was on Craig's. Liam felt his hand ball into a fist.

"Glad to hear things on the farm are going well," Craig said. Liam doubted he cared.

"And things..." Liam gestured to Kelly's engagement ring.

"We finally set a date. And we booked a venue. This classic old church on the water." Kelly had always wanted to get married on the beach. She wanted to walk down the aisle with her toes in the sand. He had even begun looking into venues before the ill-fated threesome.

"Sweet as."

"How about you?" Craig asked. He rubbed his finger over Kelly's ring. "Dating anyone?"

Liam could've reached across the table and grabbed him by the throat. Craig was always the competitive type. Even when they played squash together, Craig took it a bit too seriously.

"Not at the moment." Liam wanted to shrivel away, especially from their pitying reactions.

But he got a boost of confidence when he felt Nathan's hand on his shoulder.

Nathan

"Sweetie, don't be so bashful." Nathan gave Liam's shoulder a squeeze. He knew these bland heterosexuals in front of him had to be Kelly and Craig. Her blonde hair seemed familiar from pictures. He had seen Liam across the restaurant practically prostrating himself at their table. Nathan knew how to read a scene.

"Gidday," Kelly said awkwardly. Nathan got bored just looking at her. He was going to relish this performance.

"I'm Nathan, Liam's boyfriend. A pleasure to meet you." He kissed Kelly's hand. He squeezed Craig's hand extra hard until the guy winced. "You as well."

Liam shot Nathan a look a petrified panic, but Nathan relayed with his eyes that he had this.

"Liam's still getting used to telling people that he's

proudly bisexual." Nathan reached for Liam's hand. He pulled away, but Nathan grabbed it tight.

"Straight up? That's really awesome, Liam."

"He said he didn't know he could have feelings for another man until the last woman he slept with was such a disappoint...oh, I'm sorry." Nathan hung his head in mock forgiveness. Kelly gulped down her wine.

"How did you two meet?" Craig with the generic face and receding hairline asked.

"I'm an actor, and I came to New Zealand for a new film project. I was exploring this beautiful country. I mean, London is beautiful, but in a completely different way."

"You're from London?" Kelly asked, impressed.

Nathan gave a modest shrug. "Born and raised. I've gone drinking with Prince Harry and studied at RADA. That's the Royal Academy of Dramatic Arts. Anyway, I was exploring this wonderful country as research for my new film, and my car got stuck on the road right outside this farm. And this big, tall farmer came out in the pouring rain. Not only did he change my tire for me, but he also offered to show me around Wellington."

"I didn't know Liam knew anything about cars," Craig said with a laugh.

"Oh, he does, Kevin."

"It's Craig."

"Same difference." Nathan strolled in front of the window. He never resisted the chance to perform in front of an audience. "He drove me all around the island, showing me caves and rolling hills and making me dive off these quite terrifying cliffs. At each stop, he would pick up little bits of food, and at the final stop, he cooked a meal from scratch for me. We sat on his coat overlooking the ocean, eating the best grilled salmon I've ever eaten, completely fresh. He caught the fish in a stream with his bare hands! That was six months ago." Nathan reached across their table and took hold of Liam's hands. "Liam was gracious enough not to make our relationship public since I am a public figure in England and my publicist didn't want to make a whole to-do out of it."

"That is quite a story," Kelly said. He detected a hint of jealousy in her voice. *Good.*

"It's not a story. It's our life." Nathan came around the table and put an arm around Liam. Liam seemed to get the hang of improv because he turned and kissed Nathan, completely going with the scene.

Except in that moment, with their lips together, it wasn't a scene anymore. The kiss was sweet and tender, like it could've been a kiss Liam had been giving to him for years. It was brief but everlasting, not the makeout sessions they'd had during sex. Those kisses were about lust. This one stopped Nathan's heart and made him forget whatever he was going to say next to keep the story going. Liam gazed into his eyes, and those milky blues knocked the wind out of Nathan.

"I feel very blessed," Liam said to the table. He wrapped his arm around Nathan's waist and pulled him close. It felt like the most natural thing in the world. "Anyway, we will let you get back to your dinner. But it was wonderful seeing both of you. Congratulations on the engagement."

They walked back to their table and sat down. Nathan was still coming back to earth. It was like he was seeing Liam for the first time. He wanted more kisses like that.

"Thank you for that," Liam said. "You saved my arse."

Nathan said nothing back. The waiter had brought their food in the interim. He stared at his entree, but didn't have an appetite. What the hell was going on with him? It wasn't horniness. Or it was, but horniness of the heart?

"Liam, can you kiss me again?"

Liam creased his brow. "Excuse me?"

"Kiss me."

"Now?"

Nathan nodded to reaffirm his seriousness of the request.

They leaned forward in their chairs and kissed over the candlelit table.

Whoa.

Chapter 24

LIAM

The car ride home was full of the best kind of tension. Liam and Nathan were like magnets being kept apart at dinner, the energy of the opposing force threatening to shatter every window in the restaurant. The kiss in front of Kelly and Craig was better than a million sunrises. He imagined kissing Nathan that way over and over again. His dick was swollen and pressing against his jeans throughout the meal, but he also craved holding and touching Nathan.

As soon as he pulled up to his house and put the car in park, Nathan leaned over the console and kissed him with the same softness and heart in the restaurant.

"You're a really good kisser," Nathan said matter-of-factly.

"You, too." Their mouths opened and closed delicately. Nathan's tongue peeked inside. It was careful. He was trying to savor this moment, and Liam wanted to do the same thing. Everything between them was slower. Liam imprinted to memory the feel of Nathan's warm lips, the silkiness of his tongue, the smoothness of his jaw.

They made out like teenagers in his car, but not the type where the goal was ripping each other's clothes off—though Liam knew that was coming. It was like they'd just discovered kissing and the emotions it could unlock. Nathan climbed over the console and sat in his lap. Liam ran his fingers through Nathan's hair and inhaled his sexy scent, sending his mind spiraling with desire. Nathan grazed his beard. His fingers were their own gentle kisses on his skin.

The one thing that had remained the same were the giant erections straining against their pants. Liam hugged Nathan close to him, letting his erection press against his firm ass. He couldn't wait to feel the heat of his skin and plunge his cock deep inside him. Nathan's ass rammed into his car horn, startling them and the sheep outside.

"I think we should go inside," Liam said. Nathan nodded in agreement.

They climbed out of his car, which took a minute since they were tangled together. They kissed again and moved backwards to the door, neither removing themselves from the kiss. Liam had no idea what was going on, how much of this was lust and how much was something purer, but he couldn't deny the feelings surging in him for Nathan.

Inside, Liam moved Nathan backwards to his bed. He lay on top of Nathan and unbuttoned his shirt. During the sex of lambing season, clothes were ripped off, torn asunder, yanked off bodies in milliseconds. The faster to nakedness, the better. But tonight, Liam wanted to stretch it out like a last supper. He undid each button, kissing the warm skin he was slowly revealing, tracing the curves of his lean, defined muscles with his lips, flicking a tongue over erect nipples. Nathan shivered under his touch. He brought Nathan's shirt to his nose and inhaled the musky, soapy scent. "You are so beautiful, Nathan. I don't want to stop looking at you." Liam planted a soft kiss on his mouth. "I'm falling for you. I think I might already be there."

"Me, too," Nathan said barely above a whisper.

He kissed down Nathan's smooth chest, over the ridges of his abs, to his pants button. He rubbed his beard over the mound in Nathan's pants, eliciting moans of pleasure from the redhead that hummed through his body. Nathan gasped when he unbuttoned his jeans, his cock begging to be free. His teeth pulled at the waistband of Nathan's underwear, making his farmhand writhe underneath him.

Liam wrapped his lips around his pulsating, long cock, torturing him with slow strokes and rubbing his hand across his chest. He dragged Nathan's dick across his beard, eliciting shivers and guttural moans out of his lover. He loved feeling the warm hardness on his face.

"Liam, Liam, Liam..." Nathan said his name over and over, mumbling and muttering it like he was in the middle of a trance.

He needed to kiss Nathan. He *had* to kiss him and look into those eyes again. He had a feeling they would be up all night.

Nathan

Nathan needed Liam. Literally needed him. He didn't know he needed this feeling so badly, that his body had been deprived of a valuable nutrient.

"I want you, Liam. I care about you so much."

This was the type of shit Nathan was saying tonight, shit he never said during sex or anytime. He didn't need or care about people. He was fine on his own. But the words were the truth, mystifying even him, coming from a deep place that he had no control over. This was lust. This was...heart?

Nathan pulled off his pants. "We have a problem. You are wearing too much clothing."

Liam cracked a smile. His white teeth peeked through those full red lips and the haze of his beard. It was fucking irresistible. He took off his shirt, exposing his ripped chest, and Nathan couldn't wait to feel the bristle of his chest hair rubbing against him.

Nathan had Liam kneel on the bed. He undid Liam's pants and managed to push them down to his tree trunk thighs. His cock jutted out, thick and hot, waiting to fuck. Nathan straddled Liam, resting on his muscular thighs, and his dick hit Nathan's aching hole. He was cocooned in Liam's strong grip. His beard scratched at Nathan's neck as he pecked him lightly.

Liam held him firmly in place, locking him there with his lips, making him feel whole. Nathan was never one for making out. He wasn't thirteen. Why waste time on making out when there were so many other fun, more advanced things he could be doing with guys? Why go slow when fast was so much better? Fast didn't leave time for thinking, for doubting. That was one thing his ex-boyfriend had complained about sex-wise. *This isn't a timed event*, Eamonn would say as Nathan raced to nakedness and penetration.

But it was, because for Nathan, sex was a way to forget. It was a diversion.

Nathan wanted slow tonight. He wanted to absorb every feeling Liam was giving him, the caring and passion that blazed in his eyes.

Liam held him in his arms, his cock hovering beneath Nathan's hole. There was no sex yet. Not even ferocious making out. Just kissing. Pecks on the lips, gazing into each other's eyes. And Nathan actually liked it.

He might've liked it more than the rough, stress-relieving sex they had been having.

So much was said in the silence. Nathan tangled his hand in Liam's chest hair. His fingers trailed down the muscles in his back, then ruffled the hair just above his neck.

"This is different for us," Liam said.

"Yeah," Nathan breathed out. His cock leaked pre-come into Liam's stomach. He felt the tip of Liam's dick brush against his opening, and fuck, he could no longer take the teasing.

He leaned back and pulled out lube from Liam's night-stand drawer. They'd realized sometime in the middle of lambing season that they weren't seeing anyone else, let alone having sex with anyone else, so they decided to forego condoms. Nathan only wanted to be with Liam; it was the best sex he'd ever had. Liam moaned against his neck as Nathan lubed up his cock, and he wasn't even inside yet.

It was like that restaurant had transformed them into born-again virgins.

"Yes!" Nathan roared out when Liam pressed inside him, stretching him wide. He sunk down onto Liam's throbbing cock. It filled him completely.

"You feel so good," Liam said.

Nathan withheld his witty comments. Not for tonight. He moved up and down on his dick. He needed it so badly. The heat, the tenderness, the feeling of one person having control over his body. They continued kissing passionately, their sweaty chests rubbing together. He wanted to be connected to this man in every way possible.

"Liam, Liam, Liam." Nathan couldn't stop saying his name. Liam responded with increased thrusting. He loved the feeling of being wrapped in Liam's python arms and his thick thighs thrusting up and hitting his ass. In his embrace, he felt safe. He wasn't alone, wasn't abandoned.

Soon, the sweet, tender lovemaking gave way to full-on fucking. They were horny guys after all. It was inevitable that things would speed up the closer they got to coming. Liam held Nathan in place and jackhammered into his tight ass. Each quick hump hit Nathan in just the right spot. Liam lost control and panted wildly, the animal in him coming out. Their kissing turned to lips hovering beside each other, emitting desperate pants of breath.

Nathan's dick rubbed pre-come all over Liam's abs. He went dizzy. He couldn't believe it. He was going to have a hands-free climax for the first time. Because he couldn't celebrate this moment any longer, he shot his load against Liam's chiseled, sweaty, furry stomach.

Liam looked down at the mess and raised an eyebrow. He was just as surprised. But only for a second. He pulled Nathan close and kissed him deep as he emptied himself inside Nathan's hole.

They remained in that position and reverted to sweet, tender kisses. They looked in each other's eyes, and Liam seemed to be just as speechless as Nathan.

I love you, Liam.

Nathan felt it completely, as sure as anything in his life. In those sparkling blue eyes, he found home. Liam was his person.

But damn it, he couldn't say the words.

"What is it?" Liam wiped sweaty strands of hair out of his eyes. He kissed Nathan's cheek.

"I like being here. With you."

They lay down together on the bed, Nathan spooned by the man who had vanquished fire-breathing dragons and scaled sky-high walls to reach his heart. But as he drifted off to sleep, he thought about how quickly it could all be ripped away in a second. Love could flip to disdain like a light switch. Mariel cherished two of her children and cast away the third. Four words—*I am Mariel's son*—and then he might be abandoned all over again by the man who held him tight. Just like his mom had done. Just like his dad and family had discarded him.

Nathan threaded his fingers with Liam's and hoped an answer came to him while he slept.

Chapter 25

NATHAN

There was nothing innately pleasurable about shoveling hay, but the next day, Nathan couldn't stop smiling to himself as he scraped it off the floor of the new pen. He could feel Liam's arms around him in bed, their lips touching softly over the table at the restaurant last night. The memories had not dimmed since he woke up; they'd only gotten stronger. Even the sheep around him could see the dopey smile drawn in permanent marker.

Liam exited the shed with his own special glow on his face. Nathan watched him walk over to the pen, his broad shoulders moving under his flannel shirt.

"I'm going to make a supply run in town. Do we need anything?" Liam showed him the list he'd made.

"You forgot lube," Nathan said.

"I get that shipped here." Liam blushed. "It's less conspicuous."

"There's nothing to be embarrassed about. I doubt we're the only farmhands stocking up."

Liam cocked an eyebrow and raised his lips in an

amused grin. He massaged Nathan's back and kissed him goodbye where his neck met his shoulder.

"Be back soon."

Liam got in his truck and drove off, leaving Nathan alone with nature. He paid attention to the peaceful sounds of the farm, the bleating and crunching and steady breezes. He could hear himself think, which was something he'd specifically avoided back in London. Maybe country life could be for him.

His heart somersaulted in his chest when he heard the sound of Liam's truck pulling up to the shed about fifteen minutes later. That was a fast trip. But when Nathan left the pen, he realized it wasn't a truck he heard.

Pastor Fry looked at Nathan through his windshield. He got out of the car, his tall frame making Nathan feel shrimp-like.

"Hiya, Pastor. Y'alright?"

"Gidday, Nathan." He didn't shake Nathan's hand. Probably because of all the muck on it, Nathan thought.

"Are you looking for Liam? He just ran into town."

Pastor Fry surveyed the farm, taking in the sheep roaming around and the hoof house. His stare was impenetrable, making Nathan even more nervous.

Nathan wanted to keep talking, wanted to keep having this technically family time. But conversation was a two-way street.

"It's a nice farm he has. He seems to be happy," Pastor Fry said.

"It's hard work, but he loves it. We both do."

"A posh gentleman like you?" Pastor Fry looked him up and down. Anyone back home would be shocked to see Nathan in dirt-covered jeans and T-shirt. "You must miss London."

"Not as much as I thought."

"When do you go back?" The breeze that swept through didn't shake Pastor Fry's silver hair one bit. He seemed like a grandfather who gave bad Christmas gifts.

"I, uh…I'm still working that out. My visa is for nine months."

"Nine months." Pastor Fry smiled to himself. "Just enough time for anyone to find themselves in a heap of trouble."

Nathan gulped back a lump in his throat. Even though they were outside, he felt some kind of walls closing in on him.

Pastor Fry took a step closer, so close he could've wrapped him in a warm, grandfatherly hug. He studied Nathan, soaking in as much data as he could.

"She used to make the same face you're making," he said. "It's…I can't believe it."

Nathan thought he was going to collapse. Tears instantly came to his eyes.

"Grandfather," he said.

Pastor Fry gave a tight nod, his body stiff with awkwardness.

Nathan wiped away his tears, but more just filled their place. The levies inside him were allowed to break open for the first time since he got here. He wrapped Pastor Fry in a hug, but noticed that it wasn't reciprocated. Pastor Fry's arms hung at their sides.

"Nathan, you can't call me that."

"I'll call you whatever you like. Gramps, grandpa, papa."

"No," he said forcefully. He pulled away from Nathan's hug.

"What? I don't understand."

"You have a family back in London. We are not it."

"Yes, you are. Mariel is my mum. You said it—"

"Mark and his family have been through a lot."

"So have I. I've spent my whole life being lied to and cast aside."

"You are not supposed to be here. I don't know how you found us, but you can't stay."

Nathan felt a cannonball tear through his chest. "You knew about me?"

"It's complicated."

"This whole time, you knew I was in London?"

"I nearly had a heart attack when I saw you at dinner. I thought I was dreaming, but I kept seeing my daughter in you."

And yet you don't want me to stay? Your own flesh and blood? Another family member kicking him to the curb.

"I know I wasn't born under the most ideal circumstances, but Mark will understand. So will the kids. I have to tell them the truth."

"You will do no such thing!" Pastor Fry's eyes blazed defensively, a papa bear protecting his cubs. But Nathan wasn't a predator. He was his cub, too. "It's best that you pack up and leave immediately, before you hurt this fragile family."

"Hurt?" Nathan's shock and longing for a grandparent began turning to anger, crystallizing in his heart.

"I will pay for a flight back to London for you, and I can drive you to the airport." He put a hand on Nathan's arm.

"What? Now? Without saying goodbye?"

"Let's go, Nathan."

Nathan shrugged off his hand. "Get the fuck off me."

This was not how he wanted to kick off his burgeoning grandparent-grandchild relationship, but his new grandfather seemed as awful as his existing one.

"Why are you doing this?" Nathan asked.

"Because it's what Mariel wanted. You were a mistake, Nathan, something she wanted to forget ever happened. And she did. Did she ever try calling you or writing you or finding you on social media?"

Nathan wouldn't give him the satisfaction of a head nod.

"She wanted you out of her life. And for good reason. In and out of rehab, homosexual. You've only been here a few weeks, and you've already tried corrupting my granddaughter."

"Don't you mean my half-sister?"

"You don't belong here."

While what Pastor Fry said sounded true, Nathan could feel in his heart that it wasn't the truth.

"Go inside and pack your things, before things really spiral out of control."

"No." Nathan dug his boots into the mushy grass.

"You're trouble, Nathan, and I don't want you around my family."

"I'm not leaving." He wasn't going to be chased out like this.

Pastor Fry gave him a final, dagger-filled glare and walked back to his car. It took everything in Nathan not to fall apart on the spot.

"I'm going to tell them," Nathan said, fighting back.

Pastor Fry's expression softened. "When Mariel finally confessed to us what she did, it destroyed my wife and me. We were never the same after that. It took everything we had to keep it together in front of Mark and our congregants. We always wondered what else Mariel was keeping from us, wondered how else she could hurt this beautiful family she'd created.

"You will cause irrevocable damage to Franny and Walt. I don't think you want to do that to your half-siblings."

Nathan pictured his mother tossing him onto the front steps of his dad's flat, not looking back as she walked away, just as his grandfather now drove off the farm, tires screeching against the gravel, without a glance in the rearview mirror.

A few minutes after watching Pastor Fry's car disappear into the hills, Nathan tried returning to work. Shoveling manure was something he could do on autopilot while his mind spun out. But a familiar name buzzed on his phone.

"What?" he screamed to the caller. A nearby sheep skirted off. "What do you want?"

"Hi, son?"

Hearing his dad call him son left a sour taste in his throat.

"You keep contacting me at the absolute worst times." He threw down his shovel. "What do you want?"

"I haven't heard from you in a few weeks is all."

"Since when do you care?"

"Where are you?"

Nathan had to laugh. His father acting like a concerned parent? "I'm traveling. Just like you."

"Usually you check in or I see posts online of your journeys."

Nathan was surprised that his father checked his social media, but he shrugged it off. "I'm alive. Is that good enough?"

"Nathan, please tell me where you are. You're worrying me."

"Why would I worry you now? You've never given a flying fuck about me before."

"I brought you to a rehabilitation facility."

"You dumped me there. You didn't even bother to pick me up when it was done." He waited for his father to reply, but he seemed to still be gathering a response. Nathan happily supplied one for him: "You had reservations. Another beautiful resort."

"What has gotten into you? I haven't heard from you in weeks. You won't answer your phone. You won't tell me where you are. Are you drinking again?"

Of course. Of course it had to be his son fucking up yet again, he thought. Nathan rubbed at the spot between his eyebrows, a headache forming.

"Did you ever wonder why I acted out so much, Dad? Did you assume I was a bad seed? A mistake?"

"You've had your issues, but you seemed to have gotten straightened out." His dad struggled for answers, like he was forced to a take a test he didn't study for at all.

Nathan lost the energy to be sarcastic and obnoxious. The fight was draining him after all these years. "You've lied to me my entire life."

"What are you talking about?"

"You had a picture of my real mum in your bloody desk drawer and never showed it to me. You knew what she looked like. You knew *something* about her, and you never told me." Nathan heaved in breath, but he was too angry to cry. Angry at his new family and old family and himself.

"Nathan, I...oh, bugger. I can explain."

"There's nothing to explain. Jesus, Dad, did you ever think that I was a shitty son because you were such a shitty father? You ever heard the expression the apple doesn't fall far from the tree?"

"You're not a shitty son."

"You treat me like one."

Nathan had a catch in his throat, like maybe he'd gone

too far, but there was not too far with him. He had never told his father off before. Even though their relationship was tenuous at best, he was still Nathan's only family, and he was afraid to lose that. But he realized he never had it in the first place.

"Son, can we meet somewhere? I want to talk about this. Please."

He wanted to throw his phone into the manure pit, but stopped himself.

"I found her," he said with a defiant edge in his voice.

"You...you found her? Your mother?" His dad could barely get the words out. "Where are you, Nathan?"

Nathan clenched his jaw tight.

"Catch me if you can."

Chapter 26

LIAM

While roaming the aisles of the hardware store checking things off his list, Liam got a call from his brother (the nice one), asking him to pick up Walt from school. Mark's meeting was running late. Liam realized he could take advantage of this precious time for some uncle-nephew bonding.

"Hey pal!" he said as Walt climbed into the passenger seat. He hugged his backpack to his chest. "How was school?"

"Good."

Liam wished his niece and nephew gave him more than one-word answers, but he probably gave the same answers to adults at Walt's age.

"Listen, Walt, I want to talk with you about something, something that's... developed," Liam said before Walt could take out his phone.

His nephew had a hesitant look on his face. Kids didn't want to hear about adult things. They didn't want to think of the adults around them as real people.

"What is it?" Walt asked.

"Nathan has been a great help on the farm over the past few weeks. We've grown close, first as co-workers, then as friends, but..." Liam felt his whole face go red. *Out with it.* "But now, we are romantically involved. Which I know is probably very confusing to you. You see, usually boys and girls like each other, but sometimes a boy can like another boy and a girl can like a girl. And there are some boys, like, uh, me, who liked a girl but then liked a boy."

I am mucking this up proper. Liam had no idea how to go about this conversation. Did his nephew even know what sex was? He steeled himself for Walt's expression, but when he looked over, Walt was on his phone.

"Can you get off your bloody phone for a second? I'm trying to have a serious talk."

"You're bisexual, Uncle Liam."

"I...you know what that is?"

Walt rolled his eyes. "Of course I do. Some kids in my class are bi. Are you sure you're bisexual, or are you pansexual or polysexual?"

"I..." Liam had no idea what those were. He felt ninety years old. "I think I'm just bi."

"Cool."

"Well, this was an easy conversation. And if you ever need to discuss feelings you may be having for someone in your class, I'm here."

"Sweet as."

Liam didn't stop Walt from going back on his phone. It allowed him to breathe and get over any lingering awkwardness.

"Nathan really likes you," Liam said, thinking of how great Nathan is with the kids.

Walt nodded, but Liam noticed how he squirmed in his

seat. There was something off, something that raised an alarm inside Liam.

"What is it?" Liam asked.

"Nothing."

"You can tell me."

Walt opened his mouth to say anything, but reconsidered. "It's nothing."

"Are you sure, pal? You can tell me." Liam was two seconds away from pulling over and using his patented tickle torture moves he used on him and Franny when they were toddlers.

Liam white knuckled the steering wheel. He thought of the buzzing phone during shower sex and all of Kelly's web of lies she spun right around him.

"C'mon, Walt." Liam took a calming breath. "Whatever it is..."

Walt gave a heavy nod, like he was ready to lift a weight off his shoulders. "I'd gotten a ride home from school from my friend's mum, and when I got home, I heard a noise coming from the basement..."

NATHAN

After filling the feeding troughs for the sheep, Nathan stumbled back to the shed. His muscles were sore from the extra work he did, work used to forget that tense conversation with his evil grandfather and his dad. Knowing his father, he probably shrugged off the phone call minutes after being hung up on and set out to plan his next vacation with the step-missus. To his father, Nathan was merely an inconvenience that he'd deal with later if he chose. He didn't know if the same could be said for his grandfather.

His heart flooded with relief when he saw Liam. He was

hunched over his computer working on a graphic design project.

"Am I fucking glad to see you?" Nathan rubbed Liam's shoulders, then ran his hands down the farmer's chest, taking in the musky scent of his hair. But he felt Liam tense under his touch. "Did you get what you needed from the supply store?"

"Yeah." Liam didn't turn around from his computer, no matter where Nathan's hands went.

"That's good." Nathan took his hands back. Liam seemed miles away, and nerves took over Nathan. Had Pastor Fry gotten to him? "What do you want for dinner? I'm cooking."

Nathan had become quite the cook during his time on the farm. He tried to whip up his favorite restaurant meals from memory, and each time, he got a little bit closer. All of his food was edible, which was more than he could say in his spare cooking attempts back in England.

"Or maybe we could do take away. Eat dinner in bed."

Liam spun around in his chair. His eyes were hot interrogation lights. "What were you doing in Mark's basement the other day?"

"Excuse me?"

"What were you looking for?"

Walt. Nathan knew that secret was never going to last, and a residual wave of guilt for making Walt try crashed inside him.

"I had wandered down there by accident. I was just curious."

Liam wasn't buying it. His eyes didn't flick away from Nathan. "Why would you rifle through somebody's stuff?"

"Because I don't have any manners."

"What were you looking for?"

"I told you, nothing. Just snooping. Boxes were made to be opened."

"Then why did you ask my eleven-year-old nephew to lie about it?"

Sweat prickled at the base of his neck. They were in a tennis match. As hard as Nathan hit the ball, Liam came back with equal force.

"You should've seen his face when he told me," Liam said.

It was most likely as heartbreaking as his expression when Nathan asked Walt to keep their secret. Something had broken between them, another relationship Nathan had irreparably harmed.

"How could you ask a child to do that, a child who looks up to you?"

"I'm sorry," Nathan said. "I panicked."

"Walt said you were searching for something."

"I told you, I was just a curious little cat."

"Nathan, this isn't funny!" Liam bolted out of his chair, but then took a breath, reining himself in. He stumbled to the couch and sat on the arm. "That's Mariel's stuff. Mark and the kids are very sensitive about it. They don't want strangers rifling through it."

"Strangers."

The word was a bucket of cold water at four in the morning, a brutal wake-up call. Liam seemed to realize what he said instantly.

"I didn't mean...it's a family thing," Liam said.

Nathan nodded, the irony tugging at his chest. Liam didn't realize his new choice of word wasn't any better, a confirmation that Nathan would forever be on the outside.

"Just tell me what you were looking for. Please," Liam said, his eyes softening, the blue warmth returning to them. "Just tell me the truth."

He was giving Nathan an opening to reveal all. *Tell the truth.* He feared it would only make Liam kick him out. The truth wasn't going to set him free. It was going to make him alone. The truth had already cost him a grandfather.

But this was Liam. Liam cared about him. He wouldn't think of Nathan as damaged goods. Nathan had gotten closer to him than anyone else in his entire life. That had to count for something. That had to be worth the risk.

"Was it alcohol?" Liam asked just as Nathan was opening his mouth. "Were you looking for a drink?"

He sneered out the words, so sure of the answer.

"Yes." Nathan nodded his head.

The disappointment washed over Liam's face, his shoulders, everywhere.

"Nathan."

"I thought I could find an old bottle of anything."

"Did you?"

"No."

Liam sighed and raked a hand through his hair. "If you need help, we can get you help."

There was no we, he thought.

"It doesn't matter. I got a call from my director. They're getting ready to go into production."

Liam opened his mouth to say something, but instead gave the slightest nod.

It was another lie, one that Nathan shot out so easily, but he realized the truth at its core. This story of theirs wasn't meant to have a happy ending. He had dug himself into too deep a hole. He had messed with these good people enough.

It was for the best that his stay here come to an end before he caused even more damage. Nathan was pure trouble, just as Pastor Fry had told him. He had come to New Zealand to find out why his mother abandoned him, and it was time to admit he'd gotten his answer.

Chapter 27

NATHAN

"Tonight's the night!" Franny charged into Nathan's room two days later and paced back and forth.

"Nervous?" Nathan asked through the bathroom mirror in that artificially chipper voice that he'd been using since his fight with Liam.

"Nervous?" Franny repeated. "You're never supposed to ask an actress if she's nervous. You'll jinx me! You just say 'break a leg.' I thought you knew this."

"But what if you actually break a leg on the way to the theater?" Nathan quirked an eyebrow, which felt like a herculean task considering how he was feeling on the inside. He had to stay in character until he exited for good. He didn't want to cloud Franny's mind before her stage debut. Tonight, after the show, he would announce he was leaving.

Franny continued to pace, gaining so much speed she could start a hurricane off the coast of Maui. Nathan remembered what those butterflies felt like. When he was on stage, he wanted so bad to nail it, to make every line land with the audience.

He stopped her in her pacing tracks and looked her squarely in the eye. "Franny, you are going to amaze them. You are the dog's bollocks."

"What if I forget a line?"

"Improvise."

"Nathan!"

He tucked a lock of shiny red hair behind her ears. Her red mane glowed in the sunlight, so much better than her attempt at going brunette. Her true self shined through.

"You've been practicing for weeks. You've been off book a week longer than your fellow cast members. You *are* Cinderella." Her acting skills had vastly improved during the rehearsal process. Nathan loved coming in for nightly dinners and hearing her beautiful singing wafting from upstairs.

"You can do this," he said. "Your mother would be very proud."

Her smile held back tears. Nathan's did the same.

"I couldn't have done this without you. I'm so glad you came here. And not just for me. You've made all our lives better."

Nathan felt a lump in his throat. He wasn't used to such compliments. Usually he had the opposite effect.

"Uncle Liam really cares about you."

Nathan tensed up. His feelings crushed his head harder than any hangover.

"We should get going. You don't want to be late," he said.

Nathan waited with Walt in the living room while Franny and Mark went upstairs to get her costume. Walt played a game on his phone.

"Walt, I want to apologize. I shouldn't have asked you to

keep a secret. That wasn't right of me." Nathan knew from his past rehab visits that this wasn't a real apology. Not yet. He said he wanted to apologize, but he hadn't officially done so.

This was a hard one. He'd apologized to friends and family members for stealing, saying mean things while drunk, stealing cars and boyfriends. Yet the litany of those bad deeds at this moment paled in comparison to the breach in trust he'd created with his little brother.

"I'm sorry," he said, his voice trembling.

Walt put down his phone when he noticed how serious Nathan was being.

"It's okay, Nathan." Walt checked to make sure nobody was coming down the stairs. "You know how our remote control is broken?"

Nathan blushed. Another drunken misdeed. "I'm sorry for that, too."

"I broke it," Walt interjected.

"What?"

"It wasn't working and I threw it against the wall. I should've said something. I'm sorry."

Nathan waved it away like ancient history. "None of us are perfect."

They traded knowing smiles, two imperfect people who had each other's backs.

Liam swung open the front door. He wore a button-down shirt that tugged at his broad chest and tucked neatly into dark khakis. He and Mark had gone shopping for a special outfit for his niece's debut. Nathan didn't want to stop looking at him. He had an overwhelming urge to hug him, to feel his warmth. Liam was beautiful, every part of him.

A heavy moment weighed between the two men. Nathan

hadn't told the others that he was planning to leave. He didn't want to ruin Franny's debut.

"Are we ready to go?" Liam asked.

"Ready!" Mark called from the stairs.

"Then let's get the—" Liam mouthed *fuck*, making Walt giggle. "outta here!"

"I'm going to be acting on stage tonight!" Franny yelled as she rumbled downstairs.

"Hard out!" Liam said. She hi-fived him, then Nathan.

The five of them packed into Mark's car. Liam, Nathan, and Walt took the backseat with Walt in the middle. Their fingers met behind him, and Liam cracked a sexy smile that Nathan felt in all his pleasure zones.

"All right, Fosters and Nathan," Mark said.

"Hey! Nathan's a Foster, too," Liam said.

"An honorary one," Franny said.

Nathan fought back tears with an extra large smile.

"All right, Fosters." Mark honked his horn in celebration. "Let's go!"

THEY DROVE through fields that eventually gave way to suburban sprawl. Nathan was on a high better than drinking could ever give him. We wanted to live in this moment forever.

Half an hour later, they pulled into the theater parking lot, and the moment abruptly came to an end when Nathan recognized Pastor Fry's car parked next to theirs.

"Grandpa and Grandma are here already!" Walt exclaimed.

Yes, they fucking are.

. . .

Liam

The theater had been the old mansion of a shipping magnate a century ago, with a wide staircase leading to imposing marble columns. It was an intimidating establishment, and Liam felt nervous for his niece, but when he looked over, she had a look of confidence stamped on her face. She was going to bring the house down.

"I'm going to the cast entrance around the side," Franny said with a gleeful giggle. "You can wait there after the show and *maybe* I'll sign your programs. Kidding!" She kissed everyone goodbye and skipped off.

Nathan, conversely, looked like the nervous one. He wiped his palms on his pants; his eyes darted around when they reached the lobby. At first, Liam found it sweet that he was nervous for his niece, but he got the feeling this wasn't about Franny.

Liam slyly clasped Nathan's hand and tried meeting his eyes. "You all right?"

"I—yeah. I'm fine. I didn't realize everyone was coming to support Franny. I thought her grandparents were against theater."

"They wouldn't miss this, no matter their Christ-related objections," Mark said.

"That's sweet," Nathan said.

A layer of residual sweat dampened Liam's palm. "You sure you're all good?"

Nathan nodded and smiled. It did nothing to reassure him.

They pushed open the heavy wood doors, which led to a grand lobby with plush red carpeting and a chandelier hanging above them. Franny could've been debuting on Broadway for all Liam knew.

Mark handed their tickets to the usher who directed

them to prime seats in the center section. Liam could've found them on his own thanks to Pastor Fry's white shock of hair sticking up like a beacon.

"You know what." Nathan said, gripping Liam's arm before he could enter the theater and nearly cutting off circulation. "I'm going to purchase a drink—Coke. And maybe some candy, too. I need some kind of sweet snack. It's a British tradition, eating candy before a show. It's for good luck."

"Oh. I didn't know that," Mark said.

"I've never heard of that," Liam said, another alarm going off in his head.

"It's a new tradition. Meghan Markle started it."

"I'll take M&M's," Walt said.

"Great choice," Nathan said. "Mark?"

"Um...I'll take a Sprite, I suppose."

"Smashing. And you?" Nathan squeezed Liam's hand.

Liam stared at Nathan, trying to figure out what he was doing with this inane request. He was always figuring things out with Nathan, like he was a puzzle that kept coming up with new pieces.

"Nathan, what's going on? Why do you seem nervous?"

"I'm not."

The lie was all over Nathan's face, but before he could ask another question, Nathan interjected.

"I'll get you M&M's, too." He leaned in close to Liam's face and smirked. "I'm just craving some sugar to sublimate my urge to tear your clothes off. I'll be right back."

Nathan dashed to the concessions line. Liam joined his brother and nephew in taking their seats next to Pastor Fry and Brenda. He strummed his fingers on the chair's arm, tapping his fingernail against the strip of metal with the seat number.

Five minutes later, Nathan was still in line. Supposedly.

Liam got up to check on him. Maybe he needed help carrying snacks back. Maybe something was really wrong. The suspicion clouding his mind turned to worry.

He zoomed down the aisle and out into the lobby. There was no sign of Nathan at the concession line.

Instead, there was Callum.

"Gidday, Piglet. How ya going?"

Callum motioned for his wife Claudette, a woman fond of plastic surgery and *Real Housewives* shows, to enter the theater. James, Oliver, and their families were getting their tickets scanned at the main entrance, but the brothers locked eyes on Liam like animals in the hunt.

"It's great you're all supporting Franny," Liam said.

"We wouldn't miss our niece's acting debut for the world," Callum said.

James and Oliver joined their circle. They put on their best smiles, yet the greed in their eyes could be seen from space.

"We've been waiting to hear from you," James said.

The contract had been sitting on Liam's desk ever since they came over, staring at him in the morning and whenever he worked on freelance graphic design projects after an exhausting day in the field, his fingers barely able to type.

"We need a decision immediately," Callum said. "Grates is breathing down my neck, and his investors are breathing down his neck."

"I'm still thinking about it."

"You've thought about it enough, Piglet. Are you in or out?" Oliver asked, only wanting one answer.

"I'll let you know tomorrow."

"Unfortunately, tomorrow isn't good enough," Callum said. "He needs an answer tonight."

"It's quite a big decision."

"You've had more than enough time." Callum moved to a cocktail table and motioned for his brothers to follow him. He pulled out a copy of the contract with a pen and slid it across the table to Liam.

"You brought this with you?" Liam asked.

"We knew you'd be here," Callum said.

"Is that the only reason you decided to support your niece?"

His brothers remained coy. Liam fumed silently, furious on Mark's behalf, and his own.

"You don't need to read it over. You've already read it," Oliver said.

"I'm not going to sign something without reading it." Liam scanned through the contract, but the dry legalese wore him down, as did his brothers staring at him. He needed Nathan here. He would have a sharp remark to hurl back at him.

But Nathan wasn't around.

"Who're you looking for?" Callum asked. "Once you sign, I'll talk to Mark after the show. He said he'll do it if you do it. He's a good big brother."

Liam tried reading the terms, but he kept thinking about the good memories he had of working the farm, and how those memories now included Nathan.

"Look, bro, I didn't want to do it this way, but time is of the essence," Callum said. "Do you really want to be working the farm until it kills you, like it did Mum and Dad?"

More people crowded into the lobby, filling the tables around them. Their chatter bounced off the walls. His brothers kept staring at him. He craned his neck around for a sign of Nathan.

"Hold on one second," Liam said.

"What? No! You have to sign," James said.

"You're ambushing me."

"We're not putting a gun to your head, Piglet," Oliver said.

"Stop calling me Piglet!" Liam immediately lowered his voice so as not to attract attention. He did his best to tune out the noise and pressure and tried reading the contract. Maybe this was the right move.

He kept hearing Nathan's words from their stroll in Wellington. He chose this life for a reason. Before he could ruminate further, something caught his eye in the contract.

Musket Development Group.

Nathan had pointed it out to him. *Make sure you know what you're signing.*

"Who is this Musket Development Group? I thought the deal was with Grates Realty."

"It is. Musket is a division of the company."

"But wouldn't that be made clear in the contract?"

"You had time to have an attorney look this over," Callum said calmly. James and Oliver behind him were not as calm.

The alarm bells wouldn't stop ringing for Liam.

"Musket..."

"Development Group, yes. Grates sets up shell companies for each project," Callum said.

Liam had gotten good at detecting Callum's bullshit from over two decades of brotherhood. He got a sick taste in his throat.

"Musket, as in musketeer. You used to play Three Musketeers around the house. I always wanted to play with you, but you told me I couldn't because there were only three of them." Liam started coldly at Callum, who didn't scare him any longer. His brothers were the scared ones now. "You're tricking me into selling you my land, and you're going to sell it to Grates for an even bigger sum."

"Pig—Liam. That's not what we're—"

"You were going to screw over your two other brothers. Why? Just because you didn't have the childhood you wanted? I didn't choose to be the youngest born." Liam ripped up the contract, crumpled the pieces into a ball, and dunked it into the trash. "And we're supposed to be family."

Liam shook his head at his brothers, who all turned varying shades of white.

"It's a real shame you can't choose your family." He walked off.

NATHAN

It was a beautiful bathroom. Marble countertops. Ivory white tiled floors. And spacious stalls with full-sized walls, making it easy for Nathan to hide.

What am I going to do? What is Pastor Fry going to do?

Nathan sat on the toilet, head in his hands. He couldn't watch the show from here. He couldn't miss Franny's debut. But he also couldn't face Pastor Fry and his glare of disgust, a glare that exposed Nathan for all he was.

The bathroom door swung open, jolting him from his thoughts.

"Nathan?" Liam's voice echoed against the walls. "Are you in here?"

He opened his mouth, but nothing came out. His words were hiding like he was.

He heard Liam enter the bathroom, his shoes squeaking on the tile. He squeaked right up to the stall door.

"Nathan?"

Nathan pressed his hand against the stall door, hoping Liam felt some of what was vibrating inside him.

"My brothers are pieces of shit. Family is a really strange thing. I feel closer to you than I ever did to them."

Nathan stared at the stall door, as if he had X-Ray vision, as if he could be with Liam in his arms.

"I think I'm falling in love with you, Nathan. Oi, I'm already there."

A tear slipped down Nathan's cheek. He could list the people he'd ever said I love you to on one hand. Zero. He wasn't worthy of love. He was so scared. He couldn't make a single sound.

Shoes squeaked away and seconds later, the door swung closed. Nathan hung his head.

Minutes later, the loudspeaker crackled to life. "Attention. The show will be starting in five minutes. Please take your seats."

It was now or never. Nathan couldn't miss Franny's show. She needed him. Liam needed him. Pastor Fry would have to drag him away. Damn it, he was a Foster.

He gave himself a confident nod in the bathroom mirror.

"There you are," Liam said to him when he returned to the lobby. He peered into Nathan's eyes. "What is going on?"

"Liam, I…I have to tell you something."

"The show's starting."

"It can't wait."

"Nathan?"

It couldn't be.

"Nathan?" the firm voice said again.

Nathan assumed he'd gone into some catatonic state of shock, or perhaps this was all a dream he was about to wake up from, because staring back at him was his father, pissed the hell off.

Chapter 28

NATHAN

His dad charged into the center of their conversation. It'd been a while since Nathan had seen him. He almost didn't recognize his slimmer body and tanned face, which was scrunched and red at the moment.

"Nathan, what in sodding hell are you doing halfway around the world?"

"What are *you* doing here?" Nathan asked.

"You said 'Catch me if you can,' and I caught you. I want to know what is going on. Do I need to take you back to rehab?" His dad grabbed his arm.

"Excuse me." Liam stepped in and took hold of his dad's wrist. "Get your hands off him."

"Who are you?"

"His boyfriend." Liam tightened his grip around his dad's wrist, making him buckle under the pain.

"Well, I'm his father, and it's time for Nathan to come home."

"What? No, you're not."

"You don't believe me?"

"His father died of cancer years ago."

Nathan's dad slowly turned to his son, a mix of shock and hurt spreading on his face. "Is that what you've been telling people?"

That same mixed expression took over Liam's face, like a virus that was quickly spreading. The few theatergoers still in the lobby formed a circle around them. They were getting two shows for the price of one.

"What is he talking about?" Liam asked.

"I'm not dead. I'm alive and kicking and here to bring my son back home to London before he causes anymore trouble."

Liam went into a daze. "Your father's alive?"

"I'll do a sodding DNA test if I have to!" His booming, frustrated voice brought more people out from the theater.

"Liam, I can explain."

"Why would you lie about something like that?"

"I..." It made sense in the moment, but like a drunken night, it made him cringe in the daylight.

"Did you come here and make up a whole new identity?" his father asked, instantly thinking the worst of him.

"Guys, the show's about to start," Mark said.

"This is...Nathan's father," Liam said.

Another look of shock greeted Nathan. The room spun around and became stifling and hot.

"How did you find me?" Nathan asked his dad.

"I tracked your credit card purchase for a ticket to New Zealand, and then I got one of the IT guys from my old company to go through your computer. I don't care that it was an invasion of privacy. You had me worried sick. You were fresh out of rehab. I didn't know what kind of trouble you'd gotten yourself into this time." His dad unfolded a piece of paper from his pocket. It was a print out of

Nathan's missed connections post. "And it was so much worse."

"What is that?" Mark took the piece of paper from his dad.

"Nathan, what have you done? We could've discussed this," his dad said.

"Mark, what is it?" Liam asked.

But Mark didn't answer. He was completely absorbed, his eyes expanding in shock as he read each line, as he looked at that old photo.

"Mark," Liam said roughly.

Nathan's dad watched Mark's expression change, and as the pieces of this sordid puzzle clicked for him, he went into his own state of shock.

"Oh dear God," Nathan's dad said.

"Will somebody please explain what the fuck is going on?" Liam yelled, silencing everyone. All heads turned to Nathan.

It was now or never.

"I'm Mariel's son." The tears instantly sprung to his eyes. "She shagged my dad at a festival in the nineties when she was studying in London. Nine months later, she left me on his doorstep."

The crowd erupted in gasps. Even though most of them had no idea who he was talking about, it was still gossip to feast on. Mark went as pale as a ghost, while Nathan's dad seemed to take all of his color. And Liam...Liam's face was a block of stone, betraying nothing.

"I'm not preparing for a film role. I came here to find out more about my mum and why she chose never to have contact with me. My whole life, I've never fit in with my family. And I thought maybe there was another family waiting for me somewhere, a mother who loved me. I wanted to find out who she was, and I wanted to know what I did wrong."

Mark had a sorrowful look in his eyes. Walt clung to his side.

"All I've done since I arrived is lie, but I didn't know how to tell you the truth. How do you tell this wonderful family who took me in that I am their bastard child? I fell in love with you, with all of you, and I didn't want to let that go. For the first time, I felt part of something special. I liked who I was." He wiped tears off his cheeks. He hated all these eyes on him. All eyes on him except for Liam who stared at the wall, his jaw set and tight.

"Mark, I am so sorry," Nathan eked out.

Mark hugged Walt tight against him. He was at a complete loss of words.

"Liam?"

He reached out for Liam's hand.

"You lied to me. This whole time..."

Nathan nodded yes. It was true, and he was done making excuses.

"We should get back inside. The show's about to start," Liam said. He led Walt and Mark back into the auditorium, not once looking back at Nathan.

Two ushers came over to officially break up this scene and get people back to their seats. The auditorium doors swung closed on the darkened theater just as the first notes of the *Into the Woods* overture bellowed out.

"Let's go, son." His dad put his arm around Nathan, and they left behind the Fosters for good. At least Nathan wasn't leaving alone, but he still felt hollow.

Chapter 29

<u>Liam</u>

The post-premiere dinner celebration for Franny was cancelled. Mark waited until Franny took her bows to break the news about Nathan to her, but she'd heard whispering about the fight that took place in lobby just before the curtain rose. Liam's heart ached watching Franny absorb the shock. Mark didn't seem as hurt. If anything, he had an intense focus, like he was running on adrenaline to keep his family together.

The Fosters returned home once the show was over. Mark disappeared straight into the basement without saying a word. Liam and the kids stood around in fumbling silence for a few minutes before Walt admitted he was hungry. Liam heated up cans of soup in the kitchen for the kids, and a cup of tea for himself. It was a welcome distraction from the pain and anger colliding in his chest. He had gotten the last pieces of the Nathan puzzle.

"Mark, I heated up some soup," Liam yelled down into the basement.

"I'm not hungry," Mark yelled back.

Liam served his niece and nephew.

"So you had no idea?" Walt asked him.

Liam shook his head no. But maybe he should have. The lies started to make sense, but they were still lies. The love he felt for Nathan, their intimacy, was clouded over by falsehoods. Did he even know the real Nathan?

"I can't fucking believe it," Franny said over her bowl of uneaten soup.

"Don't curse," Liam said, though he shared her sentiment. "I'm sorry this came out on your opening night."

She shrugged. She still kicked ass as Cinderella, though Liam couldn't fully enjoy her performance since his mind was elsewhere.

"How are you guys doing?" he asked. "I can understand if you're angry and hurt. Nathan spent a lot of time with us under false pretenses."

"What would you and Dad have done if he told you the truth when he first came?" Franny asked. "Would you have let him stay here?"

"I don't know." He tried to picture Nathan as a stranger from halfway around the world ringing the doorbell and saying he was Mariel's son. And then he thought about baby Nathan on his father's doorstep all those years ago, how scared he must've been.

"I have an older brother. I think it's cool," Walt said.

"I do, too," Franny said.

Liam squirmed in his seat. "He's related to you, but I wouldn't call him your brother."

"Why not?" Walt asked.

"It's complicated. You see the relationship your dad and I have with each other and your other uncles. There's a bond. It's not just blood."

Walt shrugged. "Nathan was funny. I liked him."

"He helped me with the bullies at school," Franny said. "Didn't my dad used to stick up for you when you got teased at school?"

"Most of my teasing came from your uncles." But it was Mark who made them stop when their jokes got to be too much, or when roughhousing got too rough. It was Mark who would check on him at night, flicking his light switch on and off to see if he was still awake, or waking him in the process. It wasn't as bad as an ice bath to the ass.

Liam shook the memory out of his head. It was made of lies.

"It's going to be okay. It'll get better. Everyone is in shock. But shock wears off. And soon enough, we'll forget Nathan was ever in our lives."

"I don't want to forget." Walt didn't mince words. His assuredness, which he was too young to realize he had, rattled Liam.

"Yes you do!"

"Why?"

"Because." Liam scratched at his beard. "Nathan isn't a part of our family. He's an interloper."

"What's an interloper?"

"It's someone who doesn't belong. An intruder." Liam pressed his palms against the table, like a lawyer making his case. "Nathan intruded on our lives and did nothing but lie and spin stories. He made you lie for him, Walt."

"I get it now. He wanted to know about his mum," Walt said in between intentional slurps of his soup.

"So?" Liam swirled his spoon in his tea. "That doesn't excuse what he did."

"If I didn't know anything about my mum, I would want to know, even if I had to lie," Walt said.

"Mum was the best. I can't imagine never meeting her," Franny said.

She dipped her spoon in and out of her food. Liam was too invested in this argument to tell her to stop.

"Uncle Liam, you kind of remind me of Javert," Walt said.

"Who's that?"

"He's in *Les Miserables.*" They had watched the video of Mariel's performance multiple times since Nathan had arrived. "Javert chased Jean Valjean for years because he stole a loaf of bread. He only stole it because he was starving, but Javert didn't care. He only saw Valjean as a criminal. I've taken things from my sister's room. I don't think that makes me a criminal."

"What stuff?" Franny asked.

Walt shrugged and slurped his soup.

"Walt?" she pressed.

"Am I Javert in this scenario?" Liam asked, getting them back to the topic at hand.

Walt and Franny ate a spoonful of soup at the same time. Their slurps spoke volumes.

Life wasn't a play, no matter what they thought. Though perhaps there was a kernel of truth in there. What would Liam do to learn about his mum? What if he had secret siblings scattered around the globe? He had never been in Nathan's situation.

But was everything a lie? The nights and mornings together? The kisses? The sex? Liam didn't want to take a chance to find out. He had hit his limit with deception.

The outside screen door screeched open, then the front door. Pastor Fry and Brenda came inside, giving Liam a solemn look like they'd just come from a funeral.

"Where's Mark?" Pastor Fry asked.

"In the basement," Liam said. He didn't know what Mark was looking for, but he dared not interrupt him.

"This is awful. Brenda has been crying the whole car ride."

Her face was a red, splotchy mess. Liam handed her a tissue box.

"We need to talk about this." Pastor Fry sat across from Franny and Walt. "Kids, I understand you must be in shock. You all must be." He turned to Liam. "It's torn us up inside for decades."

"You knew about this?" Liam asked.

"Mariel panicked when she discovered she was with child. We were afraid she would try to terminate the pregnancy. We flew to London immediately, and she decided that she wanted to give the baby up for adoption. She believed God had given her this child, but that he was destined for another family. She knew about the members of our church who'd had trouble conceiving, and she wanted to help couples who wanted to be parents more than anything. She was very giving, your mother. She found a lovely family in London for Nathan."

Mariel hid a secret from Mark, from Liam, from the world. All those dinners and holidays Liam had spent with her, she never revealed anything. She carried this secret to her grave.

"Our daughter was young and scared. She'd made a mistake, but she tried doing the best thing she could. And when she left London, she knew that Nathan was not her baby, that he was with his real family now."

Franny and Walt seemed to understand as well as two kids could. Pastor Fry was trying his best with a kid-friendly explanation.

"I understand this is a great deal to take in, kids, but at least now you know what happened," Pastor Fry said.

"Except none of that is true." Mark emerged from the basement holding a dusty journal triumphantly in the air and one tucked under his arm. Streaks of dust covered his clothes and clouded his hair.

"Mark, what were you doing down there? You should be with your family," Pastor Fry said. "We need to discuss this together."

"We do. Everyone deserves to be heard."

"Precisely."

"Even Mariel."

Liam traded curious looks with his niece and nephew. "Mark, what are you talking about?"

"Your brother is under a lot of emotional stress. Mark, maybe you should go upstairs and lay down. We can talk about this in the morning," Pastor Fry said.

"No, we are talking about this now!" Mark was never one for yelling. His booming voice shut everyone up. "Mariel kept journals all throughout her life. I remember watching her write in them at school, around the house. When she died, I couldn't go through them. It was too painful to look." He showed off the two journals to the room. "I found her journals from when she studied in London."

Liam bobbed his head up. That must've been why Nathan was in the basement. He was desperately trying to untangle the mystery of his life. He caught Walt looking at him, the same thing appearing to run through his little mind.

"Mark, dear, those are personal," Brenda said.

"Not anymore."

"Mark, stop it. You are acting wild, and disrespecting my daughter's name." Pastor Fry reached for the journal, but

Mark snapped them away. He had a look of madness in his eye—or was it clarity?

Mark flipped open the first journal. "September second: Fuck. I'm pregnant."

Walt and Franny snickered.

Mark continued reading: "I am the worst girlfriend. I don't know what I'm going to do. I am so scared, but at the same time, I already feel love for the person growing inside me. He or she is a part of me. I've been thinking of holding this baby in my arms and picking out baby clothes and telling off snobby mums in play circles. But what am I going to tell Mark? He loves me. I am ashamed for doing this to him, but I love him so much, and maybe, someday, he will understand."

Mark turned a chunk of pages. "September twenty-eighth: I told my parents, and they reacted even worse than I expected. Twenty minutes of Mum crying and Dad calling me a whore." He flicked his eyes at Pastor Fry. "Telling me what a horrible mistake I made, then bringing up every mildly rebellious thing I'd ever done in my life, down to putting on lipstick when I was five. He refused to let me come back to New Zealand in this condition. He's paying for me to stay in London until the baby is born. Free holiday! The catch is I can't tell anyone back home about the baby, especially not Mark. Dad said this was for my own protection, so I could go back to my life, but I knew he was mostly worried about what his congregants would say about him. He said if Mark ever found out, he'd dump me, and the whole community would want nothing to do with a whore. There was that word again. He and Mum would disown me. How can I not tell Mark? How can I not bring this up when we chat on the phone?"

"Mark, that's enough," Pastor Fry said.

Mark ignored him and flipped to one of the last pages. "March seventh: I had my final ultrasound. There is a baby inside of me. A baby boy! I cry every day thinking about giving him up, about not knowing how he's doing. I have dreams about hearing him cry but not being able to hold him. I found the father. He's a businessman in London. He deserves to know about his son. So does Mark. Dad and I had another blowup about it, and he said he would have me committed to an institution if I uttered one word of this back home. I wasn't crazy, but that wouldn't stop him. Mum then got on the line and said Mark would never speak to me again, neither would my friends. I would never be able to act. My life would be over before it begun."

"Stop!" Pastor Fry ripped the journal out of his hands and threw it against the wall. "Your children are here!"

"What would you have done if she told you?" Brenda asked. "Would you have married her, had these two beautiful children? I meant what I told her all those years ago. Her life would've been ruined."

Liam could see the struggle on Mark's face. Hindsight was easy. The present, not so much.

"We'll never know," Mark said. "You didn't give any of us that chance. She cared about Nathan. The secret she had to live with her whole life...I don't know how she bared it."

He pulled the second journal from under his arm. "This is from seven years ago. May ninth: Another year older. I wonder what you're up to. I wonder what kind of student you are. Maybe you're in all the smart classes, unlike me. Or you're the star of your football team, unlike me. Maybe you're a straight arrow, unlike me. But I hope tonight, you do something just a little bit wild, like I would've done at your age. Smoke a joint. Stay out really late." Mark let out a tearful guffaw. He broke, and the tears fell. "I've been tempted to find you online. It's like an alcoholic staring at a liquor bottle. But I can't. It would be too painful to find you, to have to explain how I abandoned you. It's better you be with your own family and never think of me." He snapped the journal shut tossed it on the coffee table. "I always felt some distance between Mariel. I knew she loved me, but there was a part of herself she was hiding."

Liam felt the same about Nathan, and he thought about the secret he had to carry everyday, the shame. He looked over at his niece and nephew, who were crying like their dad.

"Your grandchild was out there in the world, and you didn't care," Mark said.

"He is not my grandchild! He was a mistake, a mistake that should've stayed buried," Pastor Fry said.

"He's not a mistake!" Franny yelled. "He's my brother, and you're a jerk, grandpa!"

Pastor Fry turned red with anger. "Are you going to let your daughter speak to me in that way?"

"No, no I'm not," Mark said. "Franny, do not call your grandfather a jerk."

Franny hung her head and nodded that she understood.

"Call him a fucking arsehole prick instead."

Every jaw dropped to the floor. Franny and Walt giggled in shock. Liam had never seen this side of his brother. And probably, neither had Mark.

"Get out of my house," Mark growled at his in-laws.

Pastor Fry and Brenda left without saying a word. Mark and Mariel would've worked through what happened in London, Liam believed. It would've been a tough pill to swallow for his brother, but they would've made it. They were in love. They would've made it through.

Chapter 30

NATHAN

Nathan didn't want a drink. He wanted to feel drunk. He wanted to turn the world into a blur. When he had gotten extremely drunk, he blacked out during fun moments – in pubs or in bed. Why couldn't he have blacked out that whole scene in the lobby? Why couldn't he have had zero recollection of Mark's reaction to his admission, of Liam refusing to look at him and walk away?

His dad had booked them a suite at a luxurious hotel in downtown Wellington, one that overlooked the ocean. From his balcony, Nathan could see the restaurant where Liam had taken him. Another memory for which he wanted to be blacked out. The TV blared in the background, but he couldn't pay attention. His mind kept drifting to yesterday and the mess he made of everything. His mum was smart to keep her distance. He'd found a way to ruin her life posthumously.

His heart ached over Liam, but what did he expect? All he did was lie; Liam wouldn't want to stick around for that.

Room service knocked politely at the door. Nathan

opened up, and the waiter wheeled in a cart of food. His dad walked in behind him. It was close to midnight, but his dad was starving. He was on London time. Nathan's stomach growled, too, but he got nauseous at the thought of putting food into his mouth.

The waiter set their table and pulled off two plate covers. Steam rose from their meals.

"This looks delicious," Nathan's dad said. He tipped the waiter nicely. He then hugged Nathan and awkwardly kissed him on the head, then sat down to eat. All this fatherly affection was new for Nathan, but he could get used to it. He appreciated that his dad was trying.

He motioned for Nathan to join him at the table. Nathan put the plate cover back on his food.

"I was able to book us on a flight home tomorrow evening. I got us the last two first class seats."

"Smashing," Nathan deadpanned.

"I don't know if I'm overtired or ready for another day. I think I'm on my fourth wind." His dad shoved a forkful of food into his mouth.

"What about my stuff?" Nathan asked. "My stuff is at Liam's."

A pang of hurt stabbed at him. He was going to miss that tiny shed.

"I'll...I'll go and get it." From Mark's. Mariel's two lovers would have to come face to face. Nathan couldn't imagine that would be easy for him, or would it since so much time had passed?

"How are you doing?" Nathan asked him. His dad gave him a look, surprised at the question.

"It's all very strange. Very, very strange."

"What was it like when you found me?" Nathan realized he never knew this side of the story.

"I freaked the fuck out." His dad moved his fork around the plate, but didn't take a bite. "I was so scared. The night before, I was at a pub drinking with colleagues. The next morning, the doorbell rang, and there you were with a grainy photograph from that bloody concert. I became an instant father at twenty-five. I felt like my life was ripped away from me. I was angry. I took it out on her. I never wanted you to know about your mum. That was my form of revenge for what she did. She wouldn't get to hold a place in your memory. But I wound up hurting you the most. I blamed you, because you were as close as I could get to her. I am deeply sorry." He rubbed Nathan's leg, and his voice got heavy with emotion. Nathan never saw his dad cry. Not because he was the strong and silent type, but because they'd never been together in a situation that would involve tears. Things never got emotional between them. "I threw money at you to shut you up and tried to live the life I wanted. I didn't do right by you."

"Dad, it's all right."

"No, it's not! The alcoholism, the expulsions. It's because of me, because I didn't give you what you needed." He wiped away his tears, but more came. Nathan gave him a tissue box. He had never seen his dad like this. Emotions poured out of him that were locked up for twenty-two years. "I always knew you would have questions about your mum, but I didn't want to answer them. I wanted to forget, and I tried to make you forget."

"You tried to forget in some of the best resorts in the world."

"I tried to run, but the pain I felt, the pain I knew I was causing, was always with me." He pointed at his heart. "You were suffering, and I shut you out."

It was everything Nathan wanted to hear. Justice. Vindication. But it didn't satisfy him, not when he saw that his dad had been punishing himself this whole time.

"I really hated you," Nathan said. "But you're the only family I've got."

"When you go to rehab again, I'm going to show up for every family visitation. I'm going to make sure you stay sober."

"I am sober, Dad."

His dad tried to hide his surprise. Nathan couldn't blame him. He was just as shocked saying that as his dad was hearing that.

"I can't believe it either."

"I'm sorry. I didn't—"

"It's all right. Working on that farm and being with those wonderful people made me want to stay clean."

"I know it will be a hard transition back to London."

"I think I can do it, though," Nathan said. "It would be so easy to fall off the wagon again. I would have so many people to blame for it. You, Mum, Pastor Fry, Liam. But I'm tired of blaming people." Nathan saw how great life could be when he stayed sober, when he surrounded himself with people who cared about him. He was going to miss the Fosters like hell, but he made a pact with himself to find quality people in London. "I'm ready to do this for myself. I'm going to go to an AA meeting tomorrow before we go to the airport."

"I'm proud of you." His dad patted his hand.

"You don't have to be proud of me for not being a drunken disaster. That's quite a low bar." He wanted people to be proud of him for actual accomplishments.

"I'm proud of you always. And honestly, I'm proud of you for working on a farm for more than a day. Hell, an hour."

"Right!" Though secretly, Nathan found that he enjoyed it. "I need a holiday from my holiday."

"How about we take a father-son trip? There's this Ritz Carlton resort in Costa Rica I've been dying to go to. Your stepmom has refused because of the humidity."

They laughed. Nathan ripped off a piece of a roll and tossed it into his mouth.

"What does she think about all this?" Nathan asked.

"She knew that your mother was long out of the picture and that I didn't have to pay any kind of alimony, so she was fine."

"She can channel any lingering frustration into decorating another room."

"I hope so. The woman may have her faults, but she has great taste."

Nathan looked up from his food and saw that his dad wasn't joking.

"Oh, father. I have failed you as a gay son."

NATHAN'S APPETITE came back a little bit more, and over room service dinner, he regaled his dad with tales of farming and Mariel's acting career. His dad never got a chance to see her perform. "Unless you count the night I met her, when she put on a cockney accent to fool me into buying her a drink!" He and Mariel were not soulmates, not by a long shot, but they were connected by Nathan. They always would be.

"She sounds like a wonderful woman," he said.

"She does. I wish I could've seen her on stage. When I get back to London, I'm going to sign up with an acting teacher and to go back on auditions."

"You don't sound too excited," his dad said.

"I am, but..."

"A part of you wishes you were on that farm."

"Is that crazy?" He wondered if his mum had the same tug-of-war between city and rural life. It wasn't so much the farm as the people who were there.

"I think you'll forget all about the farm once you're back walking the streets of London."

Just before midnight, the hotel phone rang, an annoying old-school clang that made Nathan want to cover his ears.

"Hello?" his dad said when he picked it up. His expression changed throughout the call. "Yes...Oh...all right...we'll be right down."

Nathan hung on every vague word. "What is it?"

"Mark Foster is in the lobby."

THE LOBBY WAS quiet save for the music coming from the hotel bar. Mark sat in a chair with a paper shopping bag waiting between his ankles. He stood when he saw Nathan walk over.

"Nathan."

They shook hands, but it didn't feel right. It was too proper for them.

"It's late," Nathan said.

"I'm sorry if I woke you. I called around to all the hotels looking for Roger Hargrove. I wanted to catch you before you left."

"I don't leave until tomorrow evening. How do you know my father's name?"

From his shopping bag, Mark pulled a black, worn

journal with dust wiped off the cover. Mark didn't have to say whom they belonged to.

"This is what you were looking for in the basement?"

Nathan nodded.

"I did some digging tonight." Pain surged across Mark's face. He had to sit down. "Nathan, I want to apologize, on behalf of my family."

"No, I need to apologize. I'm sorry for lying to you and your kids."

"I'm sorry for what happened to you. Mariel explained everything in these journals. Her parents threatened to institutionalize her and take away Franny and Walt if she ever breathed a word about you. They were so ashamed of her and...so cruel."

Nathan saw how they reacted at Franny's dress. He could only imagine what they said when their already rebellious daughter got knocked up in a foreign country.

"They never should've kept her away from you. No matter what the circumstances were."

"It wasn't too Christian of them," Nathan said.

"Mariel was forever rebelling against them. I think that's why she got into theater, so she could be women she wasn't allowed to be at home." Mark handed the shopping bag over to Nathan. "I want you to have these."

It was filled to the brim with journals, some leather-bound, some dollar-store ones, some in better condition than others. An entire life tucked snuggly into a single bag.

"Are you sure? These are Mariel's personal items."

"You deserve to know who your mother was. She never stopped thinking about you. Every May ninth, she would write an entry to you wondering about what you were up to."

"Why May ninth?"

Mark cocked his head to the side. "Because that's your birthday."

Nathan's eyes opened wide. "May ninth is my birthday? It's not May thirteenth?" He turned to his dad. "I have a real birthday!"

"I found Nathan on my doorstep May thirteenth," his dad explained to Mark. "We put that as his official birthday."

"I have a real birthday!" Nathan threw his arms open and shouted it for the entire hotel lobby to hear. He felt like Geppetto had made him a real boy.

"Hard out!" Mark said.

Nathan got quiet, his elation replaced with a different kind of warmth. "That means Mum spent four days with me."

It was a blip compared to the time most kids got to spend with their mothers, but Nathan would take it.

Mark picked up the paper bag. "I also included photographs and programs for you. I spent the past few hours digging through her possessions in the basement. Walt is going to upload her performance videos to YouTube and send you a private link. He knows more about that than I do."

"Mark, thank you so much." Nathan's throat clogged with emotion.

"We'll pack up and box your stuff and ship it to you in London, if you'd like."

"You're ready to get rid of me, I reckon." Nathan smirked.

"Just the opposite. I don't want this to be the end, Nathan. You have an open invitation to come back to our house whenever you want. You can email or call me if you ever have questions about Mariel. She was your mother, and I will never restrict information. Also," Mark cleared his throat. "whenever you want to visit or talk to Franny and Walt, that is your right. I know things are in a very precarious place currently, but they are your siblings, and you deserve to have a relationship with them, if you choose."

"I would like that," Nathan said. Inside, his heart was lighting off fireworks. He didn't get a chance to say goodbye to them. He didn't even get to see Franny perform. "Would they?"

"I think they would," Mark said with a knowing smile.

"How is everyone doing?"

"It's been an interesting few hours. My kids have asked me more questions than they have since they learned what sex was. It's the first time when I wish they would go back to reading their mobiles."

"I am sorry about that," Nathan said.

"Don't be. This whole development has been unorthodox to say the least, but I'm glad I got to meet you and know you."

"Likewise," Nathan said. He had his real father and something like an older brother in Mark, plus real siblings. There was only one person missing. "Have you spoken to Liam?"

"He's..." Mark scratched at his neck. "He's still processing."

Nathan had a feeling he would be "processing" for the rest of his life, and if Nathan ever came to the farm again, he would stay locked away in the shed.

Mark gave Nathan a hug and wished him a safe trip home.

"I hope this isn't the last time we talk," Mark said.

"Really?"

"Yeah. You're family, Nathan."

It was a nice word to hear.

Chapter 31

LIAM

The next day was rough. Not only was Liam having to work double-time on the farm but he couldn't stop thinking about Nathan not being there. He listened out for other footsteps or someone cursing in a tangy British accent, but his farm was quiet. Not even Tilly and the other sheep were giving him ambient noise. And the silence made his thoughts go to yesterday.

Nathan was Mariel's son. Nathan was lying to him this whole time. And now Nathan was gone.

His feet seemed to covered in concrete, and his body moved like mush, as if he completed a marathon without stretching. In the shed, Mark was packing up Nathan's things to send back to London. Soon, he and Nathan would be half a world apart. It would get easier, he told himself. When Kelly left, he felt awful, but it got easier. He wasn't even Facebook friends with Nathan, so that would help.

Who the fuck am I kidding? This hurts so much more than Kelly. Liam thought back to their break-up. He was angry and hurt that she'd cheated on him. But did he *miss* her like he did Nathan? Did it feel like someone had torn muscle from his bone? He'd found Mark's old ad looking for a farmhand, but he didn't have the heart to post it yet. Maybe tomorrow, when the wound was slightly less fresh.

"Do you need any help out here?" Mark joined Liam, who was shoveling at the manure pit. "I may be a bit rusty, but I still know my way around a farm."

"I'm good." Liam wiped his sleeve across his sweaty forehead. "How's packing going?"

"I'm done. He didn't bring much."

"Just a suitcase." Liam remembered the sight of him dragging that fucking suitcase through his farm in the middle of the night.

"What's so funny?"

"Nothing."

"It's good to see you smiling."

"You too, brother," Liam said. "That was pretty awesome last night. I've never seen the Pastor speechless."

"Well, now my ten-year-old son can't stop saying fucking arsehole prick."

The brothers shared a laugh, one that relieved some of the tension swirling in Liam's chest.

"Are you sure you're all good with keeping the farm?" Liam asked. "If you want to move, if you need that money, I will do it. I would do anything for you."

Liam didn't know where Mark found the strength to hold it together. Maybe it was instinctual as the oldest brother and as a father. It was in his blood to take care of those he loved. Just like their dad.

Mark hooked him into a hug.

"Every time I see you out here, working with the sheep, it's like a piece of Mum and Dad are still alive. And besides, Wellington sucks."

At family dinner, the table was quiet. Liam couldn't imagine what his brother was going through, finding out that Mariel had a child on the side, or his niece and nephew who now had a new brother.

"Franny, would you like to say the prayer tonight?" Mark asked.

Franny bowed her head. "Dear Lord, we thank you for this bounty and your blessings. If you do have time, could you please help my Uncle Liam stop being a Mopey Martha? Thank you."

"What?" Liam whipped his head up.

"Uncle Liam, you need to get out of this funk," she said, as if he were merely upset about spilled milk or a rainy day.

"It's more than a funk. It's not a funk!" Liam said.

"It's a funk," Mark said as he cut slices of meatloaf.

"How are you all not in a funk? Twenty-four hours ago, you found out that you have a brother and that your mother...you were walloped with new information."

"It's like when I get new shoes," Walt said.

Liam clanged his fork onto his plate. "This whole situation is like getting a new pair of shoes? Please elaborate."

"New shoes give me blisters at first, and they feel weird and uncomfortable, but then they feel good."

"We're very surprised, but you're the only one who's upset." Franny pointed an accusatory spoonful of mashed potatoes at him.

He looked to his brother for backup. "She's right," Mark said.

Et tu, brother?

"Nathan lied to us! Pathologically. Nothing he told us

about himself was the truth. He came here under false pretenses and weaseled his way into our hearts."

His family gave him all double-takes. The kids laughed.

"I didn't mean hearts. You know what I mean!" He slapped a heap of mashed potatoes onto his plate. For show, only. "He lied."

Walt pointed his fork at him. "Javert!"

Liam cocked his head at him.

"What would you have had Nathan do?" Franny asked. "Come here and say 'Hello, I'm your mum's secret child that she kept from you for twenty-two years. May I come in?'"

Liam missed when his niece and nephew worshipped him and never questioned anything he did or said. Why did kids have to grow up?

"Aren't you mad at your mum? Your wife?" He looked straight at Mark.

The table got quiet. Liam had an upper hand he didn't want.

"It's hard to hold a grudge with someone who isn't..." Mark cleared his throat. "I know that despite her secrets and despite what happened, she loved me. She loved us." Mark leaned over the table, closer to his brother. "People are gray, Liam."

"It's not the same as Kelly," Franny said. He would forever think her too young to talk about this. "Kelly lied to trick you. Nathan lied to get closer to us."

And to me.

"And Kelly smelled," Walt said.

"Walt!" Mark said.

"What? She did."

Liam put down his fork and pushed away from the table. He didn't need to be ridiculed or chastised by his family. Maybe they were fine with everything, but not him.

"He asked about you," Mark said.

Liam's heart paused. "He did?"

"He misses you."

"He said that?"

Mark shrugged. "He didn't have to."

"Interesting," Liam said.

"He's leaving to go back to London tonight."

"All good." Liam pushed himself back to the table. "That makes sense. That's his home."

"No, it's not. This is his home," Mark said.

Franny sighed and clanged her fork onto her plate. "Uncle Liam! Are you really going to let him go?"

Liam looked to Mark for backup, but he seemed to be siding with his daughter. "There's more to it than that."

"Is there? The only person lying here is you," Mark said.

"Javert!" Walt said while pretending to sneeze.

Liam shot him a glare. "It's too late. He's already on his plane."

"He's taking a night flight," Mark said. "That's what he told me."

In a flash, Franny and Walt were on their phones, typing and scrolling with dogged determination.

"There's a flight that takes off at ten o'clock. It's the final flight out," Franny said. "It's flying to Los Angeles, then onto to London."

"And it will take thirty-eight minutes to drive to his hotel," Walt said, showing his dad the Google Maps preferred route.

"He might not have left for the airport yet," Franny said.

"We don't know that's his flight! And he..." Liam thought about waking up with Nathan in his arms. He pictured Nathan's face when he delivered Tilly's lambs, the shock and joy and tinge of sadness glowing in his eyes and brightening his cheeks. It was pure. It was real.

Liam looked over at his brother, and after a whole life together, they didn't need words.

"I can get us there in thirty-one," Mark said.

Chapter 32

NATHAN

Nathan waited at the foot of his hotel bed, watching the weather report on the TV, silently hoping for a freak blizzard. His father was filling his toiletry bag with free bathroom soaps. Someone knocked at the door. Nathan's breath caught in his chest. He raced to the door.

"Evening, sir." A member of guest services handed him a bag of his laundry. He had bought a new outfit in the hotel shop and sent for his old outfit to be washed thoroughly.

"We washed it twice," the employee said. "The clothes had a very strong smell on them."

"It's sheep manure," Nathan said wistfully.

He opened the bag and inhaled the fresh scent. He missed the old smell. He had gotten used to it, and it had become a part of him. If he ever came across another sheep, he would think of the farm and Liam when he smelled it.

Nathan threw the clothes into his suitcase, also purchased at the hotel shop.

"Are you ready to go?" his father asked. He crammed his bulging toiletry bag into his suitcase.

"Ready." He thought about calling Liam, but he didn't know what to say. He knew how Liam felt, and that was enough for him.

"The cab will be here in two minutes."

Nathan sat on his bed and closed his eyes. He pictured all the memories he made over these past two months. He thought about Franny and him going dress shopping, laughing over family dinners, the way Liam pulled him close when they spooned. And of course, he thought of the sheep meandering around the farm, living their best lives. He could hear them now, baaa'ing in the background. It was almost peaceful, a sound he got used to as he drifted off to sleep.

"Do you hear that?" his dad asked.

Baaaa.

Was Nathan still daydreaming? His dad charged to the window.

Baaaa.

"Do they let sheep run wild in the streets here?" his dad asked.

The baaaa'ing got louder. It filled up the empty space of the room. It was accompanied by the honking of horns.

More horns and more bleating. They wafted through the hotel window. It was madness outside. And a suspicious, hopeful feeling tingled up Nathan's spine.

He ran to the window and pulled back the curtains.

Sheep. Everywhere.

They filled the circular driveway entrance to the hotel. They meandered onto the carefully landscaped lawn. Tilly and her lambs chewed on the grass. Cabs and valet drivers trying to drop off visitors honked at the stampede of livestock. He couldn't see asphalt. Just wool. A sea of wool.

With one Liam sticking up in the center of the madness.

As soon as Liam found Nathan's window, a huge smile creased his bearded face.

"Nathan!"

"Liam? What the hell are you doing?"

"They wanted to do some shopping in the city." Liam wore the blazer from their date with a rumpled flannel shirt underneath. "And they wanted to tell you not to go, that you were the best thing that's ever happened to them."

"*They* wanted to tell me that?"

"And me. Me, especially."

Even though three stories and a flock of sheep separated him and Liam, Nathan felt like there was nothing in this world right now except for them.

"But I lied to you," Nathan said. "Repeatedly."

"You told me some untrue things about yourself, but was everything you felt also untrue?"

Nathan shook his head no.

"That's what I thought." The sheep bleated around him. "Pipe down. I was getting to that part." He turned back to Nathan. "Can you take a flight tomorrow? I was hoping we could talk."

"We can talk."

"Maybe even pash a little bit."

Nathan laughed. He remembered looking up that slang word during a restless night fantasizing about his boss, Farmer Tight-ass.

"We'll see."

A manager from the hotel bobbed and weaved between the sheep, nearly tripping over one of them. He came up to Liam, and Nathan couldn't hear what was being said, but he got the idea.

Nathan ran downstairs and into the front driveway, where it was sheep central. One sheep had climbed onto the luggage cart. Two others were grazing at the flowerpots. The line of cars backed up into the street. And in the middle of the chaos was Liam, Liam who was currently being chewed out by management, Liam with his burly shoulders and bushy beard and eyes that twinkled in the light and ears that reddened when challenged by a posh Brit.

"If you don't get these sheep out of here, I'm going to call the police," the manager said to Liam.

"I can help," Nathan said. "I have experience working with sheep."

Liam's face lit up with a pure warmth that melted Nathan. There was no way he could leave that face behind.

"He's great with sheep," Liam told the manager.

Nathan helped Liam shoo his flock of sheep into his truck parked on the street. He knew to handle them delicately so as not to scare them and start a stampede. Mark stopped traffic so the sheep could cross. This couldn't have been the first sheep crossing in New Zealand. Waiting by the truck were Franny and Walt. Nathan had never been so happy to see them.

"We couldn't let you leave without saying goodbye," Franny said.

"Yeah. You're family," Walt said.

Nathan looked past them at Liam, who was herding the last sheep to the truck.

"Actually," Nathan said. He glanced back at his hotel room. His dad watched from the window and gave him a loving head nod, full of the fatherly support Nathan had always craved.

"I think I'm going to stay a little bit longer," Nathan said.

"Really?" Franny asked.

"Really," Nathan said definitively.

He walked over to Liam, who shut the back door of his truck. “Can I talk to you a second?”

He had Liam walk a few steps away from the family so they could have alone time. The moon hung low over the ocean and its light sparkled on the water.

“Liam, I’m sorry—”

Liam grazed his fingers over Nathan’s mouth, then he replaced them with his mouth. That familiar beard brushed against his face. The kiss sent Nathan into the stratosphere. He doubted he would ever tire of those lips on his, or anywhere on his body.

“No more lies,” Nathan said.

“No more lies.” Liam kissed him again. “Wait. Was that a lie?”

“Only one way to find out.”

EPILOGUE

LIAM

Baaaa.

Liam peeked out his face from under his pillow and opened one eye. Through the window, he could see it was still dark.

Baaaa.

Yeah, yeah. I heard you.

Sleep maintained its grip on Liam. He couldn't move from the mattress. He would fall back into slumber, then awake at another bleat. He opened his one eye again, but he couldn't see the window. A sexy guy was blocking his view.

"Let's go. It's already four-fifteen. The day is half bloody over." Nathan's body had gained muscle and heft ever since he began working on the farm full-time. Liam had noticed his pecs getting bigger, his abs tighter and more washboardy, and his arms, presently crossed against his chest, were turning into the ropes he used to climb in gym class. Add those to Nathan's already withering stare and husky accent, and it was officially too much sexiness.

"Stop checking me out and get out of bed." Nathan

adjusted his hat and wiped a stray piece of hay off his half-buttoned flannel shirt.

"Is that my shirt?"

"I look better in it anyway." Nathan clapped twice, the sound ringing in Liam's half-asleep ears. "Come on. Up you get. You have to refill the feeders."

"You haven't done that yet?"

"Ringo kicked a hole in his pen overnight. I've been patching it up so he doesn't sneak out." A hammer hung from one of Nathan's belt loops. "Up. Or else."

"Or else what?"

Nathan fixed his stare on Liam and unleashed a smirk that was up to no good. He walked the few steps into the kitchen.

"Don't," Liam said.

His cry went ignored. Nathan removed a glass from the cabinet.

"Nathan," he growled. His body was under the control of the bed.

Liam watched him turn the tap all the way to the right and fill the glass with the coldest water possible. Then, to add insult to imminent injury, he plopped a handful of ice cubes in and stirred.

"I mean it," Liam said. He pulled the cover up to his neck in preparation. He couldn't stop what was coming. Nor could he stop his cock from sprouting wood at the sight of his sexy boyfriend sauntering over, ready to punish him.

"I learned this from you." Nathan held up the glass.

"I was cruel back then."

"And now I usually get up before you, so perhaps your cruel methods work."

"Please, don't," Liam pleaded. Wisps of drafty morning air hit his exposed skin. He was cold enough.

"Why?"

"Because you love me."

Nathan considered this. "I suppose I do."

He drank the water himself in one long chug. Liam breathed a sigh of relief.

"See, wasn't that—"

Liam tumbled off the bed as the mattress flipped in the air. He leapt up and kicked the blankets now tangled at his feet.

"What the hell, Nathan?"

"You seemed to enjoy it." Nathan nudged his chin at the tent pitched in his boxers.

"It must be the bleating." *Or that my boyfriend is hotter than fuck.*

"Must be."

Liam's cock led the way to Nathan. He admired the beautiful guy who'd stolen his heart. When they kissed, Liam saw stars. He brushed his fingers against the patchy beard Nathan was sporting, the hair like different pieces of land slowly joining together. His hands wandered into Nathan's shirt to feel up his broad chest. They had to be careful about how handsy they were on the farm since Mark and the kids could make an appearance at any time.

"Two can play this game," Nathan said, finding his way into Liam's boxers and stroking his throbbing cock. Just as Liam moaned, Nathan pulled his hands back. "Feeding first."

Liam stared horny daggers at him. "You country fuck."

"You posh prick."

Their mouths collided with more energy than a fresh pot of coffee. Liam pulled Nathan against him. They had time for a quickie. Liam wouldn't be able to concentrate on the farm with a massive hard-on. And judging by the bulge in Nathan's jeans, neither would he.

It was one of those many times when Liam had to have Nathan, when he successfully channeled his frustration into sexual dominance. He grabbed Nathan's hands and shoved them into his boxers.

"Are you going to operate my hands like second-rate puppets, or will you let a master go to work?" Nathan asked in that fuck-you voice that made Liam want to tear off all his clothes.

Nathan pulled back from his grip, yanked Liam's pants down, and stopped his mouth just before his aching, engorged cock.

"You know what, I think I need to check on the sheep."

"Suck," he commanded.

And suck Nathan did, until Liam's knees were about to give. He took his thick rod to the base.

"You're not so bad at this," Liam said. He grabbed a fistful of hair and balanced himself against the fridge. Nathan's tongue was like a wizard. He loved watching his cock disappear into that sarcastic mouth.

The sheep bleated outside, and Liam knew they didn't have enough time to drag this out. He signaled for Nathan to stand up. They kissed again, allowing Liam to taste the remnants of his sweaty cock on his lips.

"I want you to fuck me hard. And fast." Nathan nodded at the windows where the bleating came from. Time was of the essence.

"No fucking problem." He bent Nathan onto the overturned mattress, which stuck up on its side. He ripped down his jeans and boxer-briefs. Nathan ran out of his fancy designer clothes after three months. They were not meant for the outdoors. They went shopping together, and Nathan pretended to like the selection. He and Franny made excursions to the city for fancier outfits on special occasions.

His eyes watered at the sight of that pink, puckered hole. He massaged his opening with his thumb and pushed his way inside. He gave Nathan's ass a speedy spit shine, along with a few hard spanks that left handprints. Damn, he tasted so fucking good.

"Since we're rushed for time, I'm not going to use any lube."

"Don't you fucking dare or else I will throw you into the manure pit."

Liam laughed to himself. He slathered himself and Nathan's ass with lube. He also lubed up Nathan's leaking cock, which was complete with its own bush of grown out hair. He had embraced the au natural look, which Liam found hot.

He plunged inside Nathan. Making contact with that warm ring of muscle nearly made him bust a nut on contact. Nathan moaned for him and pointed his ass in the air. It only took a few humps for Liam to spill inside him, and Nathan was not too far behind, soaking the mattress sheet with bursts of come.

"Who thought that I'd have morning sex at four a.m.?" Nathan said. "Without staying up all night."

"Welcome to being a sheep farmer."

Nathan

After Liam and his crew of sheep had come for him at his hotel, Nathan and his father had moved their flight to the next day. Nathan's father joined them for family dinner that night, and he gave Mark the whole scoop on which hotels to stay at for his next vacation.

His father left the next morning, while Nathan kept pushing back his flight. Six months later, he had yet to return to London.

He embraced the farm life. Every night he went to bed feeling productive and finding his purpose, sometimes before the sun had even set. He wasn't planning on leaving anytime soon. His timeline was looking more and more like forever. Next week were auditions at the playhouse where his mum acted for years, and where Franny received rave reviews as Cinderella in *Into the Woods*. He couldn't wait to try out for the musical, *Les Miserables*. When he'd mentioned it at a family dinner, and how he wanted to play Javert, Walt burst out laughing. Nathan still didn't get it.

He and Liam became involved with the local farmers association and got to know other sheep farmers in the area. Back in London, he never imagined he would ever meet or be friends with sheep farmers. Their lives were light years away from his. Yet here he was, in text chains about price fluctuations and having conversations about lambing. Life was happy. Sometimes he had to stop what he was doing and think about the twists and turns that took him to the edge of the world. The world was humongous. Seven billion people. Yet a guy from London and a gal from New Zealand randomly found each other among hundreds of thousands of people at a concert, and now Nathan and Liam had found each other. It was a lot to think about. And spending his days working with animals who couldn't talk gave him plenty of time to ponder.

That night, Mark and the kids made the trek across the field to their house for family dinner. Liam and Nathan hosted two nights each week. They also moved it up half an hour so that Nathan could make it to AA each night. He had really embraced it, after a while of mocking the affirmations.

Nathan let go. Every time he tried to convince himself he was fine and that he could handle one drink, he reminded himself how easily he spiraled, and that it never ended with one drink. He wasn't going to screw up what he had with Liam and his family. They kept him in line, whether they knew it or not.

They all sat down to dinner. Franny helped Nathan set the table.

"How are rehearsals going?" he asked her.

"It is going to be hilarious! Just you wait." Franny scored a role in her school's production of *Noises Off*.

"The comedic timing has to be spot on," Nathan said, passing on sage advice from when he performed in the show years ago. Since it was a play that took place backstage, the play and play-within-the-play had to be synched perfectly.

"It's going to be brilliant. Jason is so funny in it."

She blushed the second his name escaped her lips. Once she decided to become an actress, her first co-star romance was inevitable. Needless to say, Mark demanded they run lines in the living room, not her bedroom. Nathan warned Mark that this was only the beginning.

They all sat down, and Liam put out the food. He and Nathan had made shepherd's pie. Nathan figured he should be eating more of it since he was now a shepherd himself.

"Whose turn is it for the nightly prayer?" Mark asked the table once everyone sat down.

"Mine," Nathan said with a smile.

"This ought to be good." Liam arched an eyebrow across the table at his boyfriend.

Nathan clasped his hands together. "Dear Lord...thank you." He looked around the table at his family, at the picture of Mariel sitting on the shelf, at Liam. "Thank you for everything."

NATHAN AWOKE at around midnight to an empty bed. The light in the bathroom was off, too.

"Liam?" he asked the dark. He popped out of bed. "Liam?"

Nathan searched the shed, which only took a few seconds, but it was Liamless. He slipped on his shoes and went outside into the warm air. The farm was asleep, sheep snoozing away standing up.

"Liam?"

Nathan poked his head into the hoof house quietly so as not to wake the sheep. Up on the hill, under a beam of moonlight, he found his boyfriend.

"Liam what the hell are you doing out here?"

"It's a beautiful night, isn't it?"

"Technically, morning. Could you not sleep?"

A smile stretched onto Liam's bearded face. He held a small box in his hand. Nathan knew what was usually in those boxes.

"Liam..." But before he could say anything else, Liam was down on one knee.

"I couldn't wait." Liam opened the box, revealing a gleaming silver band. "I couldn't sleep. I've been thinking about the best time to do this, but the best things can't be planned."

"They just happen."

"They just wind up dragging a suitcase through your field in the middle of the night."

Nathan prided himself on not being emotional, but his

defenses couldn't stop the tears from forming. He felt exposed and loved and scared and safe all at once.

"You are sarcastic, bullheaded, caring, sweet, occasionally funny, and someone I want to spend the rest of my life with. Will you marry me?"

Nathan nodded yes. He swore he was never going to be one of those people who was so choked up with emotion that he couldn't give a one-word answer. But damnit, he totally was.

"I love you so much, Nathan. And the truth is, you're the best thing that's ever happened to me. You make me a better brother, a better uncle, a better farmer."

"You're taking all my lines." Nathan wiped his arm across his tear-stained cheeks. "But stand up. Leave the one-knee proposals to the straights."

Liam did as instructed and kissed him under the twinkling lights of their own private, sheep-filled universe.

THE END

ABOUT THE AUTHOR

A.J. Truman remembers his college days like it was yesterday, even though it was definitely not yesterday. He writes books with **humor, heart, and hot guys**. What else does a story need? He loves spending time with his cats and his husband and sneaking off for an afternoon movie. You can find him on Facebook or email him at info [at] ajtruman [dot] com.

www.ajtruman.com